Foreign Blood

Hope you enjoy reading Foreign Blood!
Bruce, April, 2017

Foreign Blood

A Novel

Will B. Ayers

A T-A-T Publication

Copyright © 2015 Will B. Ayers

All rights reserved.

ISBN: 0692436901
ISBN 13: 9780692436905
Library of Congress Control Number: 2015906636
W. Bruce Ayers, Cumberland, KY

*For the love of money is
the root of all evil.*
—*1 Tim. 6:10*

*I am in blood
Stepp'd in so far, that, should I wade no more,
Returning were as tedious as go o'er.*
—*Macbeth, Act 3, Scene 4*

ACKNOWLEDGEMENTS

Every novel is constructed with information gleaned from people and experiences that have shaped the writer's life. While I have probed my memory to feed the creative process, several individuals who read and reread my manuscript have also helped to enlighten me. Some ensured my accuracy as I described historical events, the country of Estonia, police procedures, church rituals, and drug addiction. Others helped to ensure the manuscript was grammatically correct. Still others, in all likelihood, read the manuscript simply to encourage me. I would like to acknowledge all of these individuals regardless of the category in which they might fall.

Three individuals are due special thanks. Robert Gipe, director of the Appalachian Center in Cumberland, Ky, was the first to read the manuscript and to offer constructive criticism. His suggestions led to several changes, including my choosing a new title. Professor Allen Layne, criminal justice instructor and retired state police officer, Partridge, Ky, helped me to understand and keep straight a myriad of police procedures. Finally, Dr. Gene Cornett, pastor and teaching elder at Bethany Place Baptist Church in Chesterfield, Va, was not only a great help to me in the area of church-related issues but with many other issues throughout the manuscript.

Special thanks go also to my family and friends, who kept me focused and moving forward. This was especially true of my wife, Barbara, who never ceased to encourage me and to lift me up. Many others who read the manuscript were probably too close to me to suggest that anything was amiss. But whether they did or did not offer suggestions for improvement, I am grateful to them all. Knowing they cared about me and the book I was writing was a source of great encouragement.

I want to thank the editors at CreateSpace who guided me through revisions of the manuscript. Their knowledge and professionalism were invaluable.

Finally, I acknowledge that my faith in God has provided me with a reservoir of strength from which I have drawn liberally—not just while writing this book but throughout my life.

Cumberland, Kentucky
June 2015

INTRODUCTION

The Commonwealth of Kentucky is divided into 120 counties. Each elects a sheriff who acts as its chief law enforcement official. In addition, the sheriff's duties include tax collection, election duties, and services to the courts, as spelled out in the statute. Sheriffs are able to hire deputies and administrative personnel to help carry out their duties. The Kentucky Constitution requires the sheriff to be twenty-four years of age, a citizen of Kentucky, a resident of the state for two years, and a resident of the county in which elected for one year. The term of office is four years.

The Kentucky State Police (KSP) operates from sixteen posts scattered throughout the state. The KSP requires an applicant to pass a written examination and a physical agility test. At the time of application, the applicant must possess a minimum of sixty semester hours from a college or university or be a high-school graduate with at least two years of active military duty or two years of experience as a full-time sworn law enforcement officer. An applicant is also expected to complete a boot-camp-like academy, which places emphasis on adherence to a strict honor code.

Neither sheriffs nor their deputies are required to meet any particular standard for education or law enforcement experience. Some offices have standards that are equal to or exceed those of the state police; others have only minimal requirements.

The working relationship depicted in *Foreign Blood* expresses my view of how the sheriff's office and the state police could work together. I know there is often much less cooperation between the two agencies than I have shown. In my opinion, there is no reason this has to be the case. Perhaps at some point in the future, the relationship between Al Whitaker and Hartford Ford, who head my fictional sheriff's office and state police post, will be the rule rather than the exception. Should that occur, safety and security around Kentucky would be enhanced.

PROLOGUE

Tallinn, Estonia

Hendrik and Elizabet Sepp had once again worked for almost twelve hours. They had begun at 6:00 a.m. and now were ready to close their fish processing and distribution plant on the Gulf of Finland as the clock neared 6:00 p.m.

It had been a good day for the fishermen who supplied them with fresh fish. In early September, sprats and herring were plentiful, and when reporting in, the fishermen said their nets were running over after dropping them just a few miles out into the gulf.

The day's catch filled two refrigerated trucks, which went off to restaurants and small markets within a hundred-mile radius. Estonians liked their fish fresh, and the Sepps liked making fish available to them.

The remainder of the catch had been iced down. Starting early the next morning, the fifteen employees who worked with Hendrik and Elizabet at their processing plant would fillet and package it. The packaged fish would be shipped to Finland, Latvia, Lithuania, the Russian Federation, and other nearby countries.

They were tired, but since it was Friday, they were looking forward to the weekend. They would come in late the next day, arrive at 8:00 a.m., and be finished by noon. It would be fun spending time with their two teenage children. They had planned a trip to Tartu to visit Hendrik's brother.

Family was important to Hendrik and Elizabet, both of whom came from small families. Elizabet was an only child, and Hendrik had just one brother. All four parents were deceased. The absence of other family members was probably one reason the Sepps idolized their children, Aleksander and Viktoria. At fourteen and twelve, they seemed to Elizabet to be growing up too quickly.

"Where have our babies gone?" she would often lament to her husband.

Hendrik would smile and remind her that the children would be staying around a few more years before striking out on their own.

Like parents everywhere, they had great hopes for their children. They insisted Aleksander and Viktoria go to college.

"I want them to use their minds more than their backs," their father would say to Elizabet. "The world is changing, and now Estonia is part of that world. Their futures can be as bright as those of young people anywhere."

The two of them knew their dreams for their children were tied to the success of the fishery, and that was the primary reason they worked so hard.

There was no reason to think the success the fishery was enjoying would in any way be thwarted as they turned off the lights, stepped outside, and started walking toward their Volkswagen bus, which was parked in a twenty-vehicle lot. At that moment, though, on an unseasonably cool and very dark evening, their lives and their children's lives would change forever.

Three individuals dressed in what appeared to be gray and black military fatigues stepped from behind a police vehicle. With pistols drawn, they insisted the Sepps accompany them to a speedboat tied alongside the fishery's dock. The much larger surrounding fishing boats dwarfed it. When Hendrik began to protest and demand to be told what was going on, one of the three men hit him in the face with the barrel of a nine-millimeter Makarov pistol. This knocked Hendrik unconscious, and another man dragged him toward the boat.

Elizabet screamed and started to run, but the last man quickly apprehended her, covered her mouth with duct tape, and pulled a burlap bag over her head. She and her husband were then pushed onto the floor of a Poseidon Odyssey speedboat. Powered by a 350-horsepower engine, it moved quickly out into the gulf.

CHAPTER 1

MORE THAN FIVE YEARS LATER

He carefully walked up the meandering path in Pine Mountain as if afraid his footsteps would somehow change things for the worse. He loved these mountains, respected them, and wanted them to remain intact for future generations. Pine Mountain was one of very few mountain ranges that had not been surface mined for coal in recent years. While he supported mining, he hoped it remained that way.

Pine Mountain was part of the majestic Appalachian chain that stretched from New York to Alabama. At over four hundred million years old, they were the oldest mountains in the United States. At one time they had been the highest in elevation and easily towered above the present-day Rockies. However, time combined with erosion from wind and water had reduced them to much less than half their former size. Now, Big Black Mountain above the coal community of Lynch was the highest in the region. At just over 4,200 feet, it was also Kentucky's highest point.

Sheriff Alfred "Al" Whitaker was thinking of such things on a clear Saturday afternoon when he saw it up ahead—a body sprawled on a mountain path with an ancient sycamore tree in the background. It was impossible to tell if the body had been dumped from a vehicle or shot where it lay.

Tracks could clearly be seen on the dirt road below his path. They could have been from hunters. Deer were plentiful as were grouse, turkey, and black bear. It just as easily could have been the killers, though. Al didn't want to take any chances, so he stayed off the road.

Everything seemed normal—as normal as a homicide could be. No two murders were ever alike, but there were always similarities. Maybe the thing that tied them all together was the finality of the killing itself. There would be no tomorrow for this victim, just as there was none for any other victim he had seen in his thirty-plus years in law enforcement.

He never got used to it and never could accept that one human could become so estranged from another that the only outcome was death. *Maybe estrangement doesn't fit all homicides,* Al thought. In his experience, though, it covered many of them. There was also indifference, hostility, alienation, and, increasingly, financial motivation.

There was little blood, which suggested the deceased had bled into his lungs. That happened a lot with chest wounds. Al didn't envy the pathologist who would do the autopsy. Pooled blood in body organs was always messy. Wounds like this with little blood on the surface always seemed surreal. The sheriff knew that many things in life, and at crime scenes like this, were not what they appeared to be.

He could hear the state police response team coming up the path. He had asked them to stay off the road. There would be three of them: a lead investigator, the county coroner, and a specially trained photographer who would take hundreds of shots in and around the dead man. The photos, the sheriff knew, often proved as valuable as the results of an autopsy.

Al knew the limitations of his office and often called on the state police for help—especially with complicated cases involving murder.

Detective Frank Davidson was short, stout, and without an ounce of fat on him. He looked at Al and exhaled sharply before speaking. "What do you think, Sheriff? Another drug deal gone wrong?"

It was a good guess, as dealers now filled the mountains. They sold mostly prescription drugs. OxyContin, a powerful painkiller, was the favorite. Methamphetamines were cooked up in makeshift laboratories from ingredients easily purchased over the counter and were also plentiful. Recently, heroin had been showing up too—though not much. *Whatever the amount, it's too much*, Al thought.

Al was not about to jump to conclusions. He thought things through. This was sometimes to the point of aggravating cops such as Davidson, a fifteen-year state police veteran who had studied criminal justice at the local community college before matriculating to Eastern Kentucky University in Richmond to complete a baccalaureate degree. While on good terms with the sheriff's office now, Al knew that Davidson had not always been a big supporter.

Al Whitaker had nothing against education. He had a degree in cultural anthropology from the University of Kentucky, and all three of his kids had graduated from college. Two had obtained professional degrees. He liked to joke that he had doctors, lawyers, and Indian chiefs in the family. Maybe he didn't have Indian chiefs, but his great-great-grandfather had been a Cherokee from down in North Carolina.

As much as the sheriff might have valued education, though, he knew policing could not be reduced to fancy concepts from books or DVDs. He often thought officers such as Frank Davidson were too textbook oriented. Sometimes instinct trumped what the experts had written down.

"I don't know just what to think, Frank," Al finally said, "except that's a mighty big hole in this poor fellow's chest."

Davidson nodded as though he had expected the answer Al had given him. He had worked with the sheriff on well over twenty-five cases spanning more than ten years—just a small part of Whitaker's almost thirty-three year career. He knew Al Whitaker never got ahead of himself—or the evidence—and never jumped to conclusions.

The sheriff looked at the body again. He started at the feet and worked his gaze slowly to the head. "Frank, does anything seem irregular to you with the way the right hand is positioned?" he asked.

"I see what you mean with the hand under the chin, Sheriff, but that could have occurred naturally whether the kid was shot here or thrown from a car. Especially if he landed on his elbow."

Sheriff Whitaker nodded. This suggested he understood Detective Davidson's reasoning but not that he agreed with him.

A young man Al had not seen before photographed tire and boot tracks, and a mold was made of promising tire patterns. Then the body was searched for identification. There was none. The prints on the tight jeans the deceased wore clearly showed he usually carried a wallet. Where it was now was anyone's guess. Al thought it was most likely in the hands of the killer.

As the young photographer circled the crime scene and took shots from several different angles, it struck Al that he couldn't be much older than the boy he was photographing. Since Detective Davidson had not introduced him, Al stuck out his hand after the kid had put away his camera.

"Son, I'm Al Whitaker, the sheriff. Don't think I've had the pleasure of meeting you."

"Good to meet you, Sheriff," the young man said quietly and deliberately. He was tall and muscular and had curly black hair. He chose not to look directly at Al when he replied. "My name's Josh Bledsoe. Grew up over in Ewing, Virginia, but I've spent a lot of time in Harlan County."

"Where did you get your training?" the sheriff asked.

"Just picked photography up on my own," he replied. "After I graduated from high school, I studied computer science for two years, but nothing interested me as much as photography. When I read about a job opening with the Kentucky State Police, I applied. I guess the portfolio I submitted as part of the application process was impressive. I got the job."

Al smiled at the young man and silently bet the kind of photography he was doing today was not exactly what he was used to doing and certainly not what he had submitted in the portfolio.

"You say you've spent some time over here in Harlan County?" Al asked. "Ever seen the deceased before? Looks like he would be about your age."

"Never seen him before that I can recall. Might have, though. You know, folks don't look the same when they're dead."

"Unfortunately, the fact that they might look different is the least of the changes that take place," the coroner, Dr. Jack Thornberry, volunteered.

It seemed to take a minute for the truth of the statement to sink in for Bledsoe. He dropped his head before murmuring a response. "Yes, sir. I know what you mean."

The young victim was about six feet in height, and Al guessed he probably weighed between 170 and 180 pounds. He helped Detective Davidson and Thornberry bag the body and place it on the gurney.

Dr. Jack Thornberry held a medical degree from the University of Tennessee and had worked as a forensic pathologist in Missouri for several years before recently coming home to Harlan. He was about the same age as Al. The sheriff knew he had been at scenes like this hundreds of times before.

He whistled as he pushed the gurney one hundred yards or so to a waiting all-terrain SUV specially designed for cases where bodies had to be transported over unimproved mountain roads. The going was tough on the path, but with Detective Davidson navigating at the front of the gurney, they made it without too much difficulty.

Al knew not to ask Thornberry anything. The cause of death was evident, and beyond that Thornberry simply would be speculating.

"Boys," Thornberry would say in cases like this, "we'll just have to wait until our friends up in Frankfort get the pathology report back to us. If there's something else we need to know, that report will tell us."

Long after the state police team had left, the sheriff remained behind. Jason Hightower, police chief in nearby Cumberland, and two members of the police patrol at Kingdom State Park who had called to inform him of the body earlier in the day had joined him.

The park was named after a novel written by John Fox Jr. at the turn of the twentieth century called *The Little Shepherd of Kingdom Come*, and the park contained some of the most striking views in the region.

Apparently two young men driving on the Little Shepherd Trail had first seen the body. Why other law enforcement officials had not been called before him was unclear. Maybe it was because he lived nearby in a three-bedroom, two-bath bungalow nestled in an alcove at the foot of the park and was closest to the scene. They would have known that, on a Saturday afternoon, he would be home.

That's beginning to be a problem, the sheriff thought. *Everybody knows my routine—where I am and what I am likely to be doing.* He also knew that at his age, regardless of what they knew, he was not going to change a thing.

"Jason," Al said, and he smiled at a young man he had helped to recruit and train as a deputy in the Harlan County Sheriff's Office some years earlier. "I wish you could have been here before they took the body away, but I understand you can't always drop everything to meet with me."

"Wish I could have been here too, but I just got back in town after Augusta and I were vacationing down in Gatlinburg when I got the call," Jason said.

"How is Augusta? You know, you're mighty lucky to have a wife like her," Al said.

"She's fine. Thanks for asking. I reckon you and I are both lucky, though. You've got a great wife in Ruby. I know Augusta has learned a lot from her. She considers her a great friend," Jason said.

"What do you have in mind for me to do, Al?"

"If you get a chance, will you run down to Harlan first thing Monday and check the photographs the state police photographer took? I want you to see if anything looks unusual or out of the way to you."

"Did you see something?" Jason asked.

"Just want another set of eyes on the deceased and the crime scene. You've worked a lot of homicides too. Thought maybe you would see something I didn't."

Al reckoned Jason had heard him make a similar request many times before. It was part of his philosophy that good policing required collaboration and that two heads were better than one.

Jason told his friend he would try to get to Harlan as early as possible on Monday to look at the photographs. Al had helped him out too many times to say no.

Al, Jason, and the two members of the park patrol walked back to where their cars were parked. Al Whitaker led the way with his slow, deliberate gait. The others, out of respect, did likewise.

The sheriff cautiously drove down Kingdom Come Drive in a 2009 Crown Victoria bought secondhand from the Kentucky State Police. After changing the color from gray to brown at the local technical school and stenciling it with the county sheriff's logo, it looked good. Al figured it would probably serve him well for several years, despite the more than one hundred thousand miles that registered on the odometer.

Parking under the carport attached to his house, he got out of the car and looked around a full 360 degrees. He always did this out of habit before starting down the walkway and up the steps to the door. He inserted the key and opened the door carefully. He did not want to disturb any mail that might have been slipped through the slot in his two-inch oak door.

There wasn't much today—two or three letters, a copy of the *Smithsonian* magazine, and today's *Lexington Herald-Leader*. Until recently the paper had been delivered early in the morning, but when the delivery person got sick and a replacement could not be found quickly, the newspaper people made a business decision. They stopped home delivery. Now the paper came in the mail, and he had to go through it in the evening. It was a morning paper. It wasn't the same.

Al went to the fridge to check for his evening meal. Usually his wife of almost thirty-five years would have supper on the table. However, Ruby was visiting her sister in Lexington over the weekend. She wanted to get a visit in during the fall before the winter snows started falling in the mountains.

Looks as if it will be another TV dinner, he thought, and he pulled out a lasagna entrée with mixed vegetables. It was the very kind of meal Ruby detested. *But Ruby's not here*, Al thought, *and this will have to do.*

He put the dinner in for four minutes in the microwave, and then he let it cool while he poured a Diet Coke over ice. Eating while reading the Saturday paper took about forty-five minutes.

He cleared everything from the table to the sink and pulled out a three-ring binder. After committing everything he had learned at the crime scene to his journal, he put the binder into a leather carrying case with a sheriff's star embossed on the front. It had been a gift from his youngest son, Randolph, on his sixtieth birthday almost three years before.

CHAPTER 2

Before Al finished washing the dishes and putting them away, something he did after every meal when Ruby was away from home, he heard a knock on the door. He wasn't surprised. People in the area often came by to check on him and Ruby, and in the summer, they brought them vegetables from their gardens. This time of year, they often brought apples picked from orchards near the top of Big Black Mountain above the frost zone. He recalled this had been a particularly good year for apples. As he approached the door, he expected to see someone there with a basketful of Scarlet Galas or Tangy Reds, both of which were among his favorite apples.

When he turned on the porch light outside his living room, however, he saw a young woman he didn't know. She was tall and slender and had long blond hair and penetrating blue eyes. He opened the door and asked if he could help her. She looked from side to side before fixating on Al's face.

"They have killed him," she said. "I knew they would do so."

Taking her gently by the arm, Al led her to the living room sofa, and he asked her to sit down.

"Can I get you something? A soft drink? I could heat up the coffee."

"No. I am fine. I am fine," she said.

He noticed that while she spoke clearly and distinctly, his guest did so with a foreign accent.

"Young lady, who are you?" he asked. His words clearly implied he wanted to know why she was there and also if the killing she was referring to was the one he was investigating.

"I am Viktoria from Estonia. I have come about Aleksander."

Then she started to cry. He reassured her she was safe and that he would try to help her, which calmed Viktoria somewhat. She still sobbed repeatedly as she recounted a strange story to Al.

It began, she said, when she and her brother, Aleksander, were left on their own five years before. Their parents, Hendrik and Elizabet Sepp, had owned a fish processing and distribution plant in Tallinn, Estonia, just off the Gulf of Finland, but they had disappeared. It had happened when the Russian population, which had been somewhat dormant following Estonia's independence from the old USSR in the early 1990s, started to reassert itself.

"They wanted things like had been before. They wanted in control. It was not all Russians," she added. "But some of them resent that Estonia was free and that Russia was no longer in control. They believe we take their jobs unfairly."

Viktoria spoke of a thriving commercial fishing industry that annually caught and processed thousands of tons of fish—primarily herring, sprats, and perch. While the Sepps were a small firm, they had been financially stable and able to employ between fifteen and twenty workers at any given time.

The police had done a perfunctory investigation and kept the case open for almost six months before suddenly closing it down without explanation.

"They come, the police, and say there are no leads. That our mother and father are gone from us. They don't know how. Don't know why. My brother and I cannot believe what we hear. To not know was as bad almost as the time when first they disappear."

The sheriff listened intently. He did not know what to make of this story, but one thing was certain. He wanted to know whether this young woman's story was true and if so what it had to do with the body he'd found in the park.

After finally taking a sip of water, Viktoria seemed to get her second wind. She ran her fingers through her hair before continuing. "We go, Aleksander and I, to live with aunt and uncle in Tartu. More than one hundred fifty kilometers from our home. We find that school not interest us as before. We wonder, where are our parents?"

She said her uncle was a local politician in Tartu and had inquired about his brother and sister-in-law's fishing business, since legal documents showed the two children would inherit everything.

"He tell us he works with courts to protect Aleksander and me, and we sign documents that allow him to run fishery. My uncle, he say the business is broke almost and that it is not worth all the worry."

"Sounds like some of the goings-on in this country," Al said.

"Nine months ago our uncle insist Aleksander and I leave Estonia and come to live with relatives in America. I don't know what to do, but Aleksander is fond of everything from America. He hears US music on TV. He sees famous ballplayers. He thinks everything is better here. So we decide to come to America."

Viktoria said her uncle had arranged everything for them, from passports to booking their flight from Tartu to London and then to Atlanta.

"He gives us each two thousand American dollars and sends us to live in America." What Viktoria told Al next almost bowled him over. "We come, Aleksander and I, here to live with relatives in Benham. Today we have been here almost five months."

"In Benham?" Al blurted out. "I don't know of anyone named Sepp around here, and if there are what are they doing here?"

Viktoria explained that the Sepps had come here to mine coal in the early 1900s at the same time thousands of others had come from Europe to begin new lives in America.

"Our father's great-uncle Jakob come to America in 1918. Aleksander and I live with his grandson and our cousin, Marcus."

"Marcus Smith?" the sheriff asked.

Viktoria nodded her head. Al knew Marcus well. He was a foreman for Mineral Mountain Resources, which operated several large coal mines in the Benham area.

Marcus's great-grandfather, Jakob, had apparently done what many Europeans did. He anglicized his name to sound more like the native population, and the name "Smith" was about as native as one could get.

"What makes you think your brother is dead?" Al asked.

"We hear about the body in the park, and I know without seeing him this is my brother, Aleksander."

"How did you find out about this?" Al asked.

"They talk about it in Benham already. They say it is a young man who has been shot. I know it is Aleksander," she sobbed.

Al told her a positive identification had not yet been made since the victim's wallet had been taken and there was no identification.

CHAPTER 3

The sheriff had driven down US 119 from his home in Cumberland hundreds of times, but never had he been as troubled as he was on this early November morning when he thought about the bizarre tale Viktoria Sepp had recounted.

He was so upset he heard little of the Reverend Maynard Johnson's sermon at the Trinity Baptist Church the day before as he grappled with what that young woman had told him.

He had taken her home before retiring for the night. She told him she had gotten a ride to his place.

"I heard you are an honest police officer," she said, "and would tell the truth."

When he dropped off Viktoria, Al spent a few minutes talking to Marcus Smith, who told him the young woman was his cousin, and she and her brother had been living with him and his wife, Trudy, for the past five months.

Marcus verified what the sheriff had thought about his family's name change. His great-grandfather had gotten tired of people asking about his name, so he changed it to Smith, which was one of the region's most prominent surnames. What the locals did not know, Marcus told Al, was that in Estonia the meaning of the word "Sepp" was Smith. "In reality Great-Grandfather Jakob didn't change the family name that much," Marcus said.

Marcus told the sheriff Viktoria was telling the truth about her mother and father. They had gone missing some time ago. He said he didn't know a lot about the fishery, except what his cousin Gunnar Sepp, with whom Viktoria and Aleksander had been living, had told him.

"But Viktoria and Aleksander swore up and down the fishing business belonged to their parents and that they were the rightful heirs," Marcus said.

All this was running through Al's mind as he walked into the Harlan state police headquarters, which was located beside Wendy's on the bypass. He repeated the story Viktoria had told him to two of his deputies, Jim Lucas and Gloria Strong, as well as a contingent of state police officers, including Detective Frank Davidson and Captain Hartford Ford, Post Ten commander.

Jim Lucas, a fifteen-year veteran in the sheriff's office, knew Al wasn't one to be taken in by fairy tales, but he had a hard time believing what his boss was telling them.

"Sounds fishy to me," he said. This drew a laugh from Gloria Strong and the state police officers. Not wanting to push his luck too far with the sheriff, he regained his composure and crisply said, "Go on, Al. Tell us the rest of it."

"Not much else to tell," the sheriff said. "But Marcus Smith verified she and her brother were living with him and said the story about her parents having gone missing was true. After I left them, Marcus brought Viktoria down here to look at the body we found in the park. As we now know, she identified the deceased as her brother."

Before leaving Post Ten, their responsibilities for carrying out the investigation were divided up. The sheriff's office took some, and others fell to the state police. This kind of cooperation between the two law enforcement agencies was unusual in Kentucky, but the sheriff and post commander had been friends for many years, and each knew of the other's expertise in policing and commitment to honesty and integrity in the investigative process.

Captain Ford said his office would follow up on the autopsy. The body had been sent to Frankfort, where the state pathologist would oversee it. The office would make some inquiries with the FBI about working with Interpol to see if there was any truth to the wild tale Al's lady friend had told him.

"It sounds a little strange to me." Captain Ford laughed. "But then again I've heard stranger things." The captain then said Detective Davidson would continue to be the lead officer for the state police. "We'll get back with you, Al, in the next day or two."

Al nodded and said he and his deputies would begin asking around to find out more about Aleksander—who he was running with and what he had been doing the last five months. As they walked out of Post Ten, the sheriff asked Deputy Strong to see what she could find out in Benham.

"Start at the Kentucky Coal Museum. It's in the center of things up there, and the workers might know something about this boy or Viktoria. Dig around some, but don't upset the applecart," Al said.

Deputy Gloria Strong nodded that she understood.

She appreciated that the sheriff had faith in her to "dig around without upsetting the applecart." It was a standing joke around the office that Al sometimes mixed his metaphors.

However, everyone who worked with him agreed he was a good man, one of the best, and while he might not have always said things the way they would have, they all had complete confidence in his instincts for investigating crime.

Once Al made his way from the state police post to the Harlan County Courthouse, he turned to Deputy Jim Lucas and motioned for him to follow him to his office. It was one of several spaces occupied by county officials in the three-story building constructed in the 1920s.

Al estimated 25–30 percent of the public's business with the sheriff's office was connected to taxes, since the county sheriff was the official tax collector in each of Kentucky's 120 counties. But folks came for other purposes too—most often spreading talk about crimes that might or might not have been committed. Every now and then, a solid lead would come in, but that was rare.

Two administrative assistants, both of whom wore uniforms that identified them as deputies, greeted them. This had been done at Al's insistence.

"I want them to be police officers," he'd said. "You never know what kind of crazy person is liable to come in here, and having them deputized and in uniform might serve as a deterrent."

They were affectionately known as "Al's AAs," and in the sheriff's view, they were "two jim-dandies."

Blanche Halcomb was a thirty-two-year-old single mother who had held her position for almost eight years. She held an associate degree in criminology and had also studied business administration.

The other was old enough to be Blanche's mother. Sylvia Turner was almost fifty-nine and had known Al all her life. She had grown up in Lynch not far from him. She was proud of her black heritage and often recounted that her great-great-grandfather had "come to these mountains from Alabama to mine coal, and some of us never left."

Turner and Halcomb were united in their dedication to the sheriff's office and particularly to Al Whitaker. Anyone who said anything bad about him within earshot of them was immediately challenged.

The sheriff spoke to the two women as he walked through their work area on the way to his office. "Ladies, I guess you heard about the body they found up at Kingdom Come State Park."

"Lordy, Lordy," Sylvia said with her hands on her hips. "That's all they talking about up our holler. We got any leads, Sheriff?"

"Gloria Strong is headed up your way to try to find out more about the two Sepp kids, Aleksander and Viktoria. Aleksander was the boy found in the park."

"I never heard of no Sepps, Sheriff, and I've been living up that holler all my life."

"Me either, Sylvia, but both of us have heard of Marcus Smith. His grandfather was a Sepp but changed his name."

"Marcus and his wife, Trudy, they be good people, Sheriff. I been knowing them almost as long as I have you." Sylvia said this before acknowledging she would help Deputy Strong try to get a lead on the deceased and his sister.

Al Whitaker and Jim Lucas walked into the sheriff's office, a sparsely furnished ten-by-ten boxlike space with three framed prints of mountain scenes hanging on the walls. Al sat down behind his desk, put his hat down on a stool to the left of the chair, and motioned for the deputy to take a seat.

"I asked Jason to come down and take a look at the photographs of the victim. See if he noticed anything unusual. I want you to get together with him later today and find out what he thinks, Jim."

Lucas squirmed in his chair before acknowledging Al's request. The sheriff knew Lucas was not particularly happy to continue to involve Jason in county investigations after he had left to become police chief in Cumberland. Al also knew Jason was good at seeing things others didn't, and he knew Jim knew it too and would get over his uneasiness.

"What do you want him to be looking for, Al?" Jim finally got around to asking. "Something in particular you saw?"

The sheriff picked up the Styrofoam cup of coffee Blanche had brought in and turned it in his hands before setting it back down without taking a drink.

"The way the victim's right hand was positioned under his chin. Looked almost as if it had been placed there to hold his head up. I didn't tell Jason what I saw. I didn't want to bias him. None of the state police officers thought it was unusual."

The two men walked out of the office together and headed to their almost identical cruisers. They were parked side by side in front of the courthouse. Al hollered at Jim as he got into his car. "I'm headed back up to the park to see what the two kids who found the body told the park's police patrol. Let me know what Jason says. And ask the state police if they got anything from the tire prints."

"Will do, Al," the deputy responded.

A trio of twenty-two-wheelers loaded with coal traveling in a convoy slowed the sheriff's half-hour trip back up US 119. That was to be expected on a two-lane road in a part of the country that had an economy based almost entirely on coal mining.

Al knew some of the truck drivers. Most of them were locals who had grown up in Harlan or neighboring Bell or Letcher County. Driving a truck might not have been the prestigious job they had hoped for when they were young, but like coal mining it paid well and allowed them to stay close to home.

Sheriff Whitaker was thinking he usually didn't get involved in on-the-ground investigations anymore—too many other things to do in running his office—but every now and then, a case would be of particular interest to him for one reason or another.

What with Viktoria coming to his home with her strange story, this one had definitely piqued his interest. He had made sure the deputies not working on this case continued with their assignments, and he knew his two AAs could handle things in the office.

CHAPTER 4

Al stayed on US 119 when coming into Cumberland. The highway went from two to four lanes just before the cutoff to the community college. He exited at Kingdom Come Drive and headed up into the park a distance of about a mile and a half. It was uphill most of the way. He blew his horn to alert three bicyclists as he drove around them. He pulled up in front of a small lake and walked a hundred yards to the patrol office.

The office was in a corrugated metal building, and although it was painted green to mimic the surroundings, it always looked out of place—especially now when the green it was supposed to mimic had given way to the colors of fall.

Al liked fall. In fact he liked all the seasons. He also liked living in the hills of Eastern Kentucky. More than once he had been tempted to take a position in Central Kentucky's Bluegrass region. There had been several offers, but usually at the urging of Ruby, he had always said no. Although born in the mountains, Ruby had grown up in Lexington and had several friends who remained there. However, she had never liked the place. "I always wanted to come home," she would say.

He walked in and expected to find Jonah Wright, head of the park system's police patrol. Seeing only Jeb Jones, who headed the patrol at the Kingdom Come State Park, Al tried not to show his surprise. Jones was a new hire and not more than six months out of the state police academy, which was where the state parks sent their police officers for training. Jonah Wright was a twenty-year veteran, and when something like a homicide occurred in one of his parks, he was usually there.

"Sheriff, I thought I would be seeing you today. The two guys on duty yesterday put their report together before they left last night. I made sure of that." Jones fumbled through his desk drawer and pulled out a police report that was stapled to several pages of writing on a notepad. "This is their report together with written statements from the two kids who found the body."

Al took the report and statements from Jones. He thumbed through the pages slowly before pulling the journal out of his leather carrying case and carefully looking at what he had written on Saturday. He looked at one of the written statements again before asking Jones if he thought it would be possible to talk to the two kids who had found the body.

"They live up in Letcher County. Not too far from Followell's Grocery Store. Where you turn off to go to Eolia," he said.

Al nodded. After asking him to make copies of the report and statements, he put everything in his leather carrying case, thanked Jones for his help, and headed to Eolia.

He was on US 119 again, but this section of the road had been built in the 1940s, and it wasn't as straight as the newer section between Cumberland and Harlan. It was a curvy, narrow, dangerous road, and Al always took his time when he traveled on it. He had seen too many accidents on the road to do otherwise.

For a November day, the weather wasn't too bad. It was sunny and cool, but he knew that could change in a hurry.

As Al drove toward his destination, he smiled to himself. He knew Ruby would be there when he got home with supper ready and a full report on how her relatives were doing. Ruby always said she wasn't one to talk about anyone. He chuckled. That sure wouldn't keep her from accessing her nearly photographic memory to give a play-by-play of everything that had taken place at her sister's.

Al knew he would not change a thing about Ruby. She was sweet and kind and a wonderful mother and grandmother. As a wife no man could have asked for anyone better. She stood beside him in the good times and the bad. He was mighty glad to have her.

About ten miles from Cumberland and a few miles from his destination, Al encountered a stalled pickup truck. He slowed down, rolled down his window on the driver's side, and hollered to the person he assumed was the driver. The person had pulled off on the shoulder and was looking under the hood of the truck.

"I could call someone if you need me to."

"Got everything covered. Thank you," the presumed driver replied curtly and held up a cell phone. "Think I have a gas leak. I've called a wrecker."

When he reached the entrance to KY Highway 806, which led to Eolia, Al pulled into the parking lot of Followell's Grocery, a small single-pump convenience store that had gained notoriety in the film *Coal Miner's Daughter*, which was based on the life of country music legend Loretta Lynn. She had grown up about seventy-five miles northeast in Butcher Holler in Johnson County.

The movie was filmed primarily in Letcher County with some scenes shot in Kingdom Come State Park. Sissy Spacek portrayed Loretta, and Tommy Lee Jones played her husband, Mooney. They were filmed stopping at the store to fix themselves bologna sandwiches washed down with soft drinks.

Word was that such a visit had actually taken place when Loretta and Mooney were traipsing about the country to convince DJs at small, rural radio stations to play Loretta's records. That included the song with the same name as the movie.

Al had known the store's owner, Jeff Akin, for some time. He wasn't exactly a close friend, but he was an acquaintance whom Al would often call on for information. He trusted him and knew he could count on whatever Akin told him.

Akin left the sheriff to himself for a few minutes after he walked into the store. Al knew this country store was country in appearance only. Cameras were hidden throughout the twenty-foot-by-twenty-foot storefront, and they could be monitored from Akin's office in the rear.

By the time the store owner made an appearance, Al had taken a soft drink from the cooler and was seated at one of two booths in the store.

"What's the sheriff of Harlan County doing up this way?" Akin asked as he sauntered over to the booth.

Akin was a big man and carried almost three hundred pounds on a five-foot-ten frame. When he walked he did so slowly and with great care. He always grasped a cane in his left hand, and he leaned on it noticeably.

Al always thought Akin's slowness in coming to wait on customers might have been linked to poor health. He assumed Akin used as much time as he could to rest in his office. *Why not?* he thought. *He can see everything taking place on the monitors.* He did wonder, though, how that would work if there were ever several customers in the establishment at the same time.

"Jeff, I know you've heard about the body that was found down in the state park on Saturday," Al said, and he looked directly at the big man. "I was wondering if you could point me in the direction of the two young men who found the body."

Too big to fit into the booth where Al was sitting, Akin pulled up a chair, turned it around so he could lean on its back, and sat down facing him. "Who you looking for, Sheriff?"

"Boys by the names of Luke Henson and Clayton Wright. From what they reported at the park, both were in their mid to late teens."

Before Al had finished his response, Akin's face appeared flush, and he began tapping the floor with his cane. "Them two might look like they're teenagers, but they're older than that, and they been in and out of trouble most of their sorry lives," Akin almost shouted.

"What kind of trouble?"

"Drugs mostly. They been caught twice stealing copper wire from telephone lines over around Whitesburg," Akin said. "They're cousins, and they've been in and out of jail. They spent about sixty days behind bars the last time they were caught. I've had to run them off more than once when they been nosing around here."

Al understood all too well the problems associated with the theft of copper wiring from telephone lines. When it happened—almost weekly in one part of the region or another—it shut down communications for hundreds or even thousands of people in the mountains, the majority of whom did not have cell access in the remote areas where they lived.

"Can you tell me how to get to them?" Al asked.

He was perturbed the police patrol at the park had not picked up on who these cousins were and what they had been up to. Jonah Wright would not be happy when he heard about this.

"They both live up a holler about five miles due west from the Eolia School with their grandpa," Akin said.

He added there was no good way to get there except to take a narrow dirt road he described as rough and rocky. Al paid Jeff Akin for his soft drink, thanked him for the information, and walked out into the late-fall day. It was growing much cooler, and as often happened this time of year, clouds were beginning to fill the sky.

He didn't think it would get cold enough to snow, which he would have preferred to rain—especially since he was headed up the road Akin had described.

Sure enough the road was rough. There were twists and turns with rocks jutting out of the ground. Most were not sharp, though. Al knew about roads like this. Many dated back to the late 1800s when locals were busy cutting timber and built roads like this one to transport it.

They would load the logs, many weighing several hundred pounds, on sleds pulled by teams of horses. Over time sharp rocks were worn down. Al was thankful this was the case. At least the road was passable, if only barely so.

The Crown Victoria bounced like a kid on a trampoline, and more than once Al's head touched the car's roof. He traveled for more than thirty minutes before seeing a log house ahead in a clearing to his left. Sitting nearby was a two-story barn and what he figured was a hogpen, an enclosure to fatten hogs for slaughter.

Surprisingly the house, barn, and hogpen were positioned at the mouth of a wide valley, which looked to be prime farmland. On both sides of the ridges, oak, maple, and poplar trees were in abundance with a smattering of pine standing among the almost-leafless hardwood. Al knew about valleys like this that opened up back in the mountains. He had seen several but never one this big.

He pulled the police cruiser in behind an old, rusty pickup truck, retrieved his hat from the driver's seat, and stepped out onto a gravel driveway. He straightened himself up some, ran his hands down his shirt to smooth out the wrinkles, and walked toward the house. Before he reached the porch, which ran the entire length of the house, he saw a tall, razor-thin elderly man headed his way. "What do you want, and what are you doing up this holler?"

In cases like this, Al knew the worst thing he could do was respond with the same kind of antagonism the old man was exhibiting. He smiled and stuck out his hand. "I'm Sheriff Al Whitaker from down in Harlan County, and I'm up here looking for two young men who reported finding a body in Kingdom Come State Park on Saturday."

The old man looked Al over carefully before taking his hand. When he did so, he squeezed his hand as if to say, "I might be old, mister, but there's a lot of life left in me."

"My name is Oscar Pennington," he said, "and this property has been in my family nigh on a hundred years."

"It's a good-looking farm," Al said. "This is one of the biggest mountain valleys I have seen."

Pointing to two rocking chairs, the old man invited Al to sit with him on the porch. "Now," he said, "what's this about you wanting to talk to two men?"

Al told him whom he was looking for and explained that Jeff Akin at Followell's store had told him they were cousins who lived up here.

"Luke and Clayton, they're my grandsons, and they've been with me going on two years. You say they found this feller that was killed?"

Al replied they had and asked if Luke and Clayton were home.

"Nah. They ain't here. Fact is they ain't here most of the time. They was sent here to help me after the missus died a few years back, but they spend more time in Cumberland and Whitesburg than they spend with me."

"How do you take care of this place without having someone to help you?"

Oscar Pennington lowered his head and shook it back and forth. "I don't farm much anymore. Raise a little vegetable garden and enough corn to fatten my pigs. That's about all." He said he rented out the rest of the farm to what he called distant kin, who raised soybeans, sorghum, and corn. "They do right well, and if I need anything, they're always willing to help me."

When the conversation came back to Luke and Clayton, it was apparent their grandfather was fed up with their behavior. "None of my family never stole nothing from any person," he said. "But these two been arrested more than once for stealing. I don't like it none, and I've told them, one more time and they can go back to Ohio where their folks live."

The old farmer explained that Luke and Clayton were the sons of two of his daughters who had left home right out of high school to work in factories in Dayton. They had both married, and the grandsons were the offspring of those unions.

"Not a whole lot of opportunities around here for women when my girls graduated high school. The missus and me made sure they finished school and then let them go."

Al noticed Pennington often paused when speaking. It was as if he was deep in thought, especially when he spoke of the past. That was most apparent when he mentioned his "missus," which was what he called his late wife, Rachel.

"Rachel would never have put up with Luke and Clayton. She was a good Christian woman. Took the Bible real serious. Guess I've been too lenient." He sighed. "But no longer."

Al suspected loneliness might have motivated the old man's leniency. Al found himself feeling sorry for him for just a minute, but then his position of sheriff, which had been seared into his consciousness for many years, took over, and he began questioning Pennington about his grandsons again.

"Did your grandsons mention finding a body?" Al asked.

"Nary a word. Course they don't talk much to me. Especially since I got on them over their stealing."

"Do you know where they are now?" Al asked.

"If I was a bettin' man, I'd say they was over around Whitesburg. I reckon that's where a lot of their thievery took place."

Al thanked Mr. Pennington and started back to his car before remembering one last question. "What do the boys drive?" he asked.

"I don't know exactly what make and model it is, Sheriff. All of them new cars look alike to me," Pennington said, and he scratched his head before continuing. "It's fairly new, black as a starless night, and low to the ground. They banged it up some coming up and down this holler."

CHAPTER 5

A cold rain began to fall, and the temperature dropped precipitously as Al drove away from Oscar Pennington's place. At this elevation the rain could turn to snow instantly, and that was exactly what happened.

By the time he made it back to Followell's store, the rain had turned to a wet, flaky snow. While not heavy, it came down steadily. *Just enough*, he thought, *to make driving difficult and the roads slick.*

The trip home normally would have taken forty minutes. It took over an hour. He pulled into his carport, and snow already covered the ground. It was an unusual accumulation so early in the season.

He opened the door to a toolshed attached to the carport and pulled out a coal shovel. It was much heavier and better constructed than the snow shovels available in hardware stores. He exited the carport and began to clear the sidewalk to the steps. No sooner had he worked his way to the porch than the light came on and Ruby emerged. "Where have you been?" she almost shouted. "I was beginning to get worried about you. You could have called. Your note said you would be back an hour ago."

"Sorry. I was pretty much consumed by keeping the car on the road with the snow falling."

When Al walked into the house, the demeanor of his five-foot-three, raven-haired wife changed. There was now a smile on her face that radiated outward from her deep brown eyes. "You know what

I've cooked for you?" she asked as she embraced the man whom she had been attracted to since high school.

"Smells like chicken and dumplings, and I bet you have mashed some potatoes and fixed some green beans too," Al said, and he kissed her tenderly.

"You didn't mention dessert. Got your favorite—zucchini bread. Maybe you can even have a dip of ice cream with it. All depends on how you behave."

Al smiled and thought about how many meals Ruby had prepared for him—every one with loving care. She would tell anyone proudly that her meals weren't fast food. No TV dinners or instant potatoes for her. She took pains to prepare as much as she could from scratch. For this evening's meal, it meant purchasing a whole chicken and cutting it up herself, boiling potatoes, and adding real butter and pepper before turning them into a delicacy in a twenty-five-year-old mixer. It meant cooking shucked green beans she had picked from her garden in July and dried for a week before packaging and storing them to use on occasions such as this.

After eating, Ruby caught Al up on all that was going on with her sister, Rebecca. A lot had happened in her family recently. She had lost her husband in an automobile accident, and with both her girls living with their families out of state, Ruby was the closest relative Rebecca had.

"It was important for me to be there with her," Ruby said.

Al nodded. He knew how close the two were. As much as he supported her going to be with Rebecca, though, he was awfully happy to have Ruby home.

They talked for almost an hour. Afterward Al helped Ruby take the dishes to the sink. She washed, and he dried. Once the table was cleared, Al pulled out his three-ring binder and wrote out everything he had learned that day about the Kingdom Come homicide.

CHAPTER 6

It was 2:30 a.m. when a jet-black Nissan Altima Coupe turned off US 119 and headed toward Eolia. Luke Hanson and Clayton Wright didn't like being in the hills of Kentucky. Their run-ins with the police in Dayton had gotten them exiled, as they liked to say, "to an old house up a holler."

The snow fell so heavily the Altima almost missed the turnoff to the dirt road leading to their grandfather's farm. Because it had such a low clearance, the undercarriage of the car did not escape the rocks that protruded from the path, and the blanket of snow did little to protect it.

Neither man could sit still—even Luke, who was driving. They were razor thin and talked nonstop about how they could get the money to make the next OxyContin purchase. They would be OK through tomorrow, but after that no more pills meant withdrawal would set in, and their emaciated bodies would feel as though they were going to collapse on themselves cell by cell. Their skin would feel as if it was crawling, and their eyes, always darting back and forth, would become supersensitive to light.

It was the exact opposite of the euphoria they had felt the first few times they took OxyContin. Now they no longer looked for euphoria. They just wanted to feel normal again.

Knowing the anguish that lay in their future without drugs, they would spend tomorrow securing funds in one way or another to purchase the next pill, the next high, the next normal.

CHAPTER 7

Al spent most of the next morning in his office catching up on other matters with his deputies. There was no absence of activity.

A federal drug abuse task force had cracked down on a pain clinic near Pathfork whose doctors were spending less than ten minutes with patients before prescribing high-powered pain medications, a tour bus accident had resulted in the injury of several senior citizens touring the county from Northern Kentucky, four of whom were transported to the Harlan Appalachian Regional Hospital, and the county's new consolidated high school had filed an official request with the sheriff's office to help with traffic control when classes were released in the afternoons.

The sheriff was particularly pleased to learn of the crackdown on drug-pushing doctors. Most of them had long forgotten their Hippocratic oaths and were now looking only to fatten their bank accounts. His office had headed the undercover investigation that led to their exposure.

In a 9:00 a.m. meeting with his staff, Al emphasized that the Kingdom Come case, as it had come to be called, was not to keep his officers from handling everyday business.

"After all," he said, "this is hardly the first murder we have dealt with in Harlan County."

"Might not be the first murder case," Sylvia whispered to Blanche loud enough for everyone to hear, "but when we ever had Interpol working on something we be trying to solve here?"

Blanche shrugged in acknowledgment while trying not to draw attention to Sylvia. After the meeting the sheriff talked with each of his deputies and his administrative assistants for a few minutes before walking toward his office. He motioned for Deputies Jim Lucas and Gloria Strong to accompany him. Sipping from a cup of coffee Sylvia had brought him, he motioned for them to sit down.

"Did you pick up anything in Benham, Gloria?"

The deputy took a notepad from her hip pocket and thumbed through several pages before responding. "I talked with several people. They said the kid who was killed and his sister were typical teenagers. The boy a little more outgoing. He had been seen in the company of a couple of known druggies, but you can't walk the streets around here without that happening."

"Did either of them appear to have money problems?" the sheriff asked. "Is Marcus Smith keeping them up?"

"Good question," she responded. "He obviously has to foot the bill for shelter and food, but both of them worked part-time. The boy worked at the Martin's Fork boat dock. Pretty good with anything that runs on the water, the owner told me."

"A good worker?" the sheriff asked.

"The owner said he was. Showed up late a couple of times because of the classes he was taking at the community college. It surprised me a little he was in college."

"We'll need to get down to the campus to talk with his teachers," Al said.

"I can get there later today," Jim volunteered.

"What about Viktoria, Gloria? You said she was working too."

"About ten hours a week at the Kentucky Coal Museum on weekends. Everybody there said she was great to work with, did what she was told, and always kept busy. When she graduates high school later in the year, they say she might go into museum management in college. Likes learning about the past and was especially interested in finding out about all the immigrants who came here at the turn of the century to mine coal."

"I wonder how the boy paid his tuition," the sheriff mused. "Bet it cost a small fortune, his being a foreign student."

"They told me at the boat dock he was only going part-time. Taking a couple of classes. I think he might have some kind of scholarship the school gives to foreign students. They got students from all over now."

Directing his attention to Deputy Lucas, the sheriff asked if Lucas had learned anything from the state police on the tire patterns.

"They got some good prints, Al. Actually there were two sets. One from a set of tires with a lot of tread on them, and the other looked as though the tires were almost bald."

"I also checked with Jason like you asked me to, and he said the only thing that looked the least bit unusual was the way the kid's right hand was positioned under his chin. He said it could have occurred naturally when the boy fell, but it looked strange to him. I think that's the way it appeared to you too."

Al nodded. Jason had seen the same thing he had, and now he would almost bet the hand had not come to that position naturally. If it hadn't, though, who had positioned it that way, and perhaps more important what did it mean?

"OK. Jim, you go on over to the community college. Gloria, you check at the high school. I'll be at the boy's funeral this afternoon after I stop off at Post Ten."

As usual for that time of year, yesterday's snow had all but disappeared. State highway crews were adept at getting out in front of the winter weather. They began salting in high elevations before the first snowflake fell, and when the weather was colder and the snow was more likely to accumulate, trucks with scrapers were out twenty-four seven. This was unlike the old days, when heavy snows could have pretty much closed down things for days at a time.

Sitting adjacent to Wendy's and across the road from McDonald's, the single-story brick building that housed the Harlan Post of the Kentucky State Police had been built in the 1960s. Being so close to the fast-food restaurants meant there were lots of eyes on the comings and goings at the building. Today was little different. Al got out of his Crown Victoria with his hat in hand. He could see men and women alike looking his way and probably wondering what the sheriff was up to.

Let them wonder, he thought. *It gives them something to talk about.*

When Al walked in, Dispatcher Ken Lundrum, a small, thin, fidgety man who never smiled, greeted him. Al had known him for some time, but neither he nor anyone else he knew had ever gotten close to Lundrum. Al felt sorry for him. He had no family to speak of. His life apparently centered on his job, which everyone said he performed well. From his looks, though, he didn't seem to take much pleasure from work either.

Not much of a life, Al thought.

After a few minutes, Landrum told Al in almost a whisper that the captain was waiting for him and to head on back to his office.

Captain Hartford Ford was on the telephone, but he motioned for his old friend to come in and take a seat. They had known each other since their college days. That was almost forty years before.

The captain had attended Eastern Kentucky University, where he had been a criminal justice major and a star running back on the football team in the late 1970s.

Al and Ruby had driven to Richmond for an EKU game when they first met Hartford at a campus hangout after the game. They found out he was a native of Valdosta, Georgia. Legendary coach Ray Bibb had recruited him and several others from his area to play for the Colonels. At six foot two and without an ounce of fat on him, his body looked as if it had been sculpted from stone.

The unlikely pair—an Appalachian white man and a black man from the Deep South—hit it off immediately and had been close since. Al was glad Hartford had decided to stay in Kentucky after graduating from EKU. He had been in Harlan for almost five years, after spending several years at posts around the state.

Captain Ford hung up the phone and handed Al a Diet Coke he took from a small refrigerator under his desk. The sheriff sipped directly from the can.

"Anything from Interpol on the story the Sepp girl was telling me about her family's fishing business in Estonia?" Al asked.

"The FBI said Interpol confirmed most of the story. There was a fishing business in Tallinn. Apparently it was a very successful one, and the owners, a middle-aged man and his wife, went missing and were never found."

"What about the kids?"

"What the girl told you about them was also true. She and her brother won the sympathy of much of the population. The community and the kids themselves believed the police had either botched the case or been in cahoots with whoever killed their parents. The kids—well, just the girl now—might not get much if the fishery is sold. Interpol doesn't believe the uncle can be trusted. They thought it rather convenient he convinced Viktoria and her brother to come to America. Another twist that Interpol mentioned is also something we might need to consider."

"What's that?" Al asked.

"Apparently several young Estonians of Russian descent are coming to America, and many of them end up working for the Russian Mafia in the Northeast. Peddling heroin is a major revenue generator there. The FBI believes they're trying to expand their territory into rural areas like this. I guess the Mafia figures there won't be as many eyes on them out in the boondocks."

"That's interesting," Al said. "Aleksander had been seen with some known drug users. Gloria Strong didn't think much of it, since it's hard in this area not to have some friends who are on drugs. With this information, we'll look a little closer at that angle, though."

"What else have you and your folks found out, Al? Any leads?"

"Maybe. It's another drug connection. The two individuals who found the body are transplants from Ohio. They're cousins who were sent here because of problems back home in Dayton. They are staying with their grandfather north of Eolia. The old fellow said they have been nothing but trouble since their mothers—his daughters—sent them to live with him about two years ago."

"What kind of trouble you talking about?"

"Possession and distribution of OxyContin in Letcher County and recently stealing copper from a telephone transformer on top of Pine Mountain. The old man is fed up with them, but it's hard to tell if he has any influence with them or not."

"What are your thoughts about them?"

"Can't be sure of anything until I talk with them and give Sheriff Hawkins over in Letcher County a call. I would've known more if the officers up at the park had been more thorough when taking their statements. Jonah Wright was out of town, or we would've had more information about these two. It does seem unlikely they would have killed this boy and then announced to the world they'd found the body. I wouldn't want to bet they're not involved in some way, though. If they were desperate enough to risk their lives by stealing copper from a transformer, they must be pretty heavily into drugs."

"Keep me in the loop, Al," the captain said. "If there is anything else we can do to help, give me a call."

The sheriff nodded his agreement, thanked his friend for his time, and promised he would be back in touch. As he walked back to his cruiser, Al couldn't help but wonder if Aleksander Sepp had been part of a drug distribution network. With his ties to Estonia and the influence of the Russians there, it was something he would have to consider.

He got back into his car and waved to the faces glaring out the windows at Wendy's. Rather than taking a right to head to Cumberland, though, he took a left and drove about a half mile to the Harlan campus of Southeast Community College.

CHAPTER 8

Al figured if Jim Lucas had already arrived on campus, he probably would not have been there long. It was Lucas's habit to spend at least an hour in the morning catching up on administrative matters. Since a paper trail was required for almost every transaction, there was always a lot of work to do.

Al was right. When he checked in with the campus director in the administration building, he found Lucas seated in his office.

Al didn't know the campus director well, but he did know Keith Vicini was a former coal miner who had gone back to school after being laid off to earn a couple of graduate degrees. He had always thought it was a great move for the college's administration to put him in charge of this campus, which dealt almost exclusively with technical programs.

"I told Mr. Vicini we needed to talk with the instructor of the machine tool technology program, Al, and we were just about ready to walk over to his shop."

"Well, don't let me stop you. I'm not here to get in the way, but I had a few minutes after talking with Captain Ford, and I thought I'd stop by before heading to the boy's funeral."

As the three of them walked across campus to a modern brick building about 150 yards from Vicini's office, Al whispered to Jim what he had found out about a possible drug connection. The single-story structure they walked into housed most of the college's applied-technology programs.

They found Stephen Cornett, who had taught there for more than twenty years, in front of a modern, computer-driven tool and die machine. He was explaining to the students gathered around him how a computer program they had written earlier in the day and later programmed into the machine had turned out the shiny piece of threaded aluminum he now held in his hand.

Making eye contact with Cornett, Vicini motioned for him to meet the three of them in an office adjacent to the classroom. He introduced him to Sheriff Whitaker and Deputy Lucas. Cornett apparently knew why they were there. He immediately started talking about the homicide in Kingdom Come State Park. "I hated to hear about the kid being killed up in Cumberland," he said. "He was as sharp as a tack, and despite the obvious language problems, he picked up on stuff quickly. He appeared to have a good educational background. Knew a lot about computers. In fact he was one of our best programmers."

"What about his behavior? Anything out of the ordinary you noticed?" Jim asked.

"Nah. He was pretty much a typical teenager. Had you not known he wasn't local because of the way he spoke, you would have guessed he graduated from one of the high schools around here."

"What about attendance? Was he usually here and on time?" the sheriff asked.

"He missed some but nothing out of the ordinary. So many of my students work. I have come to expect an absence or two. A lot of them have to work to make ends meet. We take that into consideration."

"Was there ever a time when you thought he might have been under the influence of drugs? Ever smell marijuana, notice dilated pupils, or see any kind of unsteadiness?" Jim asked.

"Nothing at all. Deputy Lucas, the machines we use are expensive teaching tools—not toys. They demand your complete attention. Otherwise you can mess them up or maybe even mess yourself up. I keep close tabs on all my students and never saw anything out of the ordinary from Aleksander. And I do recognize substance abuse when I see it. We've dismissed students because of drug problems."

"We've dismissed more than a dozen students in the past couple of years because of problems with drugs," Vicini said.

The deputy turned to Sheriff Whitaker and asked if he had any questions. Al shook his head. Deputy Lucas thanked Vicini and Cornett for their time, and he and Al headed back to their cars.

"If Aleksander was into drugs, it was probably not as a consumer," Lucas said.

The sheriff knew he was right. Some of the most successful drug peddlers never used at all. To them it was a business, and if they were to be successful, they knew not to use the product. These people scared law enforcement most.

Double-dippers—those who sold and used—usually tripped themselves up and were not as difficult to apprehend. He put the Eolia cousins in this category.

While they might be easy to spot, however, the double-dippers often became so dependent on drugs they would do anything to get them. That included killing. He wondered if that might have been what happened in the death of Aleksander Sepp.

CHAPTER 9

Al parted company with Jim Lucas and headed to Cumberland for Aleksander Sepp's funeral. The drive up the familiar road was uneventful. Except the wind picked up and blew what little snow remained off the pine trees along the North Slope. With heavy snows like the one that had fallen yesterday, branches would often break off the trees and sometimes block the road, but this snow had not stayed around long enough to do that.

He had learned that Aleksander was Catholic, which surprised him. His research had shown that, unlike many other parts of Europe, Estonia was predominantly Lutheran, as were its Scandinavian neighbors.

However, Al knew one's family often dictated the church or denomination one belonged to, so somewhere in the past, Catholicism must have appealed to one of the boy's forebears. *Sort of like the way I became a Baptist*, he thought.

At one time in the early part of the twentieth century, Catholicism might have been the dominant religion in these parts. When the workers came to the area from Eastern Europe, they brought their religion, primarily Catholicism, with them. And there were thousands of them.

In addition to St. Mark's, the immigrants also founded the Church of the Ascension in Lynch, and a Catholic order operated one of the area's first hospitals in the same community. Growing up here, Al had as many Catholic friends as he did from Protestant faiths. He always found it funny that Eastern Kentucky was usually portrayed in the press as WASP— white, Anglo-Saxon, Protestant. In this part of the mountains it had been anything but that.

In addition to Catholics, thousands of workers had also come here from the Deep South. Almost all of them had been African American.

He understood stereotypes, though, and had seen them applied far too often to denigrate people and regions. As often as not, they were completely off base, but then the perpetrators were usually trying to hide their own shortcomings by pointing out supposed—often invented—shortcomings in others.

St. Mark's Catholic Church was located at 102 South Street in Cumberland. It butted up against a hillside. The brick building was constructed in the 1920s and several years after its sister church in Lynch, which had celebrated its one hundredth anniversary a couple of years before.

Al had to park almost a block away. The church's parking lot was small and could accommodate thirty cars at most. In looking at the cars on adjoining streets, he estimated there were seventy-five vehicles within a block or so of the sanctuary, and he figured almost all of them carried individuals who would be at the funeral. Quite a few of the tags were from outside the county, and at least two he saw were from out of state. One was from Ohio, and the other was from New Jersey.

Leaving his hat behind—attending a funeral was one of the few occasions when he would do so—he walked with several others to the church. Some pulled the collars up on their coats to ward off the chilling wind. The conversations were routine. How was the family? Were the kids doing OK? People were usually polite on occasions like this.

It's what happens between funerals that causes the problems, he thought.

The church was not exactly Spartan but less ornate than the Church of the Ascension, which contained beautiful statuary and murals. There was some of that here, but it paled in comparison.

The sheriff sat near the rear of the church, which was almost full. He estimated more than one hundred were present. Viktoria was in a front pew with several members of the Smith family. Many seemed to be consoling her. She wore a plain black dress with a blue shawl draped over her shoulders. Its color almost perfectly matched the blue of her eyes. Her blond hair was pulled back and affixed with a silver barrette. She looked older than he remembered. She was clearly grieving the loss of her brother.

Father Michael Ornutt, who had served the parish for almost twenty years, walked in front of the linen-covered coffin as it was wheeled to the front of the church.

"Eternal rest give to him, O Lord, and let perpetual light shine upon him," he chanted and looked straight ahead.

Al noticed the chanting seemed to cut through the sadness evident on the faces of many mourners. Perhaps it calmed them. That was not the case with Viktoria, though, who kept her head down and quietly sobbed.

The coffin holding Aleksander's body was centrally positioned in the church with his feet toward the altar, which Al knew would have been his relative position vis-à-vis the priest when attending Mass while alive.

A cycle of prayers led by Father Ornutt preceded the funeral Mass. Al knew enough about Catholic funerals to rise when others did, and if he knew the words of the prayers, he would recite them with the other parishioners.

Viktoria was the first member of the family to speak. She did so haltingly and in the same broken English Al had heard at his home. Sobs seemed to interrupt every other word.

"My brother, he was so happy in America," she said. "He could not understand how people here could be so different than in Estonia.

He go to school to learn a trade. Then he said he would be trying after the American dream."

Al assumed she meant "chasing" after the American dream, but her English was pretty impressive—especially under the circumstances.

Just as Al was allowing himself to slide down in the pew to get more comfortable, Viktoria's speech began to falter. He sat up straight and almost stiffened. Viktoria raised her head, placed her right hand palm up under her chin, and looked straight ahead for what seemed a long time, if only a second or two. Then she simply broke down, her legs literally gave way, and Marcus's wife, Trudy, had to assist her from the podium.

Now Al was almost certain his suspicions about Aleksander's hand having been staged were correct. What he did not know was who had done the staging and why.

Marcus came to the podium to thank everyone for the outpouring of support the family had received. He said welcoming Viktoria and Aleksander into his family had been an unexpected blessing.

"Their coming here was a complete surprise to my family, but they have blessed and enriched our lives in so many ways since they came. And now sadly Aleksander has been taken from us." He then looked down at the podium and shuffled some papers around. He seemingly wanted to say something else but was unable to do so. After the briefest of pauses, he quietly said, "We ask for your prayers for Viktoria and our family."

On the pew opposite the one in which he was seated, Al noticed two well-dressed men in their early to late twenties he had never seen before. They sat quietly except when responding to the priest's prayers. One was about five foot ten and well built. He had long, jet-black hair combed straight back. The other was bald. Like so many others with receding hairlines, it appeared he had chosen to shave off what little hair he had left. This left only the darkened outline. He too appeared just short of six feet, but unlike his partner he was overweight.

They might be driving one of the cars with out-of-state tags, he thought.

Apparently they were either Catholic or well acquainted with the church's ceremonies and rituals. There was no hesitancy on their part about what to do or not to do as the funeral progressed. Recalling what Captain Ford had said about the Russian Mafia, Al remembered from his study of religion in college that both Eastern and Russian Orthodox churches were liturgically similar to Catholicism.

He wished he had been close enough to them to determine how well they spoke English. He made a mental note to ask Marcus Smith if he knew them.

Like almost everyone else, Al waited outside as the coffin with Aleksander's body was carried to a hearse parked in front of the church. Viktoria followed Father Ornutt in the procession, and she in turn led the remainder of the Smith family.

She saw Al as she passed by and acknowledged him with a nod. She still looked as though grief had touched every fiber of her being. Al found himself feeling sorry for her.

She had now lost all her immediate family—mother, father, and brother. Even with the comfort of other relatives, it had to be difficult for her to deal with so much in such a short time. And it wasn't as if she had known her "new" relatives that long. If all that wasn't enough, she was also in a foreign land with foreign ways.

Al did not want to become maudlin. He couldn't afford to today or any day. He had to keep his mind clear and focused if he was going to get to the bottom of who had killed Viktoria's brother. He hoped once that was determined he would also know why his young life had been snuffed out.

While he felt sorry for Viktoria, he knew he had felt sorry for individuals before—individuals who turned out to have committed the very crimes for which they were expressing grief.

As he walked back to his car, Al made sure to memorize the letter and number sequence on the two out-of-state license plates. Once back in the car, he called Jim Lucas and asked him to run the license plates through the national database.

After checking in with Blanche and Sylvia to give them an update on where he was and what he was doing, Al headed home.

Maybe it was the sadness so much in evidence at the funeral that affected him, or maybe he was simply worn down psychologically. Whatever the reason he could feel a migraine coming on.

CHAPTER 10

The distance from St. Mark's to Kingdom Come Drive was not more than a mile and would have taken only a few minutes had he not had to wait for the funeral processional to clear out. By the time he pulled under his carport, it was around five thirty, and the migraine was almost in full bloom. That was the way they usually hit him—all at once.

Ruby was happy to have him home, but she scolded him for not letting her know ahead of time so supper could have been ready—or at least well on its way.

"I'm not very hungry," he said, and he smiled as he kissed her on the cheek. "That boy's funeral and the pitiful way his sister was acting have curbed my appetite, and on top of that, I'm suffering from a migraine. Don't you go preparing anything. I'm just going to stretch out on the couch and rest for a while."

Ruby smiled. It was an understanding smile—one she often used when her husband's usually upbeat nature appeared beaten down. She was sure most of his headaches were products of his cases, as he closely identified with victims of crime—or for that matter anybody who was seriously down on their luck.

Fortunately for Al it didn't happen every time sadness confronted him. Had that been the case, he probably would have had a continuous migraine.

Al appreciated that Ruby was adept at reading his moods and knowing what to do to cheer him up when he was down. That was one of the many things he loved about her.

She knew tonight was not a time for her cheering him up. She simply needed to be there for him.

CHAPTER 11

The call from the young photographer Al had met at the crime scene came early—around 6:15.

"Sorry to call so early, Sheriff," Josh Bledsoe said, "but I've been going through the photographs I took—I think for the third time—and I found something in a couple shots I thought you would want do know about." He didn't give Al a chance to say anything before continuing. "I took four or five shots of the area away from the immediate crime scene, and in two of them, I can see someone, although not distinctly, on the ridge right beside what appeared to be a mulberry bush. It looks like a small person, but I'm not sure of that, since whoever it was remained partially hidden. I probably wouldn't have noticed it at all, except the sun is reflecting off something the individual is wearing. Maybe a necklace or something. I told Detective Davidson about it, and he said I should call you as soon as possible. That's why I'm calling so early."

Al thanked him for calling and reassured him he had been up for some time. He asked Josh to take copies of the photographs to his office in Harlan and told him he would look at them later in the day.

While it might not have been anything important, this once again confirmed the importance of taking photographs at crime scenes. He was anxious to see them, but first he had an appointment to speak with the Letcher County sheriff at 8:30 a.m. at the Mountain Grill in Whitesburg.

CHAPTER 12

Al left home just past 7:30 a.m. after eating a breakfast of scrambled eggs, a biscuit, just a tad of gravy, and a helping of fried apples. He felt much better today. The migraine had eased off around 11:00 p.m., and he had been able to sleep for at least four or five hours.

His eating reassured Ruby. Eating well, at least in the mountains, was a clear signal all was well, and he was glad Ruby had been pleased.

Since the snow, the weather had warmed some, and there were few clouds in the sky. Even though the deciduous trees were bare, there were enough pines interspersed among them to render the view striking—especially when rays of sun cascaded through them.

Al took pleasure from nature. It wasn't just the beauty. It was the predictability and structure. It was the fact natural rhythms could be counted on. He worried global warming might alter the rhythms. Spring was already coming earlier, and plants that had thrived only in the South were now showing up here. By the time any significant changes occurred, though, he figured he wouldn't be around to see them.

The traffic was light until he got to the bottom of the Pine Mountain overpass, a five-mile section of US 119 that had recently been upgraded to include passing lanes. These had been sorely needed on what was one of the region's most treacherous stretches of highway.

This morning an accident just before the turnoff to Bad Branch Falls brought traffic to a halt long before the passing lanes would have made a difference. Two state police cruisers were parked alongside a masonry building that had recently been renovated for use as a community center and meeting place. Thinking the troopers might need his help, Al hit his siren and moved to the shoulder. He drove about one hundred yards before pulling in behind a cruiser.

He took his hat from the passenger seat and started toward the multicar pileup. He noticed almost immediately one of the wrecked vehicles appeared to be a solid black late-model coupe. He thought it strange that such a late model car had bald tires.

One of the two troopers investigating the accident was Jacob Bush, a young man Al had known for several years. He had graduated from the state police academy after returning from Afghanistan with his US Marine Corps unit. Al didn't know the second officer but assumed he also was assigned to the Hazard State Police Post.

Jacob Bush saw Al approaching and was the first to speak. "Hey, Sheriff. What are you doing up this way? Not enough to keep you busy in Harlan County?" He laughed.

"Plenty to keep me busy, Jacob. In fact I'm on my way to Whitesburg to talk with Sheriff Hawkins about the two young men who found the body down at the state park on Saturday."

"I heard from Post Ten you might be looking for Henson and Wright. You don't have to go to Whitesburg to talk with Sheriff Hawkins about them. I've got both handcuffed in the back of my cruiser."

"Bet they were in the black car," Al said, and the trooper nodded. "What happened?" Al asked.

"Henson, the driver, apparently couldn't wait another minute before he got to the passing lane. He tried to pass that Equinox on the curve. He almost made it but clipped the front end of the Wrangler, which was headed for Cumberland. It rolled twice. The occupants were two coal miners headed for work. Both were injured seriously.

In fact one appeared critical. It's a miracle they weren't killed. It's a good thing that Jeep was a hardtop with roll bars. That probably saved them, along with being secured by their seat belts.

"Henson and Wright's car actually sustained very little damage except to the right front bumper and quarter panel, which clipped the Jeep. They were both banged up, but the paramedics were able to take care of the few scratches they sustained and pronounced them good to go—to jail that is. They were both stoned. I don't know how they made it this far."

"You talk about Henson and Wright as if you know them," Al said.

"Know them?" the trooper exclaimed. "I'd say so. I've arrested them twice since they have been living with their grandfather. The last time was for stealing copper from the telephone exchange just up the road. They spent several days in the county jail for that caper, but nothing short of penitentiary time will do any good for these two—at least in my opinion."

Al knew Trooper Bush was joking when he'd said he could interrogate Henson and Wright in his cruiser, but he did want to stick his head in the car and say hello to the two of them. Jacob Bush gave his OK, and Al walked back to the lot in front of the community center where the cruiser was parked.

He noticed the second trooper standing alongside his cruiser. He raised his right hand to his hat in a friendly salute as Al passed. Al acknowledged the gesture with a salute of his own and moved toward Jacob Bush's cruiser.

Clayton Henson and Luke Wright were huddled together in the backseat. Their hands were cuffed securely behind them when Al opened the car door. They both looked at him—or in his direction. He wasn't sure whether or not they saw him. They were both clearly under the influence. Their injuries, as Trooper Bush had said, were superficial. Primarily they were scratches to their faces. A couple were bleeding slightly.

Al squatted down so he could see them face-to-face. "Which one of you is Luke, and which one is Clayton?"

"How you know who we are?" asked the taller of the two.

Al wasn't sure exactly how tall the boy was since he was seated, but estimated he stood close to six feet. He was painfully thin, as was his cousin, who appeared much shorter. It was obvious substance abuse was taking terrible tolls on their physical well-being.

Al identified himself and told them he had spent some time talking to their grandfather about them. "I wanted to talk with you two about the homicide victim at the Kingdom Come State Park," he said.

"We told the park police everything we knew. Didn't we, Clayton?" the short one volunteered.

Clayton, now identified by his cousin, began to laugh uncontrollably, but between gasps for air, he was able to concur. "Yeah. We told them everything we saw."

Al knew in their current states, neither individual would be able to provide any useful information. He simply wanted to make his presence known. At some point in the future, he would be talking to them—not their grandfather.

CHAPTER 13

Al left the cousins and said good-bye to Trooper Jacob Bush, who directed him and his Crown Victoria around the damaged vehicles.

He had called ahead to let Sheriff Hawkins know he would be late, and he also informed his office it probably would be around 2:00 p.m. before he got to Harlan.

He pulled into the parking lot of the Whitesburg Grill and parked in a vacant spot beside Sheriff Hawkins's police car. He saw Patrick Hawkins seated by himself at a table in the left rear corner of the grill. He was not far from the salad bar. Al knew that, while Hawkins was enjoying a breakfast of eggs and bacon, he would have been eating a salad had it been later in the day.

Pat sure likes his salads. Al laughed to himself. *That's probably why he always sits near the salad bar, and it explains how he keeps the pounds off his five-foot-eleven frame.*

He couldn't have weighed more than 175 pounds, which was not bad for a man who was almost sixty. Between bites Hawkins motioned for Al to have a seat.

"I'm a little surprised you're not having salad for breakfast, Pat." Al laughed.

"You know darn well I never hit the salad bar before ten," Hawkins replied, and he also laughed. "Now, what happened up on the mountain?"

"You're not going to believe it, but the two individuals I'm over here to talk with you about triggered a three-car accident at the bottom of the mountain near the community center."

By the time he filled the sheriff in on all the specifics about the accident, Al had started on his second cup of coffee. "These two were completely out of it, Pat. I'm not surprised, based on what I've learned about them. But at eight in the morning?"

Pat Hawkins shook his head and raised his eyes to the ceiling as if asking for help from on high. "I know Henson and Wright well, and it doesn't surprise me. The sad thing is there are a lot of others just like them."

Al nodded in agreement and recounted what he had learned about the cousins. He looked to Sheriff Hawkins to determine what he had on the two.

"You've got everything we've been able to charge them with, but there were three or four other thefts we suspected them of being involved in, but we didn't have enough evidence to charge them. This accident on the mountain might be the thing that finally gets them. Too bad two workers had to be injured to bring it about."

"Do you think they could have killed that kid in the park?"

"You know what addiction does to people, Al. Even good people. Maybe these boys were good kids at one time. Probably were. It would have been a long, long time ago, though. Could they have killed someone? It's certainly possible."

Al knew Pat Hawkins was right. He knew that from personal experience. Pat's youngest son, Ron, had gotten into OxyContin while still in high school and battled addiction for almost four years before finally getting clean. It had put a terrible strain on his family. It almost led to divorce as both parents tried to help their son, but neither knew exactly what to do. Al remembered several times when he had received late-night calls from Pat asking him to look out for Ron.

"I'm not asking for any special treatment," he would say. "I'm just worried about where that boy is and what he might be doing."

His voice had often broken with worry for his son. Al had found Ron only once. It had been about three years into his addiction. Just a few years prior, the seventeen-year-old had been a solidly built athlete. He had stood six feet tall and weighed 180 pounds. However, he had wasted away to no more than 150 pounds.

His clothes had barely hung to his terribly thin body as he walked up and down the sidewalk outside an Alcoholics Anonymous meeting in downtown Harlan. Al knew addicts often came to AA meetings and hoped they might find people to sell them drugs.

Rather than arresting the boy, Al had immediately taken him to the Harlan Appalachian Regional Hospital for detox. He had called Pat, and he and his wife, Cathie, had been there within the hour.

The changes Ron had undergone were akin to those taking place in many others he knew. The need to acquire some addictive substance had turned their once-normal lives upside down. Unfortunately it was not just their lives that were affected but the lives of their families as well.

"Yeah, Pat," Al finally said. "I agree with you. They could have done it, but what I can't figure out is why they would report finding the body if they had killed the kid."

"When they sober up, come on back over here and talk to them," Sheriff Hawkins said. "Maybe you can get something from them that will shed some light on this."

CHAPTER 14

Later that day, in the administrative court of the third district in Tallinn, Estonia, a lawyer representing Gunnar Sepp, the brother of Hendrik and uncle of Viktoria and Aleksander, presented the judge with a stack of paperwork concerning the disposition of certain properties tied directly to the Sepp Fishery in Tallinn. As the clerk took possession of the documents and marked them as exhibits, the lawyer began addressing the court. "Your Honor, may it please the court, we come today to ask for final and irrevocable assignment of the Sepp Fishery, which has operated for the past five and a quarter years under a receivership granted to my client, the brother of one Hendrik Sepp, who, together with his wife, Elizabet, were the former owners of said fishery.

"We are reintroducing an affidavit, Your Honor, from the Tallinn constabulary that verifies Hendrik and Elizabet Sepp went missing some five and a half years ago. Further it verifies the said Sepps have not been heard from since, despite herculean efforts on the part of the constabulary and other civil authorities. Thus they are now presumed dead. This court made that presumption final on July thirteenth of this year."

The judge was a bald man who peered down from the bench over black-rimmed glasses that kept sliding down his nose. He appeared nonchalant. With a circular hand motion, he indicated for the lawyer to continue while at the same time admonishing him to move things along quickly. "We have several other cases to dispense with today,

Mr. Chernikova, and as you are aware, the court was privy to all the documents to which you refer when giving your client general operational authority for the receivership in January 2008. My concern is whether you have the additional information previously requested. Information that would allow the court to make its decision about final disposition."

"Yes, Your Honor. We have authenticated statements from fiduciary experts appointed by the court that speak to the value of the fishery and associated properties. Moreover we are submitting a copy of the death certificate for Aleksander Sepp, son of the deceased owners of the fishery, authenticated by officials in the State of Kentucky in the United States."

"Mr. Chernikova, I recall when your client was given general operating authority for the receivership, there were two children involved. Is that correct?"

"Yes, Your Honor. You are correct. Today we are submitting as Exhibit B a notarized statement from the second child, Viktoria, relinquishing her rights as the sole heir to said properties to the benefit of her uncle, my client, Mr. Gunnar Sepp, for a certain sum that will go into a trust established on her behalf where she now resides in America. Further her cousin, Marcus Smith, is to administer the trust, per the daughter's specific request, until she reaches the age of twenty-one."

Just before the judge brought down his gavel to conclude the hearing, a small, dark-haired man dressed in a light gray suit turned and quickly exited the courtroom. On the street he took a cell phone from his pocket and dialed the Interpol office in Copenhagen. "He gave him the fishery. My full report will follow," he said and then disappeared into the crowd.

CHAPTER 15

On his way from the meeting with Sheriff Hawkins, Al called Jim Lucas and Gloria Strong to ask if they would meet with him for lunch at Carlotta's in Cumberland. He had decided to work in the Benham area the rest of the day rather than returning to the office in Harlan. He also wanted to fill them in on what he had learned and see if they had found out anything else.

Carlotta's was a popular eatery in the area. Owner Russ Blankenship's grandfather had established it over fifty years before and named it for his grandmother, Carlotta Antonino. The food was good, the helpings were large, and the atmosphere was friendly. While the menu now leaned toward American cuisine, its spaghetti and meatballs was a staple that hearkened back to its Italian heritage.

The three arrived within ten minutes of each other, and just a little after noon, they were seated in their usual back booth. The sheriff and his deputies were regulars there, and Russ Blankenship knew official business might be discussed, so he always seated them away from the rest of the customers.

Al began by filling in Jim and Gloria on the funeral. He focused on Viktoria's apparent grief for the loss of her brother. "I know all of us have seen mourners who were simply putting on acts, but if that was the case with Viktoria, she was awfully good at it," Al said, and then he described her continuous crying and near collapse at the funeral.

He decided not to say anything about the way she had placed her hand under her chin—at least not now.

"If she was involved," Gloria commented, "her behavior, beginning with her coming to your home the day of the killing, has certainly not been typical."

"What did you find out when you traced the license plates, Jim?" Al asked.

"The Ohio tag belonged to a Victor Smith, and I assume that individual was in some way related to Marcus and his family, but the New Jersey tag was registered to the Star Mortgage Company in New Jersey. I called Post Ten and asked them to see if they could find out anything about the company."

"When did they say they'd get back to you?" Al asked.

"They think they can have something by Monday at the latest."

"That will give me time to check with Marcus to see if he knows anything about the two strangers. I'll bet they came in that car," Al said. "Gloria, why don't you and I go on up to the Smiths' tomorrow? I'll ask Sylvia to see if she can set something up for us. We need to talk to Viktoria too. I believe she was honestly grieving, but there are still some things that bother me. Especially after getting a call from Josh Bledsoe—that new photographer who took shots at the crime scene."

"What did he have to say?" Gloria asked between bites of chicken salad.

"He called early this morning to say he and Detective Davidson had seen what appeared to be someone—a small person—standing on the ridge beside a mulberry bush. Bledsoe also thinks he saw something shiny around the person's neck. If it was a person," Al said.

"What kind of shiny something?" Jim asked.

"He has no idea. Just something the sun reflected off of," Al said. "It might not have been anything."

"If it's someone wearing something shiny around the neck, wouldn't it most likely be a woman? Maybe Viktoria?" Gloria asked.

"That was my first thought too," Al said. "Especially since, on the two occasions I've seen her, Viktoria has had a necklace on, including yesterday at the funeral. But let's not jump to any conclusions. If it was a person, it just as easily could have been a boy or a small man. Luke Wright can't be more than five seven or five eight, and both he and his cousin Clayton wear shiny chains around their necks too."

"What have you found out about those two?" Gloria asked.

"They were responsible for a three-car wreck at the bottom of Pine Mountain this morning. They tried to pass a vehicle before getting to the first passing lane and clipped the front of a Jeep with two miners headed for work. One of them is in critical condition at the hospital in Whitesburg."

"I'll bet they were under the influence," Jim said.

"You're right. I got to speak to them after they had been apprehended, and they were clearly high."

"Where are they now?" Jim asked.

"Jacob Bush with the state police said they would be taken to a holding cell at the Letcher County Detention Center. Pat Hawkins told me they would probably be transported later today to the detox center in Prestonsburg, though."

"You and I can head over that way next week, Jim. It'll probably take three or four days for them to dry out."

"We don't know anything more about the men who were hurt in the accident?" Gloria asked.

"Not a thing," Al replied. "I've told you everything I know. Now, what else have you found out?"

"I've continued to check on Viktoria in and around Benham and at the high school," Gloria said. "Haven't found anything that would suggest she is anything but a typical teenager. Her teachers at the high school say she is bright, engaging, and well liked by everyone." Gloria pulled a small notepad from the pocket of her uniform and scrutinized it carefully. "Her teachers like her, and so do her classmates. One interesting point. Mr. Edwards, her political science teacher, said she already knew more about how the government works in America than most of his other students. He said he was definitely surprised she knew so much but not that the others knew so little. Viktoria runs with a couple girls about her age. I've talked with both of them extensively, and they say she is a super kid, and they've never had a better friend."

"What else have you found out, Jim? Anything that might help us?" Al asked.

Like Gloria had done before him, Jim Lucas plucked a small notepad from his shirt pocket before responding. "We got lucky. Our friends at the crime lab in Frankfort got right on this case. They recently hired several new people to clear out a backlog. Looks as if they finished up quicker than they thought they would and were able to get to several new cases, including this one," Jim said. "But they're having trouble identifying the round that killed Aleksander. It appears to be a nine-millimeter slug, but they aren't sure. Although it flattened some when penetrating the kid's rib cage, they say it looks as if the tip—at least the area where they think the tip would have been—might have been black."

"Are they working with the feds' ballistic people?" Gloria asked.

"They're supposed to turn the slug over to the FBI. They'll probably send it to the forensic center at Quantico. We should know something soon if that's where they send it. Obviously there was no question about the cause of death," Jim continued. "The pathology report said there was no other evidence of trauma except for the gunshot, which did extensive damage to several of the kid's organs. As we might expect, he was in great shape otherwise."

"We've got a lot of work left to do, but tomorrow let's get into the office and look at some other things. Maybe a short hiatus will help us see things a little clearer in this case," Sheriff Whitaker said.

Both Jim and Gloria agreed. They added that it would give them an opportunity to catch up on some paperwork.

"But you know, Al, if not front and center in our minds, this case won't be far off," Gloria said.

Al Whitaker smiled in acknowledgment before laying down a generous tip for the server. Both deputies did likewise. Tipping was something the sheriff took seriously. When he and Ruby were in college, his wife had worked at a local pancake house, and a lot of their income had come from the tips she received. On more than one occasion, he had told his employees that story to encourage them to be generous.

As the three friends walked out together, Al reminded his deputies that he and Sylvia Turner would be working at the local food bank in Harlan the following morning.

CHAPTER 16

The Harlan food bank, called the House of the Good Samaritan, provided food for more than 250 individuals each week, many of whom had been steeped in poverty for some time. Others were just down on their luck because of layoffs in the coal mines.

When Al Whitaker was elected sheriff almost nine years before, there had been many things about the administration he was replacing he didn't like. Giving all employees an opportunity to work at a food bank once a month was not one of them. In fact he thought it should be mandatory for law enforcement employees.

"It gives them a chance to see how the other half lives," he often said.

He knew Harlan County and much of Eastern Kentucky had long suffered from a boom-and-bust economy. The region was almost totally dependent on the mining of coal for job creation, and when the mines were going full bore, jobs were plentiful. When the demand for coal lessened, though, mines laid off employees and sometimes closed down, and that led to long unemployment lines.

As Al and Sylvia walked into the gymnasium of a long-closed high school where the food bank was housed, they carried their coffee with them in a thermos Sylvia had filled before leaving home in Lynch.

Once inside they joined half a dozen other volunteers who bagged and boxed forty to fifty food items ranging from spaghetti to potatoes to a variety of meats. Donations from local merchants and churches along with purchases from regional food distributions centers determined what was offered.

In the office Sylvia talked almost continuously, but at the food bank, she was unusually quiet. Every now and then, though, especially when kids came in with their parents, she would open up. "You going to school, honey?" she would ask the child. "Now, you look to me as if you smart as can be. You stay in school, and I know you'll do good."

Sometimes when Al looked closely, he could tell she had been crying.

"Lordy, Lordy," she would say to family and friends back home or to her coworkers in the office. "You all can't believe how bad off some of these poor people be. I feel so sorry for them that sometimes my heart almost breaks."

The sheriff didn't say much either, but when he did he expressed sentiments similar to those of Sylvia. Many of the people he worked with in law enforcement knew very little about the true face of poverty. What little knowledge they did have often came from the poor people they apprehended.

He could tell from the looks of many of the people who came to the House of the Good Samaritan that they had had run-ins with the law. Some shied away from him. He could see the fear in their faces. It was palatable, it was real, and he felt bad about it.

That was one reason he and Sylvia wore their uniforms. He wanted the people who came there to see a different side of people in uniform—smiling faces, encouraging words, and people who could see the good in them. Al knew not everyone who came to the food bank went away feeling more positive about law enforcement officials, but he hoped some of them did. That made it all worthwhile.

A line began forming outside the door around 8:15 a.m., and by the time the workers started giving out the food, more than a dozen had gathered. One of the first to come in was a paper-thin elderly woman with cottony white hair pulled back into a bun.

Her eyes were restless and darted from one person to another. After signing the registry, she received a box and two large plastic bags filled with food. Offering to help her, Al grabbed the two bags.

"Why, I be a-thankin' you," she said so quietly it was hard for anyone other than Al to hear her.

"You are welcome, ma'am," Al replied.

The two of them walked outside, and she pointed to a Chevrolet pickup that looked at least twenty years old. She asked him to put the box of foodstuff in the back.

There was little room in the bed of the truck. Several pumpkins and six or eight used tires took up most of the space. It was obvious, however, enough space had been cleared for the food. Al placed the bags in the truck along with the box of food the woman was carrying, and he moved some of the tires around so everything would be secure. He could see a man in the front seat who looked as old as or older than the woman he was helping.

"My old man got busted up a-loggin' and now can't do much of anything except work with his wood."

Al nodded and started back to the building when he heard a child crying. He stopped and looked into the cab of the truck. A baby sat in a car seat beside the old man.

"Who's that?" Al asked.

"My grandgirl's youngin," she said. "She be in jail up thar at Evarts a-waitin' to go to LaGrange fer three years."

The sheriff knew she was referring to the Roederer Correctional Complex in LaGrange, Kentucky, but almost everyone in these parts simply called it LaGrange. It was one of the oldest and largest penitentiaries in the state, and it seemed a lot of Eastern Kentucky residents ended up there.

Al was reluctant to ask what the "grandgirl"—her granddaughter he assumed—had done. The child couldn't have been more than ten or twelve months old.

The old man raised his head, focused his cloudy, hollow eyes on the vicinity of the sheriff, and said, "We told her, the old woman and me, hit was a-goin' to happen a-messin' around with that outlaw up thar at Evarts."

He then dropped his head and didn't say another word, but his wife continued. "Maude, she got caught a-stealin' three times. Her and that no-good she was a-runnin' with, this baby's pa. They was a-stealin' hot-water heaters and copper from churches. Got away with it twice, but I figure the good Lord done took offense to what they was a-doin' and put a stop to it."

Knowing the baby would not be able to eat much of what had been given to the family, Al asked whether they had formula and baby food for the child.

"Nah. We be a-givin' her some milk, and I mash up vegetables and fruit fer her. We feed her a lot of mashed taters. She's a good young one. Don't cry much a-tall."

Al asked the woman to wait while he went back inside to inform the team leader, Rolene Sturgeon. "We got some baby formula and two or three different kinds of baby food, which we give to families when we know they have little ones," Al said.

Rolene and Sylvia put together a box of formula and baby food for the child, and the two of them joined Al as he took it back to the truck.

"We've got you enough formula and food to feed the child for a month or so, Mrs. Stuart," Rolene said, "and you be sure when you come back next month to remind us you have a child."

"Why we be a-thankin' you, ma'am. I reckon you a-helpin' us is the Lord's way of a-takin' up for this here youngin regardless of what its ma and pa done," Mrs. Stuart replied.

"We be a-thankin' you," her husband said quietly, but he didn't raise his head.

Al saw this more and more these days—grandparents raising their grandchildren because the parents were in jail or dead.

In this case it was grandparents raising a great-grandchild. Al wondered what had happened to Maude's parents. He decided not to ask.

However, the Stuarts intrigued Al for another reason. The quaint way they spoke reminded him of native Appalachian speech from the turn of the twentieth century. Many of the people living in the area at that time were descended from Scotch and Irish settlers who had arrived in the late 1700s and throughout the 1800s.

Al had studied these early settlers as well as their children and grandchildren during his time as a cultural anthropology major at the University of Kentucky. Some of these pioneering families had recently become famous with the release of books and even a television miniseries on the Hatfields and McCoys from nearby Pike County.

He made a note to call Dr. Thelma Mattingly, his adviser and thesis director at the university, to tell her about the Stuarts. She was always interested in finding and chronicling evidence of the continuous use of these speech patterns.

As a recently appointed assistant professor and a newly coined PhD, Dr. Mattingly was just a few years older than Al when she had taught him in the early 1970s. She treated him with respect, unlike some of his other instructors who were fond of denigrating the culture of Eastern Kentucky, and Al had immediately taken a liking to her. The two of them had been good friends ever since.

He seized every opportunity to keep her abreast of anything that might reflect positively on the culture. He hoped she could use these examples to buttress her arguments against what she called "the Blue Bloods of the Bluegrass," who thought anyone or anything outside of Central Kentucky was somehow inferior.

Ruby, a little jealous of the professor before getting to know her, had become fast friends with Thelma. Soon Thelma was no stranger to the Whitaker home in Cumberland. Al would be sure to call Dr. Mattingly about the Stuarts.

The remainder of the morning at the House of the Good Samaritan was routine. The individuals who showed up were pretty much evenly divided between those who had been coming for some time and others who were new. Some were the families of miners whose unemployment compensation had run out. Most of them, the old and the new, didn't want to take handouts, but when their families didn't have enough to eat, some of them swallowed their pride and asked for help.

Al and Sylvia went out of their way to be friendly to everyone who came in the door. While many receiving food expected this type of acceptance from most of the volunteers, it was obvious respectful law enforcement officials surprised some.

This scenario reminded Al of a sermon the Reverend Johnson had delivered at his church one Sunday. He had used a poignant example from the Book of James in the New Testament to make his point. The apostle James had asked what good it was to have faith without works. Did it do any good, he had asked, to simply tell a brother or sister who was naked and in need of food that you wished them well and would pray for them? Al knew talk was cheap. Many folks were like those James had called out in his epistle.

Many are almost ready to elevate a lot of people to sainthood, he thought at the time, *until looking at them closely. It's then evident the only individuals they are helping are themselves.*

Al and Sylvia left the House of the Good Samaritan just before noon and headed to lunch at Gene's Sandwich Shoppe in downtown Harlan before returning to their offices in the courthouse. Gene's was a popular spot for county officials, and several were already crowded into the restaurant when the two of them arrived. Pleasantries were exchanged as they waited for a front table that was being cleared.

Al relished the opportunity to have some time to talk with Sylvia. Their paths had crossed many times since growing up in the adjoining communities of Lynch and Benham. Both were extremely proud of their hometowns and vividly remembered when both communities had top-notch schools that were fierce competitors in athletics. Now both communities were much smaller than when Al and Sylvia were young, and the schools they had attended had closed years before.

However, local residents still told stories about the athletic prowess exhibited by the Bulldogs and Tigers in their day, and that was exactly what Al and Sylvia did when they got together on occasions such as this. Each would accuse the other of having a selective memory when it came to his or her stories, and there was no denying some exaggeration was often involved.

Al knew this was the way memories worked. The good got better, while the bad was downplayed. At times such as this, there was nothing wrong with that.

On and on it went. They could have continued their trip down memory lane for hours—if Deputy Jim Lucas hadn't interrupted them.

CHAPTER 17

Jim told Al that Hartford Ford had called and said he needed to meet with him about the Kingdom Come case. As he and Jim headed out the door, Al told Sylvia to call Gloria and ask her to join them at Post Ten. Sylvia reminded Al he and Gloria were supposed to be at the Smith residence in Benham between 4:00 and 4:30 p.m. and wanted to know if she should call and postpone.

"I think we can make it up there by that time, unless the state police have an awful lot of information to share with us," Al said.

"Now, if you find out you can't make it, don't wait until fifteen minutes before you be due up at the Smiths to let me know, Sheriff."

Al nodded his understanding. Sylvia was right, and nothing else needed to be said. He had worked with her long enough to know she always got the last word.

The sheriff and Jim Lucas rode together down the bypass. Traffic was light, and they were pulling into the Post Ten parking lot within a few minutes of leaving their offices. Gloria Strong pulled in at about the same time.

"You know anything more than what Sylvia told me on the phone?" she asked as she got out of the cruiser.

"Not a thing," Al replied. "We've been speculating some, but you know how that goes. One guess is as good as another."

Once inside they saw Detective Davidson talking with three other troopers. Al knew the state police post had several other cases they were working on. He figured Davidson's conversation with these officers was likely about something other than the Kingdom Come case. It was a minute or two before Davidson acknowledged the sheriff and his deputies. He left the table and walked to them with an outstretched hand.

"You know all these folks?" he asked.

Al, Gloria, and Jim acknowledged they knew everyone present except one young female officer.

"Now, who is this young lady, Frank? We haven't had the pleasure of meeting her," Al said.

Davidson introduced Trooper Yvette Weatherspoon. He explained she was a recent graduate of the state police academy and had just been assigned to the Harlan post.

Based on her tall, slim build, Al figured she was around five foot ten.

You can see confidence oozing from this young woman, he thought.

"Ms. Weatherspoon, I'm Sheriff Al Whitaker, and my two deputies are Jim Lucas and Gloria Strong. We're glad to have you in Harlan County."

"Happy to be here, Sheriff."

"She comes from a long line of lawmen from down in West Kentucky, and now there's a law woman in that line." Davidson laughed. "I know one thing. We're glad to have her."

Al had seen officers of the law come and go over the years, but he had to admit those coming into the region now were probably better prepared than he and most of his friends had been when they first pinned on their badges.

Captain Ford was waiting for them when Al and his deputies walked into his office and took their seats. Frank Davidson stood and leaned against the paneled wall.

"We heard from the FBI again this morning. Interpol reported the fishing business owned by the Sepps has officially changed hands. An administrative judge in Estonia took the fishery out of receivership and sold it—they believe at about fifty percent of its value—to Viktoria's uncle. And get this. A release supposedly signed by Viktoria and a notarized copy of Aleksander's death certificate determined the judge's ability to take this action."

A pin drop could have been heard as the sheriff, his deputies, and Detective Davidson stared at the post commander.

"Any other bombshells to drop on us?" Al finally asked, and he shook his head from side to side.

"One more. Marcus Smith will administer a trust setup on Viktoria's behalf until she reaches the age of twenty-one."

"And Viktoria signed off on this?" Gloria asked.

"That's what is being reported. What's really got me puzzled is the death certificate. We called the pathologist who did the autopsy in Frankfort, and he said it had not been released yet. This case keeps getting weirder and weirder," the post commander said.

"You and your folks find out anything else, Al?" he asked.

Al filled in Ford and Davidson on the accident involving the cousins from Eolia and told them Luke and Clayton were now drying out in a drug rehabilitation center before being returned to confinement in Letcher County. He also described the two strangers present at Aleksander's funeral.

Davidson told the captain about Josh Bledsoe discovering something or someone in a picture taken at the crime scene. He said he had asked him to notify Sheriff Whitaker, and Al nodded that the young man had done so.

"Hartford, we'll be back in touch with you and Frank as soon as we find out anything else. This latest information just adds to several leads we've got to check on now."

"Keep us in the loop, Al," Captain Ford said, "and we'll do the same."

The sheriff gave a nod as he and his deputies left Post Ten and headed to their cruisers.

CHAPTER 18

Al and Gloria were in the sheriff's Crown Victoria and headed to Benham to talk with Viktoria within minutes of leaving Post Ten.

"Gloria, things seem to be breaking a little too quickly in Estonia. It sure looks as if Viktoria and Aleksander's uncle had everything ready to take over that fishery on a moment's notice, and Aleksander's death looks both convenient and timely," Al said.

"Especially if the kid was opposed to the sale of the fishery," she said. "And what was Viktoria's role in all this? Or Marcus Smith's, for that matter?"

When they crossed the bridge on Route 160 that separated Cumberland from Benham, Al noticed a funeral procession snaking out of the parking lot at Mianchi's Mortuary. As was customary he pulled the cruiser to the shoulder of the road to show his respect for the deceased. He didn't know who had died. He had been so busy with this case he hadn't been paying much attention to the obituaries in the local papers. It probably wasn't anyone he knew well, or he was sure Ruby would have told him.

As the last of the vehicles in the funeral procession passed him and Gloria, Al eased back out into traffic. Several other vehicles had pulled off the road, so he took his time. As they passed the mortuary, the community of Benham began to take shape. The International Harvester Company, which used coal to fire steel mills in Gary, Indiana, founded Benham in the early 1900s. Benham contained very few houses that had not been constructed in the early years. Most were two-story wooden structures that had been privately owned since the company allowed the miners to purchase them in the early 1960s.

Aluminum siding covered several of the houses, and many had metal roofs. All of them without exception were well kept. Benham was a beautiful mountain village—one that defied the stereotypes about coal camps in Appalachia.

Al turned right on Pine Street and began the climb up a steep hill to the Smith residence. He was glad the day was warm and clear, since the street could be slippery when covered with rain or snow.

He pulled into the Smiths' driveway, and he and Gloria got out of the car and walked the fifteen yards to the front porch of the brick facade. It was one of only a few in Benham. When he rang the doorbell, Marcus's mother answered.

Beulah Smith was a large woman and not just in size. The matriarch of the Smith clan wielded considerable influence in Eastern Kentucky political circles. Some argued her influence was every bit as impressive as her five-foot-five, 190-pound frame. Al was awfully glad she had been on his side during the past election.

"Glad to see you, Sheriff," Beulah said in a bellowing voice. It reminded Al of the sound from a muffled megaphone. "The family appreciates you being at the funeral for Aleksander. Now, I know it was somewhat business on your part, but we appreciate it just the same."

Al liked that Beulah said what she thought. Some might try to sugarcoat things, but there was no pretense in this woman.

"The girl is waiting for you in there," Beulah said, and she pointed to the dining room. "Why don't you and your deputy go on in? There's some coffee already made, and you're welcome to it."

Al had expected to also talk with Marcus Smith, but he smiled and nodded his thanks. He decided he would ask about him at an appropriate time.

Beulah Smith had pretty much ignored Gloria, even though Beulah had known the deputy for several years. Gloria and Al found Viktoria seated at large oak table with eight matching chairs. Viktoria stood and extended her hand to the sheriff. Al took her hand. While maintaining the clasp, he introduced Gloria. The young woman smiled as told Gloria haltingly she was glad to meet her.

Although he was still inclined to believe Viktoria had no hand in her brother's death, Al began what he knew was an important interrogation.

"Viktoria, I know you have been through a lot in the last few days, but there are some developments in your brother's case that have us confused. Are you aware the courts in Tallinn have ruled your father and mother's fishery can be sold to your uncle?"

The blood drained from Viktoria's face. "How can that be? Uncle Gunnar always told us, my brother and I, this cannot happen without our approving. And he said we, Aleksander and I, must be paid. They say some special fund, a trust, I believe, would be set up for my brother and me. But only when we are older. Aleksander and I agree Uncle Gunnar will run business for us, and we sign documents to approve this."

"We understand the fishery was placed into a receivership with your uncle Gunnar in control at the time your parents went missing. Is that when you signed documents?"

"Yes. We sign documents after our parents disappeared, and our uncle also signs with us since he says we are minors," she whispered.

"And you haven't signed anything since? Is that right?" Al asked.

"No. We only sign one time."

"Did your uncle say anything about you and Aleksander giving or selling him the fishery at any time?"

"He say before we leave Estonia that the business is bad. It needs more money to operate. He asks if we would sell fishery. I trust my uncle Gunnar, but I do not know what to do. Aleksander wants to go to America, but he says we should not sell. He tells Uncle Gunnar he will not sign to sell business. That if he is forced, he will stay in Estonia to operate the fishery. Uncle Gunnar, he just laughs at Aleksander and asks how can he, a boy, operate a business? But he tells us we should go to America. That he will not sell the fishery."

"You didn't mention this to me when we spoke earlier, Viktoria," Al said. "Is there a reason why?"

"It did not seem important to me. I do not see how it causes anything to change."

"Viktoria, did Aleksander ever talk with you about what might be happening to the fishery under your uncle Gunnar's direction after you arrived in Benham?" Gloria asked. She smiled as she looked at the teenager, who had begun to appear frightened.

"Aleksander never says much to me about fishery, but I hear as he speaks to Marcus about it. Sometimes they shout."

"What were they shouting about, Viktoria?" Gloria continued.

"The fishery and Uncle Gunnar. How he operates the business. I hear Marcus say the business, it is going bankrupt, but Aleksander, he does not agree."

"Did either Marcus or Aleksander ever discuss this with you?" Al asked.

"No," Viktoria replied, and then she dropped her head and began to sob.

Al was not sure what to believe. It could be Viktoria was in this thing up to her beautiful blue eyes, which were now overflowing. If so she was a consummate actor. However, there was one thing he did believe. Marcus Smith was involved a whole lot more with the fishery than he had let on. He wanted to talk with him—and soon.

There was another matter he needed to clear up with Viktoria before he sought out the Mineral Mountain Resources mine foreman. Al decided this called for a direct approach. "Viktoria, were you in the park when your brother was killed? The photographs taken around the crime scene show someone about your size standing on a ridge above where you brother lay." He paused and looked her directly in the eyes. "Was that you?"

Viktoria lowered her head while continuing to sob. For what seemed like an eternity, she didn't say a word. Al asked a second time if she had been in the park. Finally she raised her head, wiped her eyes with the sleeve of her blouse, and spoke calmly. "I see my brother after he has been shot. I go to him and kiss him."

Al and Gloria looked at each other. Their past experience with interviews told them they should remain quiet and let Viktoria talk.

"I hear Aleksander say he will go to the park to meet with some men. I worry because I see him around people before who I believe sell drugs. I ask my friend to drive to the park. I walk from the lake to the big tree. I know to go to the big tree because Aleksander and I, we come here before. It is a favorite place. I walk up the path and hear *bang, bang*. I know it is shooting. When I get to the tree, I see a car driving away very fast. A big, dark car. I also see someone on the ground on the road below. I pray it is not Aleksander, but my heart, it tells me it is my brother. I run to the spot where I see the body. I pray every step I take. But it is. It is my brother who is dead before me. He does not breathe. His eyes, they stare at me. I close his eyes and kiss my brother. Then I run to the hill above the tree. I sit there, and I cry."

Al and Gloria remained quiet and still. Viktoria continued. "I see then another car. This time a small car. Also black. It comes in the opposite direction from the big black car. Two men, one small and one large, they get out and look at my brother and then all around him. It is as if they search for something. But then they run back to the car and drive away very fast."

Al noticed Viktoria now seemed almost serene. It was as though a terrible weight had been lifted off her shoulders. He still had questions for her—especially about how Aleksander's right hand had ended up under his chin, but he and Gloria had gotten important information, so he decided to wait until later to tie up all the loose ends.

As they prepared to leave, Al asked Gloria to stay with Viktoria while he spoke with Beulah Smith. He was pretty sure Beulah was not mixed up in the death of Aleksander, but after listening to Viktoria, he was not so sure her son, Marcus, was not.

He found her sitting in a large leather chair in the living room where she looked to be dozing. Al cleared his throat to awaken and alert the old woman. She looked up at him and appeared not the least bit concerned she had been found sleeping. She asked how the talk with Viktoria had gone. Al told her Viktoria had been very helpful, and he was beginning to narrow down the list of suspects.

"I'm glad you are making progress, Sheriff. There was no reason for anyone to kill that boy. He was just a kid. Had his whole life in front of him. I liked him from the start. Though, he was a bit sassy." She laughed and said, "Or maybe that was what I liked most about him."

"I didn't know him, Beulah, but I agree with you. He was just a kid and didn't deserve to die—whatever the reason he was killed. Beulah, we had hoped to talk with Marcus while we were here. Do you know where he is? He told Sylvia Turner he would be here."

"He left here in kind of a hurry this morning, Sheriff. Something about a problem up at the coal tipple. You know, as a foreman he's always on call. I'm sure he wouldn't have stood you up if he didn't have a good reason." Al nodded, and Beulah continued. "Why do you need to talk with Marcus, Sheriff?"

"We're trying to run down another lead. You tell Marcus to give me a call, either at the office or at home, and I'll set up another time to speak with him on Monday."

Al and Gloria left the Smith residence after spending a little more than an hour there.

"There was a definite change that came over Viktoria after she told us about being in the park," Gloria said once in the cruiser. "I don't know if she is entirely at peace with what happened. In fact I'm sure she's not, but telling us about being in the park seemed to take a lot off her mind."

"There are still a couple things she needs to help us understand, but I think we got most of what we need from her—provided she is being truthful. And, Gloria, I'm like you. I believe she is telling the truth."

The sheriff dropped off Deputy Strong at the Cumberland Police Department on Main Street. Cumberland Chief of Police Jason Hightower, who was headed to Harlan on an official call, told Al he would give Gloria a ride to her office. It would save Al a round-trip to the county seat, and he was happy for that.

CHAPTER 19

When he walked in the front door of his Cumberland home, Al could immediately detect an absence of cooking aroma, which didn't surprise him. He had seen Thelma Mattingly's SUV parked in the driveway and figured Ruby might have skipped cooking supper in favor of reminiscing with her friend.

After talking with her late yesterday, he had been sure Dr. Mattingly would come over at some point to further discuss the Stuarts, but her being here this quickly meant she must have been very interested in his report.

"Al, I know you are surprised to see me so soon," the petite redhead said, and she jumped up to kiss him on the cheek. "But I was so excited by what you told me about the Stuarts. I couldn't wait. I talked one of my graduate assistants into doing today's lectures at the university, and here I am. I did call Ruby when I left Lexington to let her know I was coming."

"Thelma wants me to go with her tomorrow to visit this family, Al, and we were thinking you might want to come along too, since you've already met them," Ruby said with a pleading expression.

"I'd love to go with you tomorrow. I told Gloria Strong after we finished talking with some folks up in Benham a few minutes ago that I would be taking the weekend off," Al said.

"Based on your description of their speech patterns, do you know who the Stuarts remind me of? And just a hint, it was from one of your required readings during your senior year at UK."

Al had picked up on the similarities the minute he heard the Stuarts talking. It was the characters in James Still's novel *River of Earth*. It probably helped he had read the novel a couple times since his college days—not just in appreciation of the quaint way the characters spoke, but because Still had woven one of the saddest, most poignant stories he had ever read.

Writing with an insight born of firsthand knowledge, Still told about the efforts of a poor mountain family steeped in the ways of their Scotch-Irish ancestors to adjust to a changing world at the turn of the twentieth century. The introduction of coal mining into what to that point had been an agrarian society accentuated the change.

"Why don't we get up around six, cook us a good breakfast, and try to get under way no later than eight?" Ruby volunteered.

Once the agenda for the next day had been set, Ruby and Thelma took off to get some takeout for supper, and Al took out his three-ring binder and meticulously wrote down a summary of what had been a very eventful day.

In addition to his log of events, he started making a notation that Marcus Smith would be questioned on Monday, but something told him it should be done sooner. Maybe it was Viktoria saying Marcus and Aleksander had frequently argued about the fishery. Al suspected a connection, coming as it did after learning from Interpol that Marcus had been appointed to administer a trust setup for his niece. Maybe it was that Marcus had been less than forthcoming on the three occasions he had spoken with him since Aleksander's death.

Like he wants to tell us something but just can't bring himself to do it, Al thought.

He called Jim Lucas to ask him about setting up a meeting with the mine supervisor on Saturday. "Sorry about asking you to work tomorrow, Jim, after promising the weekend off, but the more I think about it, the more I think we need to speak with Marcus."

Al explained why he and Gloria hadn't gotten a chance to question him yesterday and said some answers were needed about why and how he had gotten appointed as administrator of a trust for Viktoria.

"Especially," Al continued, "after Viktoria told us Marcus and Aleksander frequently argued about the financial status of the fishery." He asked Jim to call Gloria to get her reading of the interview with Viktoria earlier in the day. "Maybe she can add something to what I've told you."

Jim told Al he would call Gloria immediately and that he would be at the Mineral Mountain Resources to question Marcus early the next morning.

CHAPTER 20

Al, Ruby, and Thelma left Cumberland right on schedule on Saturday morning. They stayed on US 119 until it intersected with KY 38 in Harlan. It led them near the Kentucky-Virginia border. Al had found out that the Stuarts lived up a mountain path about three miles from the state line.

Thelma had packed recording devices, cameras, and notebooks, which she referred to as the tools of her trade, into a 2008 Buick Rendezvous.

The traffic was light on this unseasonably warm day. Thelma and Ruby sang along with the oldies on a '70s station. Al thumbed through his three-ring binder in the backseat and reviewed everything he had written in his journal since first being called about the Kingdom Come homicide a week before.

When the station started playing hits from the Eagles, though, it didn't take long for Al to sing along with Ruby and Thelma to "Peaceful Easy Feeling" and "Hotel California." Before he knew it, they were on the Harlan bypass and preparing to turn left to head toward Evarts.

Like the other "major" highways in Harlan County, Route 38 was a two-lane, heavily traveled road. Several miles had been rebuilt in recent years with paved shoulders, but most of the road was in poor condition—especially between Evarts and the Virginia state line, where they were headed.

Once the trio had had its fill of music from their youth, Al began filling in Thelma and Ruby on the Stuarts. He had already told them about the baby the old couple was caring for while their granddaughter awaited transport to LaGrange. What he had not told them was that the Stuarts had been coming to the House of the Good Samaritan for several years—long before the sheriff's office started volunteering there.

"Up until two years ago, Mr. Stuart was able to get around fairly well. He was injured in a logging accident back in 2003 and has gradually gone downhill. Now he can barely get around."

"How old is he, Al?" Ruby asked.

"According to records at the food bank, both the Stuarts are in their mideighties. Mrs. Stuart is apparently a year or so older than her husband."

"If they have been in this region most of their lives, how have they held on to the speech patterns they use?" Thelma asked as much to herself as to Al and Ruby.

Both shook their heads in question. As they approached Evarts, the mountains seemed higher and the valleys narrower than they were in Harlan. Like other communities in the region, Evarts had tried to reinvent itself once coal mining went into decline. In recent years it had become a mecca for all-terrain vehicles and attracted visitors from several states to explore the hundreds of off-road trails in and around the area. Yet it still remained a shadow of what it had been during the boom years of the mid-twentieth century.

As Al and Ruby pointed out community landmarks, Thelma asked dozens of rapid-fire questions, many of which they could not answer. She appeared most curious about early settlement patterns in the region in the late 1800s and early 1900s. That was before a flood of newcomers was attracted to coal mining.

"I know the Scotch-Irish families who were original settlers to this area came largely from the Eastern Seaboard, and some of them struck out right after arriving here from their home countries. What is intriguing," Thelma continued, "is how pockets of the original settlers remained isolated and kept newcomers from corrupting their language."

"I take it you are thinking the Stuarts are representative of the early settlers, and you are wondering how they have been able to keep talking like their ancestors," Al asked.

"You're right. The Stuarts' way of speaking would not have been that unusual fifty years ago, but to find them now is nothing less than extraordinary."

"I guess we won't have to wait too long until we get some of the answers. Maybe not all the answers but enough to help you unravel this mystery, Thelma." Ruby laughed. "I know the suspense must be about to kill you."

About ten miles out of Evarts, the evidence of surface mining high on the ridges appeared. The multinational company mining in this area took responsibility when it came to reclamation, and where it had stripped away the earth to reach the coal deposits, there was now acre upon acre of grass growing. It was reasoned that trees and shrubs native to the area would gradually spread over time, and in fifty or so years, it would be impossible to tell where the mining had taken place. Unfortunately, Al had seen several instances where this theory never became a reality, and ugly scars were all that remained.

Going farther up the hollow, they were nearing the Virginia border when Al noticed a gravel road that led to the right. Although there were no markings, the road was about where he had been told to turn to get to the Stuarts.

Thelma admitted she wasn't used to traveling off-road. She slowed the Rendezvous to a crawl and clutched the steering wheel tightly as she made the turn onto the roadway. After about a half mile, the gravel ran out, and the dirt road began to run alongside a small stream that meandered down the hillside. The valley was even narrower than they had experienced when traveling on KY 38, and the mountains seemed to rise straight up from the landscape. From time to time, the road would cross the creek, and Al cautioned Thelma to put the SUV in low gear before fording the stream.

"The water doesn't look deep enough to worry about, but some of the rocks might be slick. It's best to take it slow and easy," he said.

Not taking her eyes off the road, Thelma merely nodded that she understood. All the while Ruby was nervously looking back at Al. Apparently she sought some assurance that everything was OK.

As the vehicle exited the creek for the last time, they started climbing toward a small clearing about an acre or so in size with a log cabin sitting behind a rock face that jutted out of the mountain on the right. Al reasoned the cabin had been positioned here to protect it from the cold winter winds that would come roaring down the valley from the north.

The pickup truck the Stuarts had driven to the House of the Good Samaritan was parked under a shed attached to the cabin, and Thelma pulled the Rendezvous in behind it.

As had been agreed, Al got out of the vehicle by himself to approach the house. Since he had met the Stuarts, Thelma and Ruby felt his going alone to explain why they were there was preferable to walking up with two strangers alongside him. As he knocked on the sturdy oak door, Al could hear a baby crying inside and someone singing, perhaps to quiet the child.

It was two or three minutes before Sarah Stuart opened the door. She wiped her hands on a checkered apron as she spoke. "Well, I'll be," she said, and she looked Sheriff Whitaker over thoroughly as if she wasn't really sure it was him. "I sure didn't reckon on a-seein' you up our holler. Is thar somethin' the matter?"

"No, ma'am. Not a thing," Al replied. "I'm here with my wife, Ruby, and a friend of ours who studies the way people in our region speak, the speech patterns they use, and how long they have been using them."

"Well, don't that beat everything? We ain't had nobody like that up here in nigh on a year or two, I guess it's been. Used to come here pretty regular. 'Bout four times, but nary a one has been here fer a while," Sarah Stuart said.

Al was pleasantly surprised to hear what Mrs. Stuart had said. Apparently they were not the first to notice that the family's use of the language hearkened back well over a hundred years. The old woman instructed him "to get the women folk" and come in. Al did as she requested, and he, Ruby, and Thelma gathered up the recording devices and walked into a spacious living room with an open fireplace located along the south wall.

The baby had stopped crying, but someone continued singing a beautiful lullaby.

"The birds sing a glutting song. They sing to thee the whole day long. Wee fairies dance o'er hill and dale, for very love of thee."

When it became obvious the three visitors, especially Thelma Mattingly, were curious about the singer, Sarah Stuart smiled and said, "That be my girl, Roady. She be a-singin' to the little one day and night."

When Roady, a quaint pronouncement of the name "Rhoda," stepped into the living room, she continued singing with the child clutched closely to her breast. Several things were immediately obvious. Roady appeared to be around fifty, suffered from Down syndrome, and could sing like an angel. She continued until she had finished all four verses of the lullaby, and then she dropped her head in a greeting to the three strangers. Their presence didn't seem the least bit intimidating to her, but she didn't speak a word.

"Roady don't talk none except in her singin'," Sarah Stuart said. "She been a-singin' ever since she was four or five years old. Knows 'bout every song she's done ever heard."

Al noticed Mr. Stuart was not present and asked about him.

"Lonzo be behind the house in the outbuilding. Sits out there 'bout all the time a-workin' with his wood, I reckon," Mrs. Stuart replied. "He'd done worked all his life a-carvin' out bowls and figures and a-makin' furniture. Ain't nigh as fast as he was afore he got busted up a-loggin'."

Pointing to the table, chairs, and several beautiful carvings, Sarah told her guests Alonzo had made most everything they saw in her living room. Al could tell she was proud of her husband's work and rightly so.

After inviting Thelma, Ruby, and Al to sit down, Sarah Stuart insisted on serving coffee. It was strong and black the way Al liked it, but he noticed neither his wife nor former teacher seemed to enjoy it. They sipped politely.

Thelma began to explain once again why she was there, what she did at the university, and how important it was for her to be able to find out more about the Stuarts and the way they spoke the English language.

All the while, Mrs. Stuart nodded that she understood. Finally she said, "We done had some school people up here before a-studyin' the songs we be a-singin'. They done got Roady on a record, which they played to us. Couldn't believe it was my girl a-singin'. Made me and Lonzo and Maude—that be my grandgirl who's in jail—mighty proud."

When Thelma inquired about who had done the recording, Sarah took a Bible off a shelf and pulled a piece of paper from it. She handed it to Thelma. "This here is what we done signed."

It was a contract granting East Tennessee State University's Appalachian studies program the right to copy sheet music in the Stuarts' possession as well as record Roady's singing of several songs.

She knew ETSU was among the nation's best at collecting and preserving folk music, but she was curious why they would have made four trips to this mountain cabin.

Roady sat quietly while her mother explained the family's experience with the university, and then she got up and walked out of the room. After a minute or so, she returned clutching several pieces of what appeared to be sheet music.

She smiled and sat down on the sofa beside Ruby. Ruby had not said a word as she slowly sipped her strong coffee. Roady motioned for Ruby to take the music. Al figured Roady had found a soul mate in his wife, probably because of Ruby's apparent reticence. If only she knew how atypical this behavior was for her. He laughed to himself.

Al could see Dr. Mattingly was astounded. Collecting English folk songs was not her specialty, but he could tell she recognized a treasure trove when she saw one.

Ruby, whose grandmother had sometimes sung these old songs to her when she was a child, began to pull out one page after another and read the names at the top of each page: "Pretty Saro," "Wayfaring Strangers," "The Nightingale, Arise! Arise!," "The Two Sisters," "Jack Went A-Sailing," "Black Is the Colour," "Soldier," "Won't You Marry Me?," "Pretty Polly," and several others. She stopped when she got to "Barbara Allen."

"I heard my grandmother sing this song so many times!"

By the time Ruby and Thelma were finished, they had counted more than seventy pieces of sheet music. Some were duplicates, but Thelma said she had never seen a collection as complete as this.

Al recalled that in Thelma's classes, students studied some of the earliest collectors of Appalachian ballads. That included Kentucky-born John Jacob Niles. According to textbooks, he was among the best known. He also remembered reading about British folklorists—he had forgotten their names—who toured the Appalachian region in the latter years of World War I.

The pieces of sheet music the Stuarts had were not copies. Most dated back to the 1700s and 1800s. Mrs. Stuart said the original settlers had brought the collection here.

"I now understand why East Tennessee State University has been here four times," Thelma said.

As fantastic as this collection was, it alone did not explain why the Stuarts talked the way they did. *It might have been influential,* Al thought. He could see some similarities between the lyrics and the Stuarts' vocabulary. However, Sarah Stuart's account of her family's life on the mountain made everything much clearer.

Using the expressions and dialect that had drawn Thelma Mattingly to her home, Sarah Stuart detailed her family's immigration almost one hundred years before. At the time there were four other families living up the hollow. All of them were involved in timbering and woodworking.

They were from Scotland, she explained, and had traveled here from Charleston, South Carolina, their port of entry. They purchased wagons to carry the few belongings they had brought with them there. Oxen pulled their wagons, but the wagons required frequent repairs as they came up through the Carolinas and Tennessee before making their way through Big Stone Gap in Virginia and finally to Harlan County, Kentucky.

These first settlers worked from dawn to dusk, according to Mrs. Stuart, and their only means of entertainment was singing the songs they had grown up with—the songs they had brought with them.

The only musical instruments they were able to bring with them were dulcimers, an ancient stringed instrument mentioned in the Bible. The settlers became adept at constructing dulcimers, and they were still being built today, she said. She pointed to an hourglass-shaped dulcimer that hung over the fireplace.

Mrs. Stuart recounted coming to this hollow as a young child with her mother, father, and two brothers. They came to cut and process timber with their neighbors. She recalled very few passable roads that came this far in the mountains.

"I married when I were a young girl, a-givin' up my family name of Donaldson fer Lonzo's name of Stuart. We all stayed up this here holler, a-livin' air lives and a-raisin' air families. And a-singin' these here songs," she added and pointed to the sheet music. "They were air entertainment."

By this time it had become evident to Al why the Stuarts spoke the way they did, and he was sure it was clear to Thelma and Ruby too. They lived in a remote, isolated region cut off from the coal mines operating throughout the region and more important from the influence that miners from outside the region were bringing to the mountains.

The Stuarts were the last of the original five families. The other four—the McDonalds, Grahams, Shaws, and Donaldsons—had left years ago. Mrs. Stuart said the demise of this isolated mountain settlement began when the families started sending their children to a school about halfway between their settlement and Evarts.

"Once the youngins learned 'bout the mines and the money they could be a-makin' away from here, most of 'em just up and left when they come of age," she said. "That were what happened to Maude's ma and pa—my boy, Frank, and his wife. They just up and left. Said they was a-goin' to find work and would come back fer Maude. But they never did. Left her fer me and Lonzo and I guess Roady to raise. Airs was a hard life," she continued and recounted how they had grown or raised practically everything they ate. "My ma and pa would be a-workin' from daylight till dark. Us youngins too just as soon as we growed up enough. We canned from air garden and orchard and cured meat from hogs in air smokehouse. We got water from air spring and milk from air cows."

"What did you do for clothing?" Ruby asked.

"We bartered quilts that our women be a-makin' and bowls and baskets the men be a-makin'. Took 'em to the dry goods store in Evarts and traded 'em fer britches fer the boys and calico to make dresses fer the girls. We got wool from air sheep and spun it into shawls and sweaters. We managed to get by, but many be the time when my pa would say we was 'bout pushed to the limit."

The most difficult time, she said, was when sickness befell a family member.

"We used a lot of home remedies fer colds, the fever, cuts, and bruises. It were the diseases—whooping cough, measles, and diphtheria, them kind—that took their toll. My ma lost two youngins afore they was five years old to whooping cough. My little sisters, may God be a-holdin' 'em in his hands."

Sometimes, she recalled, doctors on horseback would make the trip from Evarts, but that hardly ever happened in the winter when the snows were deep and the creeks frozen over.

"We always be a-prayin' that if'n we were a-goin' to git sick, hit would be anytime but the winter."

When Mrs. Stuart finished recounting about her and her neighbors' pasts up this hollow, it was lunchtime, and she insisted Ruby, Thelma, and Al stay for dinner. In the mountains the three meals were not breakfast, lunch, and dinner but breakfast, dinner, and supper.

Al felt a little guilty about eating the vegetable soup and corn bread knowing the Stuarts were clients at the House of the Good Samaritan, but he also knew refusing the meal would have been a sign of disrespect. However, he ate sparingly, and he noticed Ruby and Thelma did likewise.

After the meal Thelma went into her official mode. She had Sarah and Alonzo, whom they had called in from his workshop, sign a release that looked a lot like the one they had signed for ETSU. It gave the University of Kentucky the right to use the information that had been gleaned today and might be gleaned in later visits for scholarly purposes only. Moreover, so long as Dr. Mattingly continued to work with the Stuarts, they would be paid the sum of three hundred dollars per month.

Thelma had told Al and Ruby after leaving Cumberland that should their visit prove fruitful, such an agreement with the Stuarts would be executed. She had made this decision based in part on Al's account of what a difficult time the Stuarts were experiencing. She explained on the return trip that she had been even more intent on doing so after seeing the Stuarts in person.

It was almost 3:00 p.m. by the time the Rendezvous pulled into the Whitaker driveway. The wind had turned much colder, and it was howling down the valley when Al unlocked the door and stepped back to allow Ruby and Thelma to enter before him.

He hoped the cold was all Thelma would face on her trip back to Lexington in the morning. Since cell service was spotty at best on their trip to Evarts and the Virginia state line, Al had waited until he got home to return a rather cryptic message from Jim Lucas. "Al, call me when you get home. We can't find Marcus Smith."

CHAPTER 21

Thelma Mattingly left early on Sunday morning. She wanted to be on I-75 before the NASCAR fans who had attended the Saturday-night race in Bristol, Tennessee, would be headed north in their huge RVs, many of which seemed to travel in a convoy.

After seeing her off, Al and Ruby went to Carlotta's for breakfast. This gave them an opportunity to talk with many of their friends before heading to the 11:00 a.m. service at the Trinity Baptist Church.

They had long been members of the church. In fact their memberships had exceeded the tenure of five pastors. Once running over with worshippers, churches in the area had suffered huge drops in attendance as employment in the mining industry continued to decline, and family after family left to find work.

Their church was no exception. In a sanctuary built to accommodate a congregation of four hundred, only a little over one hundred were present on most Sundays. It wasn't because the Reverend Maynard Johnson didn't work at attracting people to the church. There just weren't that many people to go around.

Al and Ruby took the same seats in the same pew they had occupied for over thirty years. They nodded and greeted others who had likewise seated themselves in seats they had long claimed as their own.

The Reverend Johnson was a humble man and one of the most accommodating individuals when he wasn't preaching. Once he got behind the pulpit, though, he considered himself a messenger of God—a responsibility he took with utmost seriousness.

Johnson was seminary trained with multiple degrees, but the country preachers under whom he sat as a child influenced his sermons more than his theology instruction.

Al knew and appreciated the importance of education, but education had taught him about the pervasive influence of culture and how that influence was especially strong in one's youth. It established constructs and patterns that often reemerged in adulthood.

Today's sermon was taken from Mark 8:36. "'And what do you benefit if you gain the whole world but lose your own soul?' We are confronted in the modern world," the preacher said, "with a focus on self, and this self-centeredness is usually manifested by our desire for things we believe to be bigger and better than those we have. We want a bigger house or a more luxurious car. We want the latest fashions. Most of all we want more money. Money, we believe, will buy all the other things we desire. But will money or the things it allows us to purchase bring happiness?"

Of course, the Reverend Johnson illustrated with several examples that the answer to this frequently asked question about money was an emphatic no. In Al's business, however, he confronted a number of individuals daily who apparently had never heard this message. They seemed to be seeking things that always remained just outside their grasps.

I don't think they ever get so far as to think about what happens to their souls, he thought. *Their interest is entirely on the here and now.*

Ruby spent the rest of the afternoon reading while Al watched NFL games on television. Calls to the kids and grandkids were something they always looked forward to on Sunday afternoons—especially now FaceTime was a feature on their iPhones and laptops.

All three kids lived out of state. Their daughter, Andrea, was an elementary school principal. She had strayed farther from home than her brothers. She lived in Michigan with her husband, Keith, and their two kids. Randolph, their youngest, was in Nashville. He was still unmarried and had been pursuing a career in country music for what Al felt was far too long. Their eldest was Chris, a lawyer, who had been in Atlanta for the past eight years. He and his wife, Sydney, also had two kids.

Al and Ruby had discussed the Reverend Johnson's sermon at some length after coming home following lunch.

"Ruby," Al said before their phone calls to the kids began, "we might not be rich in terms of material possessions, but I wouldn't trade my family for all the gold in the world."

As much as Al had enjoyed the day, Marcus Smith's whereabouts had never left his mind. He was thinking of him when he finally went to sleep.

CHAPTER 22

No sooner had Al walked into the office on Monday morning than Jim Lucas cornered him to talk about Marcus Smith's disappearance. The last they knew about him, Jim reported, was when he had left on Friday to go help work out a problem at the tipple, where the coal was loaded into the gondolas, or "gons" as they were known in the coal fields.

"Beulah and Trudy are worried now. Both said it is completely unlike him to be away without letting them know in advance, and they can't remember him ever doing that in the past."

After calling Gloria Strong into the office to join the conversation, the three principal investors of the Kingdom Come homicide case plotted the next steps in the investigation. They realized an individual who was now front and center in that investigation had gone missing.

"Gloria, give Post Ten a call and fill them in on what we found out when we talked with Viktoria on Friday. And let them know what little we know about Marcus's disappearance," Al said. "Jim and I will head back up to the mine in Benham to talk with company officials about what Marcus was doing on Friday. We'll try to determine if they know anything about his disappearance."

As they got ready to leave, Sylvia cornered her friend. "What on earth done happen to Marcus, Sheriff? You know this is not like him. Trudy and Beulah must be worried sick."

How she had found out so much about Marcus's disappearance Al wasn't certain. *Sometimes.* He laughed to himself. *I think Sylvia must have extrasensory perception.*

Al assured her he didn't know any more than she knew about Marcus's disappearance. Sylvia's raised eyebrows suggested she did not entirely believe him. He didn't have time, however, to reassure her he wasn't hiding anything.

Before leaving he took a few minutes to listen to Deputy Oscar Banks give an update on the cases he and the rest of the staff were working.

"Nothing major going on," Banks reported. "A couple burglaries, both of them up on Catron's Creek. A few domestic disputes. We also have another drug bust scheduled with the Harlan and Cumberland Police Departments on Thursday of this week."

"Thanks, Oscar. I appreciate the good job all of you are doing. Hopefully this case will be over before too long."

The sheriff and Jim then headed to the deputy's car for another trip up US 119. En route they went over everything they had learned about the death of Aleksander Sepp since his body had been found in the park.

The Interpol report from Estonia had introduced something that had been on Al's mind since Viktoria had come to his home the day her brother was killed—that being the role the fishery might have played in the homicide. It was looking more and more as if there was a connection.

When they arrived at the Mineral Mountain Resources headquarters, located in a two-story brick building in Benham that had once been a school, the superintendent, Jeff Lockhart, met them. He took them directly to a meeting room near the east end of the building. It didn't take Lockhart long to express his concern about the whereabouts of Marcus Smith. "Sheriff, Marcus is one of our best employees. He's worked here most of his adult life, and everyone likes and respects him."

"What exactly was he doing down at the tipple on Friday, Mr. Lockhart?" Al asked.

"We had a breakdown in one of the loaders that empties the crushed coal into the coal gons near the end of the shift on Thursday. Found out it was a broken gear and made plans to repair it on Friday."

"Was Marcus there the entire day?" Jim Lucas asked.

"Yeah. He oversaw the entire operation. He was supposed to be back on Saturday morning to test it out as we began to load the coal again. When he didn't show up, which was not like him, we called Trudy. We thought he was sick or something."

"Hadn't Trudy called you when he didn't come home after work on Friday?" Al asked.

"No, but that's not unusual. Sometimes when we have an equipment breakdown like we were dealing with here, especially something that affects our bottom line, Marcus would work sixteen to eighteen hours consecutively."

"Without calling home?" asked Al.

"Well, it's not more than a mile from Marcus's home to the tipple, so it's not as if he had left the country." Apparently realizing what he had said, Lockhart added, "Except in this case maybe he did."

Al nodded, picked up his hat, and started toward exit with Jim Lucas beside him. When he got to the door, he stopped and walked back to Superintendent Lockhart. "How much does Marcus Smith make in a good year?"

"In a good year, Marcus could easily take home one hundred ten to one hundred twenty thousand dollars. And, Sheriff, the last two or three years have been good ones."

It was only ten minutes before Al and Jim were pulling into Marcus Smith's driveway. Waiting for them on the porch were his wife, his mother, and Viktoria Sepp. All looked seriously worried.

Trudy explained they had called every place where they thought Marcus might have gone and reported him as a missing person to the Benham Police Department. Al and Jim sat down with the family members to review exactly what they remembered about the last time they had seen Marcus on Friday. Trudy recalled she had seen her husband before she left at 5:00 a.m. for her shift at the Harlan Appalachian Regional Hospital. She worked there as a nurse in the emergency room.

"He told me he anticipated a hard day ahead. A gear or something was broken in the apparatus that loads coal into the gons. He said he didn't know what time he might be home."

"I drove down to the tipple around lunchtime on Friday," Beulah volunteered, "just to see how things were going. Talked to one of the men helping Marcus, and he said they still had a lot of work to do."

"Is there any indication he took anything with him—clothes, personal hygiene items, or anything like that?" Jim asked.

"No. Nothing is missing. And if he came back to get anything, he would have had to slip in during the night, and Beulah's a light sleeper. I'm sure she would have heard him," Trudy said.

"So it's just Marcus and his vehicle that are missing?" Al asked.

There was no reply, but it was obvious the answer was yes. There was a lot more Al wanted to ask Trudy, but he didn't want to do it in front of her mother-in-law. It involved finances, and he didn't know whether she would want Beulah to know about personal things such as that. However, he expected that, with her influence and contacts, the old woman probably already knew.

He asked Jim to take Beulah down to the tipple to point out the individual she had spoken with on Friday since she could not recall his name. He knew Jim would understand what he was doing, but he also knew someone needed to talk to the people who had worked with Marcus on Friday.

After Jim and Beulah left, he sat down with Trudy at the kitchen table. Both of them held mugs of freshly brewed coffee.

He had known Trudy almost as long as he had known Marcus. She had grown up on Collier's Creek. It was just over the Letcher County line on the road to Whitesburg. She had helped put Marcus through a two-year mining technology program before going back to school herself to become a registered nurse. They had two boys. One had followed his father into the mines, and the other had taken up broadcasting and was now a meteorologist at a regional television station in Hazard.

To break the ice, Al asked about the boys. "How are Sean and Troy doing?"

"Right now both of them are worried about their daddy. You know how close they are to Marcus. Both of them are doing well with their jobs," she continued. "We worry some about Troy. There have been a lot of layoffs recently in mining. It's worrisome."

Al nodded. "Trudy, I hate to get so personal with you, but I need to know how you and Marcus were doing financially."

Appearing somewhat taken aback, Trudy was slow to answer. "Sheriff, I don't know what our personal finances have to do with Marcus's disappearance," she said.

"We think there might be a connection between his disappearance and Aleksander's death."

"But why? He cared for that boy. We had grown to think of him and Viktoria as our kids."

"Are you aware of any communication that might have taken place between Marcus and the kids' uncle in Estonia, Gunnar Sepp?"

"The only time I know of was before the kids came to stay with us. At that time Marcus talked with him several times on the phone."

"Nothing since then?"

"Not that I know of. I'm still confused about where this is going."

"Late last week in a court proceeding in Estonia, a judge ruled the fishery owned by Viktoria and Aleksander's parents would be sold to their uncle Gunnar. We haven't seen a copy of the written order yet, so we aren't exactly sure what all is involved, but we do know a few things. One, a copy of Aleksander's death certificate was presented in court. We know it can't be real since the medical examiner has not released a certificate yet. Two, a release purportedly signed by Viktoria allowing Gunnar Sepp to take control of the fishery was introduced into evidence, and three, the court designated Marcus Smith to administer a trust setup for Viktoria, which she can tap into when she reaches twenty-one. Chances are a lot of money will be involved."

"What on earth? Marcus never mentioned any of this to me. What does Viktoria say about all this?" Trudy asked.

"She doesn't know anything about it," Al said, "and she also says she hasn't signed anything that would give her uncle control of the fishing business."

"And you think Marcus is involved? Is that where this is going?"

"It looks awfully suspicious. Viktoria also said Marcus and Aleksander argued about the fishery. Marcus apparently took the side of Gunnar Sepp."

"This is too much," Trudy said. "I don't know what to say. I don't know what to think."

"Let's get back to my question about personal finances," Al said.

"Marcus handled the finances," she said. "He paid the bills, did our investments, and made sure everything was OK at the bank. We usually took in between one hundred seventy and two hundred thousand dollars annually," she continued. "His income varied some at the mine, depending on bonuses and the like, but we were always in good shape financially."

"Did you see your bank statements regularly?"

"Yeah. We always maintained a balance in our checking account of five to six thousand dollars. Marcus never let it get above that. He took everything over that and invested in CDs and savings," Trudy said.

"Do you know how much you have invested in CDs and what your savings balance is?"

"No. The only thing I ever saw were the checking balances. Marcus picked up all our statements each month at the bank."

"The statements didn't come through the mail?"

"No. He said since he had to go right by the bank several times a week, it would be easier for him to pick them up. He took them to his office at the mine. That's where he paid the bills and took care of all our finances."

"You didn't find that strange?"

"Not at all. He's been doing that since we were married, and we've never had any problems," she said.

"So, to the best of your knowledge, you and Marcus were well-off financially. You maintained a balance of up to six thousand dollars in checking along with a savings account and money in CDs."

"Yes. That's right."

"But you don't know how much money you had in the savings account or in CDs?" Al asked.

"No. I don't, but Marcus said we were doing well. I had no reason not to believe him," Trudy said.

Al noticed the questions appeared to be causing doubt in Trudy's mind. She seemed less sure about their financial situation than when the questioning had started.

He asked about financial obligations the two of them had, and Trudy replied they were making payments on two vehicles—Marcus's 2011 Chevy Tahoe and her 2009 Buick Enclave. They also had a duplex at Cherokee Lake in Tennessee.

None of this seemed out of line for a couple with an income as high as theirs. Al knew from his observation of the family over the years they were not big spenders. They didn't seem inclined to make a show of their salaries—salaries that were much higher than what most folks made in Benham and the surrounding area.

He asked Trudy if there was any chance Marcus might have gone to their place on the lake. She indicated that was one of the first places she had called. Dennis Sellars, who ran the dock near their place, said he had not seen anyone at the house since Trudy and Marcus had been there several weeks ago.

Al assured Trudy he would do everything he could to help locate her husband.

Something was amiss in regard to the family's finances, and it wasn't just that Marcus controlled everything. Although, he was sure there was no way Ruby Whitaker would turn over all their finances to him, despite loving and trusting him. Marriage was about sharing, and it wasn't healthy to shroud parts of it in secrecy. *Unless*, he thought, *one of the partners has something to hide.*

He knew he didn't have nearly enough evidence to get a court order to open the Smiths' financial books at the bank—especially since Marcus had been missing for just over forty-eight hours. There was so much they still didn't know about the court proceedings in Estonia, so Al decided to ask Trudy if she would do her own checking and let him know what she found. She agreed to head to the bank in Cumberland later that day and relay her findings to Al. Once again she appeared nervous and uncertain.

Al called Jim once he had finished talking with Trudy. He told him he would walk down to the Kentucky Coal Museum and wait for him there. He liked going to the museum at this time of the year. They had begun to decorate for Christmas. Several organizations participated in the Christmas Around the World decorating contest, and they painstakingly prepared trees for judging, which would occur over Thanksgiving weekend.

When he arrived Trish Overton, curator, and Barbara Anthony, a volunteer who oversaw the annual Christmas tree competition, greeted him. He marveled at the work that had already been done and at the size of the trees. Many were at least ten feet in height.

"How many trees this year, Barbara?" Al asked.

"Don't know yet, Al. We think well over twenty, and by the way we are expecting another entry from the sheriff's office," she responded.

"I've got Sylvia in charge of that, and Ruby will be helping her. You can be sure we will be well represented."

Al was seated in one of the rocking chairs made available for guests when Jim walked in and sat down beside him.

"Find out anything, Jim?" he asked.

"I talked with three people who worked with Marcus to repair the loading apparatus, and they all said, as usual, Marcus worked hard. However, he seemed preoccupied with something. Didn't have any idea what it was, though."

After telling the museum workers they would be sure the sheriff's office had a first-rate entry in the Christmas tree competition and promising to be back for the grand unveiling of all the trees in late November, Al and Jim took their leave and headed down KY 160.

"In what way did they say Marcus was preoccupied?" Al asked.

"Marcus missed a couple things he normally would have been on top of such as not remembering which side the damaged gear mechanism was on. They said they had taken a similar part out on at least two occasions in the past six months." Looking at his notepad, Jim said, "One of them remarked, and these are his words, 'Marcus was off his game. His mind seemed to be somewhere else.' Beulah also seemed to take offense at some of the things the workers said. She said she had seen him that morning before he left the house, and other than being concerned about the long day in front of him, he was completely normal."

Immediately after getting to Harlan, Al and Jim drove directly to Post Ten to fill in Captain Ford on what they had learned. The Benham Police Department had notified all the local law enforcement agencies about Marcus Smith's disappearance, and Captain Lockhart said the state police had put out an all-points bulletin, what with there being a possible connection to a homicide.

The post commander also had news to share. "Quantico identified the round that killed Aleksander. It came from a nine-millimeter Makarov pistol—a model used by the Russian military until a few years ago. Thousands of them are still in use in Europe, and many of them have shown up in the United States, especially in the Northeast in Russian expatriate communities."

"That possible Mafia connection you've been talking about, Hartford, is beginning to look more and more plausible," Al said.

CHAPTER 23

Up bright and early on Tuesday, Al was in the office well before 8:00 a.m. He had a pot of coffee brewing by the time Sylvia and Blanche showed up for work.

"We're not used to having anybody make our morning coffee for us, but that don't mean we don't appreciate it," Sylvia said. "Ain't that right, Blanche?"

Blanche smiled and nodded. Al was certain the two of them would find the coffee stronger than what they were used to, but since he got to make it only once in a blue moon, he was going to make it the way he liked it.

It was almost 9:30 a.m. before the last of the deputies not on assignment reported to work. Al used this time to pore over the written reports filed on the other cases his office was investigating. His staff members did a solid job of recording the specifics of whatever case they were working on—something that had proven valuable when they were asked to testify in court proceedings.

At approximately 10:15 a.m., Al came out of his office and motioned for Jim and Gloria to join him.

"Nothing has been reported about the whereabouts of Marcus Smith. At least that was the case when I came in around seven thirty this morning," Al said. "I'm not convinced he isn't holed up somewhere near his place on Cherokee Lake. Jim, why don't you give the Hamblen County Sheriff's Department a call and ask those officers to do some snooping around down by the dock?" Al continued.

"They already know about the missing person's report, but they don't know some of the other things that are going on. Fill them in a little without sharing everything we got."

"Be kind of hard to hide a vehicle as big as a Tahoe, Al, so if he's in the area, don't you think the people at the boat dock would have seen him?" Jim asked.

"Maybe. Maybe not. Trudy said their duplex was within sight of the dock, but nothing says Marcus had to park there. He could have stashed his vehicle and either walked or caught a ride to their place."

"And we don't know if we can trust the guy at the boat dock. What was his name?" Gloria asked.

Al took the notepad from his shirt pocket and turned a few pages before responding. "Dennis Sellars. Jim, you might want to ask the sheriff's department about him too when you contact them. He could be in cahoots with Marcus."

By the time they went over what they had learned from Trudy Smith and the information Captain Ford had shared with them, their assignments had been set for the remainder of the day. Jim would work on trying to track down Marcus Smith through his contacts in Tennessee. Al and Gloria would be back in Benham talking with Marcus's family and coworkers.

"I've got a suspicion people up there know more than they're telling us," Al said.

Trudy and Beulah Smith were expecting them when they knocked on the door. Al could tell almost immediately something was amiss. His first thoughts were that Marcus had been found and was either hurt or dead. That wasn't the case, though. Trudy said they hadn't heard anything.

"We are all worried to death, Sheriff."

However, she had found out about their finances, and from the looks of things, she had been discussing her findings with Beulah.

"Marcus cashed out our last CD more than six months ago, and our savings account, which I know at one time had almost fifty thousand dollars, is down to two hundred dollars," she said.

"How much total is missing?"

"I'm not entirely sure, but at one time about a year and a half ago, he told me we had around one hundred seventy-five thousand dollars. I remember because he was concerned about the bank not paying enough interest to grow the accounts."

"You told me earlier you didn't know how much was in these accounts," Al said. He looked Trudy straight in the eyes as he spoke.

"Well, I remembered!" Trudy said curtly.

"All this questioning has confused me," she continued, dropping her head.

"Do you think he might have taken the money out to invest in something else? Stocks? Bonds?"

"I don't know. I just don't know," Trudy said. "He was always afraid of losing money with other investments."

"Sheriff, there was reason for Marcus's concern about the stock market," said Beulah. "His daddy lost a lot of our money in the market. Of course, I always thought it had more to do with him not knowing what he was doing than anything being wrong with the stock market. Marcus probably heard my husband say at least a hundred times that the stock market was not a safe place for your money."

"Trudy, was there any indication the funds were transferred to other banks or accounts?" Gloria asked.

"They told me at the bank he took it all out in cash," she responded.

After determining that all existing financial records were not at the house but in Marcus's office at the mine, Al asked if Trudy knew the password to his computers and the other information needed to access the financial records.

He was not surprised when her answer was no. However, she did give the sheriff permission to take Marcus's computer and all his paper records with him. Al thanked her but knew her permission wouldn't be enough. The computer was property of the mine company.

He also knew his office did not have the expertise to unlock the information stored on the computer. That was something specialists would need to do—specialists who worked for the Kentucky State Police.

When he and Gloria Strong walked into Superintendent Jeff Lockhart's office at Mineral Mountain Resources twenty minutes later, he asked for and received permission to take Marcus's computer to the state police in Frankfort. They would try to unravel some of the questions concerning his personal finances there.

Lockhart cautioned him, however, that any proprietary information related to his company's coal holdings should be held in confidence. Al assured him the police would do that. Al then called Hartford Ford to tell him what was going on and ask if he could send someone up to Mineral Mountain Resources to pick up the computer.

"We can do that, Al. Tell the superintendent we will have someone there by four o'clock this afternoon," Captain Ford said. "Tell him to secure the computer until we get there, and assure him we will protect any proprietary information we find."

Al asked the superintendent about other employees Marcus was close to.

"He was probably closest to the other members of our management team. Particularly his fellow foremen."

"How many are we talking about?"

"If you include all three shifts, the number would be around eighteen or twenty. I can get you a list of all of them if you want."

"I would appreciate that. He had to have been closer to some of them than others, though," Al said. Then he mentioned something

Trudy had said about their friends Vic and Joanne Hughes. "She said they spent some time together at the lake."

"Vic is one of our section foremen on the evening shift. I do recall they hung out together at our family get-togethers. He would be about Marcus's age."

Gloria got the Hughes family's home address from the personnel office, and when she and Al left the mine office, they headed to Leatherwood in a neighboring county. They hoped they would be able to catch Marcus's friend before he left for the mine portal to begin the evening shift.

KY Route 160 was narrow and curvy. It passed the entrance to Little Shepherd Trail and led to the back entrance of Kingdom Come State Park and Tornado Gap Quarry, which supplied the area with most of its crushed stone and gravel.

Traffic was light and the weather conditions ideal as they pulled up in front of the town of Dephia's last remaining gas station and asked where Vic Hughes lived.

"You need to travel on down the road for about a half mile before you come to a big red barn," the clerk behind the counter said. "Vic's home is the next one on the right. It's a white house with a two-car garage."

They found Hughes sitting at his kitchen table. He was a small, wiry man. He stood no more than five foot seven or eight and weighed 135–140 pounds. His wife, Joanna, answered the door. She was no taller than five feet and weighed less than a hundred pounds.

She offered Al and Gloria coffee, and both of them took her up on it as they sat at the table alongside her husband. They had already heard from Trudy that Marcus was missing, and both seemed concerned.

"We've been friends with them for twenty years or more. Our kids grew up together," Joanna said, and she shook her head.

"Do you have any leads, Sheriff?" Vic Hughes asked. "It's not like Marcus to just up and run off like this."

"That's why we're here. Trudy told me you were close. Said you vacationed at the lake a couple times together. We just thought you might be able to give us some idea about anything different going on with Marcus," Al said.

"I don't know whether this means anything or not, but Marcus started playing online poker several months ago. I know he won some initially. Said he could do a lot better risking a little by gambling—and he always said he wasn't risking much—than he could by leaving his money in the bank. He hadn't said anything to me about it recently. I just assumed he'd either given it up or was still risking a little. Sort of like some of us do when we play the lottery."

Gloria asked if he had noticed any difference in his work demeanor. "Did anything seem to be bothering him?"

"I don't know if there was anything I could put my finger on, but his attitude seemed to be changing. Marcus had always been what we called 'a company man.' He believed if you worked for a company, you owed that company your loyalty as well," Vic Hughes said. "Lately he had said some things that were out of character for him."

"What sort of things?" Gloria asked.

"That Mineral Mountain Resources was making all the money, and they didn't value or pay their employees like they should. All they ever looked at, he said, was their bottom line. In fact he and I got in an argument about a week ago about this. I told him Mineral Mountain was one of the best companies I had ever worked for. I said I didn't know what had come over him," Hughes said.

"How did he take your response?" Al asked.

"He just shrugged his shoulders and said I didn't know as much as I thought I did."

"What about performance? Was he the same worker he had been in the past, or was his performance slipping?" Gloria asked.

"It's hard to say. Like me, he's a supervisor. We don't do a lot of manual labor. The primary job is to oversee production, except when something breaks down and has to be repaired. Like the loading apparatus Marcus was working on. Usually our focus is on meeting our production quotas. The company has contracts that call for a certain amount of coal to be shipped out of here each day to power plants throughout the South. There was no indication in our weekly production meetings we weren't producing as much coal as we needed to."

"Could those production figures have been misrepresented?" Gloria asked.

"It's possible someone could have bribed our load-out crew to report higher figures for the tonnage they were running through the tipple and shipping to the power plants. Remember, though, the coal is also weighed upon receipt, and any weight differences would be reported to Mineral Mountain Resources. I think you're barking up the wrong tree with production. Chances are, even if Marcus slacked off some, his crew didn't. Most of his people liked him. I think, at least short-term, regardless of how he might have been acting, they would have worked hard for him."

"Do you have the names of his crew?" Al asked.

"Most of them. I'll make a list for you when I get to the mine and have someone take it to the mine office," he said.

Knowing it was almost time for Hughes to leave for work, Al thanked him and his wife for their help.

CHAPTER 24

By the time Al and Gloria got back to Tornado Gap Quarry on KY 160, they had received two calls from the office. The first was from Jim. He said he had not been able to find out anything about Marcus from his law enforcement officials in Tennessee. The second was from Sylvia to tell the sheriff she had received a call from Beulah Smith, who wanted to talk to him.

"The woman seemed highly excited, Al. I think she got something important on her mind."

He told Gloria it looked as though they would be working well into the evening. She immediately called her mother in Wallins to look after her kids until she got home.

What had started out as a clear, cool morning had changed into one that was overcast and downright cold. By the time they drove off the mountain into Cumberland, snow had begun to fall. The wind picked up and swirled the snowflakes back and forth and up and down. It looked at times as if they were suspended in the air—wanting to land but unable to do so.

When they headed up Pine Street in Benham, a thin coating of snow was already sticking to the blacktop. Al slowed down after making the turn off KY-160 and eased the transmission into low gear to climb up the hill to the Smiths' residence.

Despite the weather, Beulah Smith waited for them on the porch. She sat on the swing with her coat pulled tightly around her. She got up to greet Al and Gloria and wasted no time in getting the conversation started. "It's like Marcus just up and disappeared off the face of the Earth. It's not like him, and I got to thinking about what a good boy he had always been. Never getting in any trouble. He was always kind and respectful. I guess it was my thinking about him when he was growing up that reminded me of the cabin."

"What cabin?" Al asked.

"His daddy built a cabin for him and his brother, Brad, when they were teenagers. It was probably more for him than the boys, but he always said he was doing it for them."

Al wanted to hurry Beulah up, but he could sense a kind of sadness in the old woman. She had been transported into the past to a happier time. He let her move at her own pace.

"The cabin is up on Slope Holler, Sheriff, about halfway between Cumberland and Evarts. If I remember correctly, it's at least a mile or two off the main road. The boys and their daddy used to ride horses up to the cabin. They would head up Machine Shop Holler until they got to the top of Benham Spur and then stay on the ridgeline all the way to Slope Holler. Then they would head farther back into the mountains."

"You think Marcus might be at the cabin?" Gloria asked.

"I got to thinking about him when he was a teenager, and I remembered if he was troubled about something, Marcus would often head out for the cabin. He would ask me to prepare enough food for a day or so, and off he would go. He always came back acting like nothing was bothering him."

Al asked if Marcus had gone up to the cabin recently.

"Not in a long time. He used to take his boys up there like his daddy had taken him and his brother, but that was a few years ago."

Beulah didn't know where the road to the cabin cut off from Slope Holler. Al and Gloria left hurriedly and hoped they could find the location in the hour or so of daylight remaining. If they succeeded they could set out for the cabin first thing tomorrow.

It was approximately 6:30 p.m. by the time they reached the halfway point between Cumberland and Evarts on the mountain road. Using the spotlight on the cruiser, they inspected every foot of ground for a mile or so before noticing what appeared to be a beaten-down path. It didn't look big enough to be a road, but Al figured it might open up farther back on the mountain. If the Smiths didn't want others to know about the road, they had probably camouflaged the entrance so it would not be noticeable.

Al pulled the cruiser off the road and onto the shoulder. With flashlights in hand, he and Gloria began to search the area. At least two inches of snow had accumulated at this elevation, and Al knew it would not be long before it was much deeper.

Although the snow covered any tracks that might have otherwise been visible, it looked as though there had been recent activity on the trail. That included a broken limb and a sapling with the bark missing. It looked to Al as if something the size of an ATV might have been what disturbed things here. The trail was certainly wide enough for people on horseback and maybe even to accommodate all-terrain vehicles.

"If Marcus went to the cabin, he wasn't driving his Tahoe," Gloria said.

The snow fell more heavily as they retraced their steps to the Crown Victoria, and by the time they reached the foot of the mountain, the accumulation had easily reached four inches. The only way to get to the cabin tomorrow would be either by horseback or ATV. The sheriff's department didn't own any horses, but it did have several ATVs, and the plan was to be back on the mountain by daylight the next day on three such vehicles. They were stored locally at the state highway garage. Jim Lucas would be joining them.

When the sheriff rolled into the parking lot of the Cumberland Police Department, law enforcement officials from throughout the area had gathered and awaited his return. He made sure his office kept the state and city police apprised of Marcus Smith's standing as a person of interest in the murder of his young cousin Aleksander Sepp—not necessarily as the shooter but as someone who could have been involved on some level.

Neither he nor Gloria told anyone except Jim and the state police about the missing funds from the Smith bank account. It might not mean anything, and he didn't want to reveal this kind of information unless it appeared germane to the case.

He and Gloria Strong walked into a veritable task force of law enforcement officials. In addition to officers from Benham and Lynch, Deputy Lucas, Detective Davidson, Chief Hightower, and several officers from the Cumberland Police Department were present. Al and Jim led a briefing focused on finding Marcus Smith.

"We believe," Al said, "although we are by no means sure, that Mr. Smith might have been involved in some way with the death of Aleksander Sepp. We can't be definite until such time as we find and interrogate him."

Frank Davidson went over several other leads his department and the sheriff's office had been investigating. "There are still some things that need to be nailed down, but I can tell you we are close to clearing a couple suspects we pursued early on. At this point we consider our best bet to unraveling this homicide is Marcus Smith."

"Whether or not Marcus is holed up in the cabin, we simply don't know, but we'll be headed to that location at daybreak to check it out," Al said. "If he is at the cabin, we're assuming Marcus traveled there via ATV. When Gloria and I were up on Slope Holler an hour or so ago, we saw evidence that something had been on the trail recently."

It was almost 10:00 p.m. by the time the meeting in Cumberland ended. Al and Jim headed to their respective residences in the city, while Frank Davidson and Gloria Strong were en route to Harlan in the detective's four-wheel-drive SUV. Al tried to convince Gloria to spend the night with him and Ruby, but she needed to get home to her kids.

"Don't worry about me. I'll get a few hours of sleep, jump in my Jeep, and see you bright and early in the morning," she said.

Al had called Ruby before heading up Slope Holler to tell her he would be late. She had been worried—especially because of the snow. As a ten-year-old, Ruby was a passenger in her mother's van when it had careened off the highway in a snowstorm. It had injured her and her younger brother. Since that time she had been terribly afraid of traveling in the snow.

Ruby was used to her husband not sharing everything that happened at work. He didn't want to worry her with things that seemed more dangerous than they actually were.

However, he did share what Beulah had told him and their hope Marcus would be holed up in the cabin.

"I hope you're right. I can't imagine what Marcus's family is going through," she said.

Ruby had kept his supper warm. He showered and rested for a few minutes before sitting down to eat. He felt his eyelids getting heavy, and after helping Ruby wash and dry the dishes, he was definitely ready for bed. He was sound asleep by the time his wife came to bed at almost midnight.

CHAPTER 25

Al kissed Ruby at 5:30 the next morning and left to rendezvous with Deputies Gloria Strong and Jim Lucas before heading up Slope Holler Road. He walked out into a blinding snowstorm. It had added not only to the seven or eight inches that had already fallen but also, he was sure, to Ruby's worry.

The three had agreed yesterday evening to meet at the Cumberland Police Department. Jason Hightower had three ATVs waiting there. The chief would follow them up Slope Holler Road in an emergency rescue vehicle that would also serve as a command post to maintain communication with Al, Gloria, and Jim as they traveled off-road to the projected location of Marcus Smith's cabin.

Jim led the trio of ATVs through the streets of Cumberland to Slope Holler Road. Dressed in coveralls and helmets with visors, the three looked more like contestants in an extreme winter sports event than law enforcement officers.

The snow had slackened by the time they arrived at the base of Slope Holler. This left the view of the treacherous road they would be traversing unencumbered. Al was thankful that was the case. He had been on ATVs when falling snow made it almost impossible to see, and he knew these vehicles were dangerous enough on a clear day. They were OK on the snow or any surface as long as they stayed on the ground. Far too often, though, they became unstable when encountering obstructions such as rocks, tree branches, or anything that might cause them to go airborne. They would have to be careful when going off-road. The snow would be covering many of these obstacles.

Al, Jim, and Gloria agreed to stay about twenty feet apart when traveling up Slope Holler Road. Jim remained in the lead. Gloria followed, and Al brought up the rear.

Some distance behind but close enough to keep them in view, Jason Hightower, accompanied by two officers, drove the specially equipped command center built on the chassis of a Chevrolet Silverado. It was complete with four rear wheels for stability and a turbo-diesel V-8 engine.

Travel was slow in the deep snow, but the ATVs and Silverado maintained their grip as they hugged the inside lane. The drivers chose not to take chances by getting too close to the road's edge. From the air the vehicles that traveled up the snowy surface looked like three small fish swimming furiously to escape the clutches of a larger predator.

It took approximately thirty minutes for the four vehicles to reach the assigned staging area. There was barely enough room to get all of them off the pavement, but once the three ATVs were gone, it would be more than large enough for the command center. Not that it mattered much. It was highly unlikely anyone else would be traveling the road in this weather.

Al, Gloria, and Jim shook off as much of the snow as they could before stepping inside the command center to speak with Jason Hightower. This included pounding their boots against the Silverado's tires, but they succeeded only minimally. Each still brought a dusting of the white stuff inside the vehicle.

Jason was the first to speak. "Al, you said Beulah Smith thinks the cabin you'll be looking for is a mile or two back into the mountain?"

"That's what she recalled, but she wasn't really certain. It has been a while since anyone in the family has been there—at least that she knew of. We'll just have to wait and see."

"Regardless of the distance, it's going to be slow going," Gloria said. "We had trouble finding the path yesterday."

"I know, but you've marked the entrance," Al said, "so we know where to go in. With Jim's hunting skills, he ought to be able to figure things out once we get off the main road."

Jim had been following trails since he was a boy, and he had hunted all over this area. Although, he could not remember seeing the cabin.

"We'll stay a little closer together since we will be moving slowly," Al said.

Jason asked them to check in with him every twenty minutes or so at the command center.

"If anything happens, I can have additional ATVs here within forty-five minutes," he said.

"I don't expect anything to happen, Jason, but if it does, we'll be ready."

Jim was in the lead, and the three ATVs entered the woods at the point Gloria had marked with a small orange flag tied to a twig. Today's temperature was much lower. That left little accumulation on the trees and bushes. The fine, powdery snow that remained caused the riders little trouble as it blew through the trees. Even though the path was not hard to follow, the three drove their vehicles slowly. Al knew better than to hurry. Mistakes, sometimes costly ones, were made when people became overly anxious—especially in weather like this.

Since the snow completely covered the surface of the path, Jim stopped to look closely at a broken twig protruding through the snow. He was almost sure a vehicle had caused the breakage. It was probably another ATV. *Maybe even one driven by Marcus Smith.*

After they had been on the path for about twenty-five minutes, Jim raised his hand to signal the other riders to stop. He had chosen a wide spot underneath a tall pine tree. It was obviously very old, and its sprawling limbs had kept the snow from accumulating deeply around it. The limbs buffered the wind that had been blowing steadily since they first got on the path.

"Have either of you seen anything other than a broken twig or two?" Al asked.

Both Jim and Gloria shook their heads.

"I'm really surprised how easy it is to follow this path," Gloria said. "It might mean others than the Smiths have been using that cabin."

"It might also mean there is someone up there now, and it might not be Marcus Smith at all. It could just as easily be a bunch of kids out having fun," Jim added.

Several small birds chirped as they moved from limb to limb high up in the pine tree. *Probably mountain chickadees or snow buntings*, Al thought. Both could tolerate cold and wintry weather well. Contrary to what many believed, these birds as well as many other varieties did not go south in the winter but lived comfortably in the North while foraging for berries, seeds, and nuts. They seemed especially fond of the wild grapes that were now dry and shriveled like raisins. They grew in abundance, and despite the snow they were easy to get to.

Al made radio contact with Jason Hightower at the command center and reported their ability to travel the path with little difficulty. He told him there was nothing else of note.

The three were performing weapons checks. They had brought only their service revolvers, .40-caliber Glocks. Then Al got a call from Jason Hightower.

"The state police just informed me Marcus's Tahoe has been found parked in one of the coal company's storage facilities. The building wasn't used much anymore. About all it contained were some old continuous mining cutting machines. The coal company sold a couple machines to a firm down near Black Star and had gone to the building to pick them up when someone spotted the bumper of the Tahoe. It was almost hidden behind several boxes of roof bolts."

"That means the likelihood of Marcus Smith being in the cabin just went up," Gloria volunteered.

"He could have slipped out of Benham on an ATV, traveled along the back roads to Slope Holler, and then taken this path to the cabin without being detected," Jim said.

"Especially if he was wearing a helmet with a visor," Gloria said. "Someone might have seen him, but it would not have registered who he was."

The three pulled their ATVs from beneath the pine tree and back onto the path. They moved slowly toward what they hoped would be a rendezvous with Marcus Smith.

The wind had picked up while they were stopped, and the powdery snow blew off the trees and shrubs when gusts shook them violently. The wind also eroded the most recent layer of snow along the path, and animal tracks were now evident. It could have been any number of critters that lived here year-round. That included white-tailed deer, raccoons, and beavers.

They had traveled almost twenty minutes, and Al was thinking it was time to check in with Jason Hightower when Gloria spotted smoke up ahead swirling above the top of the trees.

"It looks as if it might be coming from a chimney since it's that high up," she said.

"I think you're right. If it was coming from something burning on the ground, it wouldn't be rising like that," Jim said.

Just as Al pulled out his phone to let Jason Hightower know about the smoke, two shots were fired. A slug careened off a tree a few yards to the right of Jim's vehicle. The three riders leaped off their ATVs and hunkered down behind them. Al whistled to get Jim's and Gloria's attention, and he motioned for them to move behind a coppice of pine trees a few yards off the trail.

Keeping the vehicles between them and the direction of the shooter, they crawled to the spot Al had pointed to and searched for movement among the trees. Al immediately recognized the sound of the shots as those from a high-powered rifle. If that was the case, the shooter was probably some distance from them. *More than likely*, he thought, *the shots came from a hunter.* He hoped that was the case.

Heavy snows often brought out locals who hunted rabbits with rifles rather than shotguns to make the kill more difficult. Al guessed they saw sport in that. He didn't.

However, he was not going to take any chances that someone other than hunters might be out there. Using hand signals, Al motioned for Jim and Gloria to hold their positions, which were secure behind the trees. They watched and listened. There were no sounds except the howling wind as it blew through the underbrush, which clung close to the ground. Ten minutes passed before Al gave the signal to head farther back into the woods.

Some twenty yards from their original spot, the three gathered behind an outcrop of sandstone that jutted up from the forest floor.

"Where did the shots come from?" Al asked.

"Off to our right," Jim said. "Not anywhere near where the smoke was coming from."

"It sounded to me as if they came from a rifle," Al said.

Jim nodded his agreement. While Jim and Gloria kept their eyes trained on the perimeter, Al called Jason Hightower at the command center.

"We heard the shots," Hightower said. "Are the three of you OK?"

"Just a little shaken up. One of the two rounds came within a few yards of Jim's ATV. But no harm done. We've hunkered down behind a big piece of sandstone."

"Can you see or hear anyone moving around?" Hightower asked.

"No. We haven't seen or heard anything since the shots were fired."

"Do you want us to bring in reinforcements? We could have someone there in no time at all."

"No. We'll stay where we are for a few more minutes and then head back to the trail and the ATVs."

"Are you sure?"

"Yeah. The shots didn't come from the direction of the cabin. I was just about to call you when they were fired. We saw smoke a short distance away. Maybe coming from the cabin. The shots probably came from a hunter," he added. He was not completely convinced that was the case but hoped it was. "We'll walk the rest of the way to the cabin. No need to alert anyone with the ATVs, if the shots didn't do so already."

Jim and Gloria heard the discussion and were ready to move back to the trail. There was no need to discuss how they would proceed. Their training had prepared them for situations like this. Even in the deep snow, they would keep low to the ground and move slowly and deliberately with their eyes peeled for signs of activity.

However, there was nothing except the sound of the wind moving through the trees. In about fifteen minutes, the cabin came into sight. Al was happy to see it. He was tired. *I'm not as young as I used to be*, he thought.

Noticing Jim and Gloria were also breathing heavily suggested his fatigue probably had more to do with traipsing through the heavy snow than his age, though.

The cabin was a good size—about ten feet by twelve feet. It had a small porch and a single window to the right of the door. Since a frontal view was all they had, there was no knowing if there was a rear exit. Al doubted there was. Most folks worked hard to keep buildings like this as airtight as possible since they were so hard to heat, and doors were notorious for letting the heat out and the cold in.

They took their pistols out of their holsters as they came closer to the cabin. Smoke was now bellowing from the chimney. This suggested someone was definitely inside.

Al motioned for Gloria to go to his right and Jim to his left. By moving his left arm in a circular motion, he indicated for Jim to go behind the building. Crouching and proceeding as quietly as possible, they moved within ten feet of the cabin. It was obvious someone had been coming and going. There were footprints on the steps and porch. What troubled Al was the presence of more than one set of prints.

Jim was now behind the cabin, and Gloria was on its right side. Al could still see her. After a few minutes, Al motioned for Gloria to come to him.

"See a window on that side of the building?" he asked.

"No. Just a solid wall," she said.

Within a couple minutes, Jim was beside them as well. "No openings in the rear of the building," he reported.

Al was pleased. This meant the front door was the only way in and out, and the three of them were in a position to control this single opening.

"There's an ATV behind the cabin," Jim said. "Don't know what to make of it. It could be Marcus's, or it could be someone else's. Guess we will know in a minute or two."

Fortuitously there were several large needleleaf conifers close to the front of the cabin that provided good cover. They would need that once they announced themselves, which Al intended to do.

Al motioned for Gloria and Jim to move with him behind the trees. They had no sooner gotten in position than he hollered, "Anybody inside, come out with your hands up. The police are surrounding the cabin."

He repeated the message twice more. Given their proximity to the cabin, he was sure whoever was inside could hear him. He asked both Gloria and Jim to take turns shouting out the same message.

Again there was no response. While the smoke continued to billow from the chimney, the cabin was eerily quiet. There was no curtain on the window, and this allowed the three of them to see partially inside. There appeared to be some source of light illuminating the space.

They saw no movement through the window, no shadows, and nothing to indicate it was inhabited. Still the smoke billowed out into the gray sky. Knowing their shouting had alerted anyone who might have been in the cabin, Al brought Gloria and Jim to the tree he was standing behind and outlined a plan to enter the cabin.

The only way shots from inside could be directed toward them would be through the window. Al told Gloria to take up position directly under the window. He and Jim would then storm the door while she remained outside in case they were unsuccessful and inadvertently allowed the occupant to escape.

It seemed to take forever for them to get into position to make the assault. Their movements were deliberate and precise. Jim kicked the door hard just to the left of the handle. The lock gave way, and a second kick opened the door completely. He and Al rushed in. While the breach had seemed to move in slow motion, their entry to the building was executed exactly the way they had practiced hundreds of times. Once inside Jim's eyes took in everything from the floor to waist-high, and Al's focused on everything from the waist up.

What they found told them there had been no cause for alarm. A lifeless body sat in a rocking chair near the potbellied stove, so hot it was glowing red. The victim's chin rested on his chest just above a gaping hole, obviously made by a round from a high caliber pistol. There was no gun at the scene, so it was evident they were looking at a homicide. Marcus Smith had been found.

He had been killed in a cabin deep in the Appalachian Mountains—a cabin he, his brother, and father had built many years earlier as a place of refuge. He would now escape life's toils and troubles for sure, but Al was certain this was not what the family had had in mind.

Al was curious about the stove. *Why is it burning so hot? Who has stoked it?*

There was a pile of block coal in a wooden box near the stove. It easily could have been procured with a pick and shovel at several outlying coal seams in and around the cabin. When he opened the stove, Al saw it was completely full. Not another block of coal would fit. It looked as though it had not been burning long, since the black color of the bituminous coal still shone through the bright-red embers in several places.

"Gloria, I'll bet this fire was stoked with new coal about the time you first saw the smoke up over the tree line," Al said.

"Yeah, and whoever killed Marcus would have been the one to do the stoking. But when was he shot?" Jim asked. "We didn't hear a shot."

"And where did the shooter go?" Gloria asked.

"I saw what appeared to be ATV tracks at the back of the building," Jim said, "and it looks as if the path we were on continues on down the ridge. It might connect with some of the surface mining roads cut into the hillside."

"If the killer exited on that ATV, he couldn't have been gone long, or the fire would not still be burning so hot," Gloria said. "I'll take a photograph of the ATV that's still behind the building and get it to Sylvia to see if Trudy can identify it as belonging to Marcus."

Al got on the phone with Jason Hightower to tell him what they had found. Hightower contacted Post Ten in Harlan to get the state police homicide response team up to the cabin. He figured it would be at least two and a half hours or maybe more before they would arrive.

In the meantime Al, Jim, and Gloria began treating their surroundings like a crime scene. As was the case with Aleksander Sepp, the serrated wound in Marcus Smith's chest had little outward bleeding. There was no blood anywhere except near the entry wound. Jim said there were several footprints out back, and there was a clear trail from the front of the house to the rear.

Inside the cabin there was a small area that served as a basic kitchen. It had a sink, two overhead cabinets, and a small table with two chairs. With no range present, the kitchen was obviously used for eating rather than cooking. Any cooking was probably done on top of the potbellied stove. That was also where coffee was brewed. The pot, which looked like something used over an open fire on a cattle drive, sat on the hearth in front of the stove.

There were several coffee cups in the sink. When he opened the cabinet below the sink, Al found four gallons of water and some soap, which he figured were used to wash dishes and utensils. There was a five-gallon bucket under the sink's drain to catch the water. He opened the other cabinets and found several cans of food and beans along with two loaves of bread and a couple six-packs of beer—enough stuff for about a weeklong stay, which might have been what Marcus had planned.

He refrained from touching both the cups and coffeepot in case they contained the prints of the killer, or killers. He also made sure not to touch the door handles.

After they had done everything they could to secure the crime scene, Al, Jim, and Gloria pulled out two chairs and a wooden crate and sat down to await the arrival of the state police response team. Al called Jason Hightower and asked him to inform his staff about what they had found at the cabin. He also asked him to tell Sylvia Turner to head up to Benham to inform Marcus Smith's wife and mother that he had been found dead.

"Sylvia should let them know to go to the morgue to make the official identification before the body is transferred to Frankfort. I would imagine it will be there no later than four o'clock."

Al knew it would not be easy on Sylvia. She had known the Smith family most of her life, but he also knew she was a professional. As difficult as it might be, Sylvia Turner would do it. She was tender-hearted but a police officer first and foremost.

It was at least two hours before Detective Frank Davidson; the coroner, Dr. Jack Thornberry; and the young photographer, Josh Bledsoe, arrived on the scene.

Like Al and his deputies, the state police delegation had ridden ATVs to the cabin. One of the vehicles pulled a two-wheeled metal wagon covered by a water-resistant tarp. Inside the wagon was a gurney on which the body of Marcus Smith would lay as it was transported back through the snow to a waiting SUV.

As Josh Bledsoe pulled the gurney inside, Al wondered if it was the same one which had carried Aleksander's body. *We've got to solve these homicides soon*, Al thought, *before someone else ends up dead.*

"Sheriff, it wasn't that long ago we had another meeting like this. Was it?" Davidson said.

"It's happening too often for me, Frank," Al Whitaker replied. "And this one looks eerily similar to what we saw in the park."

"We've got what look like good prints on coffee cups and maybe on the door handles," Jim said. "We also have boot prints—it looks like two sets—that lead from the side of the porch to the back where an ATV was parked. There are also tire patterns from the ATV someone rode away on."

Dr. Thornberry took out a magnifying glass and peered at the entry wound. He mumbled to himself as he did so. He lifted and lowered the arms of the dead man, grasped his upper arm, and ran his fingers across his forehead and along the other parts of his face. After his examination was complete, he stepped back from the deceased. "This man has been dead for eight to ten hours in my estimation."

That meant Marcus Smith had likely been killed late last night. It raised the question of why the killer, or killers, had stayed around for almost half a day before leaving. The thought ran through his mind that they might have left when they did because they had been tipped off someone was coming. *Who would have told them, though?*

Al made a point of saying something encouraging to Josh Bledsoe. Had he not continued to pore over the photos he had taken in the park, he never would have found a person among all the underbrush.

After his interview with Viktoria Sepp, he now knew the identity of that individual.

Al called Jason to tell him they were turning over everything at the cabin to the state police, and he and his deputies would be tracking the ATV that had apparently left the scene of the crime just before they arrived.

Jason said he would move the Silverado to a site about two and a half miles from the cabin where he figured the path they would be traveling on might intersect with an old surface mining road.

"The road we will be taking is in pretty good shape, and I think we can make it without too much difficulty. I expect we will be there before the three of you."

Al, Gloria, and Jim walked back to where they had left the vehicles when they started toward the cabin on foot.

"We can't be in a hurry, folks," Al cautioned. "When you are you start overlooking things."

Both deputies smiled and nodded. Their progress was a bit faster than earlier. That was probably because the other ATV had packed down the snow and made the ride less bumpy and the pathway easier to follow. The cloud cover had broken just enough to allow the sun to shine through the trees, and this warmed things up a little.

As they had earlier in the day, they stopped about every twenty minutes or so to rest and take stock of things. At the second stop, Gloria got off her ATV and dug a finger into the snow. When she held it up, Al and Jim could see what appeared to be a brown liquid.

"That's oil," she said. "I thought I saw some earlier. Chances are the ATV in front of us is leaking fluid."

The farther they went up the trail, the more oil they saw. Al expected to come across a malfunctioning vehicle with a killer or killers at any time. That being the case, they took extra caution. They slowed their progress to a near crawl and paid close attention along both sides of the trail. While there was noticeably more oil the farther they went, though, no ATV came into sight.

As they neared what they figured would be the end of the trail, the path became wider and looked more like a surface mining road. They spent another twenty minutes on the trail before seeing the command center. It was parked directly ahead on a gravel road built to transport miners to and from parts of the mountain where coal could be extracted by stripping off the covering of earth and rock. Jason was waiting for them when they parked their vehicles and walked up the steps to the command center.

"We found ATV tracks up the road a hundred yards or so along with the tracks of several large trucks. It's a good bet that a truck picked up whoever was on the ATV."

"And chances are the truck would simply disappear among the twenty or so large vehicles in and around the mine site," Jim said. "If you want to get out of here unnoticed, you could not have chosen a better vehicle."

"I wonder what happened to the ATV," Gloria said.

"From the oil stains, it looks as if it might have been loaded on a truck. Probably the same one that took its rider away from here," Jim said.

It was now well into the afternoon, and despite the best efforts of the sheriff, his deputies, and the Cumberland chief of police, a killer, or killers, had eluded them.

Beulah Smith had been right. Marcus had sought refuge in his mountain cabin. His hideout, though, had proven unsuccessful. He was dead, and the knowledge of the role he might have played in the death of his young cousin had died with him.

One homicide had turned into two. Rather than being closer to an answer, Al Whitaker knew things had suddenly gotten more complicated. After sitting with Jason for a few minutes and listening as he informed Post Ten and Al's office personnel about where things now stood, the sheriff and his deputies followed him off Slope

Holler Road to his office in Cumberland. There they got out of their cold-weather gear and sat down for sandwiches and lots of coffee to combat the cold that seemed to have crept into every part of their bodies.

Al called Hartford Ford, and the two agreed it wouldn't make much sense to search for the killers by checking every coal truck in the area. There were just too many to make that feasible. This was especially true since whoever was running from them could have taken any of the twenty or so surface mining roads cut into the mountain.

They agreed that starting tomorrow they would focus their attention on the two strangers who had been present at Aleksander's funeral. They had moved to the top of the suspect list. While there was nothing to point to their involvement in Marcus's death, Al was not so sure about Aleksander, and he was convinced the two homicides were connected.

Before calling it a day, Al took a call from Sylvia Turner. She told him the news of Marcus Smith's death had shocked his family.

"Sheriff, I kind of got the idea that they be thinking he might have done something wrong, but they surely didn't think he would be dead. His old mama, Beulah, she looked as if each breath was going be her last. Trudy finally had to put her to bed."

Al asked if the boys were there. Sylvia said they were not, but their mother had called them.

"You could hear the wailing over the phone. This family is grieving mightily. They going on down to Harlan to identify the body. The boys going to meet their mother there," Sylvia reported.

Al told Gloria and Jim he would see them in the morning and headed home. He was perplexed and as frustrated as he could remember being in many years.

CHAPTER 26

When he pulled off Kingdom Come Drive, Al saw that his driveway, like the road, had been cleared of the heavy snow that had fallen in the last twenty-four hours. Ruby had probably hired local kids to shovel it.

A lot of them would be out on their snowmobiles and looking to make a few bucks clearing driveways on a day like this. School had been called off before daybreak that morning and probably would be called off tomorrow as well. The highway crews would have the major highways cleared, but many of the secondary roads would be slick and slippery for a couple more days.

It was 4:00 p.m. by the time Ruby opened the front door to welcome her husband home. It was obvious she was relieved to see him. He knew she worried about him every day, but snowy weather just added to her concern.

"Did you find Marcus?"

"We did but too late. Took a bullet to his chest. Much like the boy, Aleksander Sepp."

"Oh my Lord. I am so sorry. I know this is going to be so hard on Trudy and the boys," she said.

"Sylvia said it was Beulah who took it the hardest."

Al gave Ruby the rundown on where things stood. He had had someone from Jason Hightower's office call Ruby to let her know not to prepare a big meal since he would be eating sandwiches in the police chief's office.

Al spent ten minutes in the shower with the hot water cascading over his tired and sore body. He was beginning to feel his age. He tired more easily now, and the fatigue lasted longer. The doctors said he had the beginnings of rheumatoid arthritis, which accounted for swollen joints that ached.

He hated to take medication but had reluctantly given in to an ibuprofen regimen, and the doctors told him it would not be long before he would need something stronger.

He knew one thing. It would never be OxyContin or any of the other powerful painkillers that had wreaked havoc on the people of his region.

CHAPTER 27

The tip line at the Harlan County Sheriff's Office usually caused more trouble than it was worth. Like a few other things, the tip line had been in place when Al was elected. While he didn't like it, the voters did. So closing it down was never an option.

Most of the individuals who called the tip line complained about personal concerns—everything from spousal infidelity to barking dogs. There were a few valid tips from time to time, but more often than not, a call was made to impugn the character of someone the caller didn't like.

Despite the fact that most tips proved useless, the sheriff's office listened to every call received, and when a tip appeared to have any validity at all, they followed up on it. One such call was logged at 2:35 a.m. It was obvious the caller was trying to disguise his or her voice, but there was no mistaking the message.

"Sheriff, I know you're investigating Marcus Smith. I also know he's missing. I expect you are hearing everything was OK with him and his wife, and they were getting along well. That just isn't the truth—at least not recently. I have personally witnessed them arguing more than once in the past couple weeks, and before Marcus went to work the day he ended up missing, they almost came to blows in their driveway."

Blanche Halcomb, who was responsible for checking the tip line, had played the message twice for Al when he came in.

"Guess we will find out if there is anything to this when we're up in Benham talking to the neighbors later today," Jim said when Al told him about the message.

Before they left the office, though, Al and his staff would be welcoming Captain Ford and Detective Davidson at 10:00 a.m. to go over everything they had learned about Aleksander Sepp's murder and now the murder of his cousin Marcus Smith.

Trudy Smith had shared information about her family's finances with the sheriff's office. Al was content to accept what she had given him at this point, but later on officials at the bank might need to confirm this information. That would take a court order.

"We might have to ask the court to give us more than access to their finances at the bank," Gloria said. "I'm thinking we are at the point where we need to access their phone records as well."

Jim and Al nodded.

While awaiting the arrival of their cohorts from Post Ten, Al took out his three-ring binder and wrote down everything that had happened yesterday and the day before. He had simply been too tired to do it last night.

Jim and Gloria met with Sylvia to get her take on the Smith family's reaction when she broke the news about Marcus's death.

"It's like I told the sheriff yesterday. Trudy and Beulah were shook up. Both were kind of glassy-eyed, like they heard me but couldn't believe what I was saying," Sylvia said.

"You didn't mention Viktoria. Did she react pretty much the same way?" Jim asked.

"That girl seemed upset. Tears and all. But not like the other two. Remember, though, Viktoria, she not nearly as close to Marcus as the other two. She spent more time petting on Trudy and Beulah—I guess trying to console them—than she did grieving on her own."

When Captain Ford and Detective Davidson arrived, they followed their usual routine when visiting the sheriff's office. They asked for coffee and headed to the conference room. In a matter of minutes, Al, Jim, and Gloria joined them.

Al asked Jim to take a marker and go to the whiteboard, which stretched all the way across one of the room's interior walls.

"Let's make a list of what we know and what we don't know," Al said.

"We probably know a whole lot less than we think we know." Jim laughed.

"Not necessarily," Gloria said. "We have some solid evidence. It's just not linear. What we've got to do is fill in the gaps. Get the evidence in a straight line that takes us someplace."

The five law enforcement officers took an hour and a half to agree on the following points:

- ✓ Two individuals had been killed in Harlan County in the space of two weeks.

- ✓ The two individuals, both males, were distantly related and lived in the same house.

- ✓ Both individuals were shot at close range in the chest.

- ✓ The younger of the two, Aleksander Sepp, was shot with a nine-millimeter Makarov pistol—standard issue in the Russian army until a few years before.

- ✓ Two cousins from Eolia reported the homicide to the Kingdom Come State Park police patrol. Both cousins were deep in the clutches of prescription drugs.

- ✓ It appeared a weapon similar to the one used to kill his young cousin had been used to kill Marcus Smith. They were waiting for the crime laboratory in Frankfort to issue its report.

- ✓ Two unknown males were in attendance at the funeral of Aleksander Sepp. They drove a vehicle that was registered to a mortgage company in New Jersey.

- ✓ The Russian Mafia has been active in and around New York City and northern New Jersey.

- ✓ One of the Mafia's largest sources of income was derived from the sale of drugs—particularly heroin.

- ✓ Heroin had begun to catch on in the mountains of Eastern Kentucky. This has been especially true since law enforcement officials have clamped down on prescription painkillers.

- ✓ Aleksander Sepp's sister, Viktoria, reported she was present immediately after her brother was shot, at which time she saw a relatively new black car speeding away. It was possible the two employees of Star Mortgage Company were in this vehicle.

- ✓ Viktoria Sepp reported she was near the crime scene when her brother was killed because she had overheard him say he would meet some men at the park, and she was afraid drugs might be involved and he would be in danger.

- ✓ Viktoria Sepp reported she saw a second car speed away from the crime scene. Either Luke Henson or Clayton Wright, the Eolia cousins, possibly drove that car.

- ✓ At a recent court hearing in Estonia, ownership of a fishery—previously owned by Viktoria and Aleksander's parents, who had disappeared without a trace well over five years ago—was transferred to Gunnar Sepp, the brother of the missing man.

- ✓ In the same hearing, an affidavit purportedly signed by Viktoria Sepp gave her permission for the ownership of the fishery to be transferred. This was introduced into evidence as was a copy of the death certificate of Aleksander Sepp, who had been dead at the time for just a little over a week. Had he been alive, Aleksander's permission would have been needed before transferring ownership.

- ✓ Viktoria Sepp denied having signed an affidavit allowing ownership of the fishery to be transferred.

- ✓ Viktoria Sepp reported in the days and weeks prior to his death, Aleksander Sepp argued with his cousin Marcus Smith about the value of the fishery.

- ✓ During the hearing in Estonia, a trust was set up on behalf of Viktoria Sepp, from which she would receive benefits when she reached twenty-one years of age. Marcus Smith would administer the trust.

- ✓ A little over three days before, Marcus Smith went missing. His body was found yesterday in a family cabin a few miles from Slope Holler Road. He had apparently traveled there on an ATV.

- ✓ An ATV apparently carried Marcus's killer, or killers, away from the cabin before Al, Gloria, and Jim arrived. The culprit or culprits might have rendezvoused with someone at a surface mining site and escaped in a large truck—one of several in the area.

- ✓ Marcus Smith's wife, Trudy, reported that certificates of deposit belonging to the couple had been cashed in at the bank, and a savings account had been depleted before his disappearance.

- ✓ Friends and coworkers reported that Marcus Smith was well liked and that he and his wife seemed to get along well. Although, a recent call to a tip line said they had been arguing the day he went missing.

"What about the shots fired near you yesterday as you were headed to the cabin?" Frank asked. "Shouldn't we list that?"

"I don't think so," Al said. "I believe those shots came from a hunter some distance away. If whoever fired them wanted to harm us, we were easy targets for several minutes."

The detective appeared satisfied with the answer.

After everyone had looked over the list, Al asked, "Where does all this lead us? Let's take it one person at a time. Hartford, what do you think?"

"First, I suppose, like all of you, I believe the two homicides are connected. I think the connection is related in some manner to the disposition of the fishery in Estonia."

"We need more information from the court hearing," Al said. "What was the appraised value of the fishery? Was it appraised too low? If so, who benefited? I think it probably was appraised too low, but we don't know that for certain. We also need to know how much was in the trust Marcus was to administer for Viktoria. And what, if anything, would he get out of the deal?"

"We hope to hear from the FBI anytime now with news about what Interpol has found out about the final court order. It should include the dollar figures we are looking for," Hartford said.

"Gloria, what do you think?" Al asked.

"I think Viktoria is back in the picture. Like most everyone else, I want to believe she is a victim in all this, but with Marcus's death, I think we need to talk with her again. Maybe get a court order to look at her phone records."

"I agree," Frank said. "But wouldn't it be best to wait to talk with her until we find out the specifics of the court order from Tallinn?"

"Yeah. You're right," Gloria responded. "That way we can approach her with knowledge she might not know we have. Don't we have probable cause to get access to her phone records, though?"

"I think we do," Hartford said. "The inconsistencies in her stories together with the death of Marcus Smith should be enough for Judge Wilson. He's not going to make it easy for us, but I'll see if we can get the commonwealth attorney on this today."

"Frank, what's your take on things? What do we need and from whom?" Al asked.

"We've got to get some information from the mortgage company. If that company is bogus, if it's a front for the Russian Mafia, drugs probably are involved. I know we asked the FBI to look into the company, but sometimes outfits like this operate off the radar, and information might not be readily available."

Seeing Al looking in his direction, Jim didn't wait to be asked what he was thinking. "We need the ballistic report on the slug that killed Marcus Smith. If it's from the same pistol that Aleksander was killed with, in all likelihood we have one killer."

"It's obvious we still have a lot of work to do," Al said, and he shook his head at the complexity of what lay before them. "I think we've covered most of what we are going to need to proceed. After the call to the tip line, we need to look more closely at Trudy Smith's relationship with Marcus. Hartford, your folks should look at his computer to see if anything interesting shows up. Remember, he supposedly kept everything concerning the family's finances to himself. If he did that with finances, were there other things he also kept secret?"

"OK," the captain said. "Let's divide our responsibilities up and get started on trying to close this case—these cases. Our folks at Post Ten will be in touch with the crime laboratory in Frankfort to make sure they get the autopsy and ballistic reports on Marcus Smith to us as soon as possible. Since we now have two homicides that appear related, they're likely to move these cases to the top of the list. As soon as I find out something, I will be in touch with you immediately.

"I've also asked our IT people to put a rush on finding out what's on the hard drive of Smith's computer. You'll get that information as soon as we do. I'll also drop by the commonwealth attorney's office before I leave the courthouse today to see if we can get something to take to Judge Wilson.

"One last thing. All of you know that working with the FBI is sometimes not easy. One of the things I have tried to do is never butt into their business." He laughed and shook his head. "They can be serious turf guarders, but I think we need our own boots on the ground in New Jersey to find out more about the mortgage company and its possible Mafia connection. Why don't we send Frank and Gloria up there to snoop around a little?"

The sheriff nodded his agreement. He knew the captain was going to suggest this. The two had spoken on the phone before Al left home earlier that morning. He had agreed on a plan to send Frank and Gloria to New Jersey. Al had suggested it, but believing Frank might not like being sent out of state on the county sheriff's recommendation, he had asked Hartford to make the suggestion.

Throughout his law enforcement career, Al's relationship had never been as strong with the state police as it was now. Hartford Ford had gone out of his way to cooperate with his office and had instructed his troopers to do the same.

That had not always been the case. Under past leadership it had been made clear the sheriff's office couldn't be trusted, and as a trooper, Frank had made it clear he didn't think the sheriff's department operated with the degree of professionalism needed in law enforcement. Al knew there were occasions when that had been the case.

He had changed his tune remarkably since Captain Ford became the post commander, but Al suspected he still harbored some of the same feelings about him and the sheriff's office.

Al had planned to have Gloria go with him to talk with Marcus and Trudy's neighbors, but now she would be headed off to Hoboken tomorrow, and he figured she would need time to work out things with her mom and kids. So Jim would go instead.

"What we've found out thus far, except for that call we got on the tip line, suggested everything was going OK with them," Al said as he and his deputy headed to their cars.

There was no plan to talk with Viktoria, but that might change, depending on how soon they got through interrogating the neighbors.

Once again the snowplows had been out en masse, and US 119 was relatively clear. Every now and then, Al would see an abandoned vehicle pulled off on the side of the road. Sometimes conditions got too slick and dangerous to be driving around. This was especially so if the driver was not used to driving in the snow or was simply afraid to do so. Al had no way of knowing for sure, but his experience told him that a lot of the drivers leaving vehicles behind were youngsters. *Probably didn't want to take the chance of being involved in accidents, especially if they were driving a car belonging to their parents*, he thought.

He remembered how he and Ruby had worried themselves sick when their kids first started driving. When any of the three were out, the tension in their house became palpable every time they heard a siren. Nothing would get better until the kids were safe inside the house—usually at the kitchen table and eating something special their mother had prepared.

"You can't keep kids tied to their mother's apron strings," Ruby used to say. "Taking chances is part of life. It's the way kids learn and grow up."

Al laughed to himself when it occurred to him he was almost to Cumberland, and his entire thought process had emanated from cars abandoned on the side of the highway.

Before leaving Harlan, Al and Jim had agreed to stop at Carlotta's for a quick lunch when they got to Cumberland. By the time Al arrived, Jim was already there and sitting in their usual spot near the back of the restaurant. Al spoke to the people he knew and nodded respectfully to those he did not. He had been accused of always being political and playing to voters, but the truth was Al had behaved in exactly the same way since long before he became involved in politics, and he would continue to do so once out of office.

When he got to the booth where Jim was seated, he noticed his deputy had already ordered him a Diet Coke and was looking at the daily specials, which were written on a centrally located chalkboard so it would be easy to see. Al immediately saw what he wanted—baked chicken, coleslaw, and green beans. Jim ended up ordering the same thing.

Russ Blankenship, as usual, was meeting and greeting his customers as he bussed the tables. He had decorated the restaurant with Christmas lights and a small tree, and carols were playing in the background.

Thanksgiving was a week away, and Al wondered, *Why the hurry?* It was almost as if Thanksgiving had been merged into Christmas and had lost much of what made it special. He knew large and small businesses drove this in their desire to extend the buying season, but that didn't make him like it.

After they finished lunch, Al and Jim rode together in the deputy's car to Pine Street in Benham. They had agreed to work in tandem as they interrogated the Smiths' neighbors. Al knew the interrogations needed to be conducted now, despite Marcus Smith's death. He also knew some might misunderstand and choose to be uncooperative.

They started near the top of street. That was some five houses above the Smiths'. Al and Jim knew the owners of the first two houses they visited. Both visits were uneventful. According to one neighbor, "Trudy and Marcus always got along well. Good neighbors. They were always willing to help you out. Just good-hearted folks."

After walking away from house number three, Jim Lucas was shaking his head as they approached the next one in line. "Al, these folks are just saying things you would usually hear when someone is dead. They're remembering only the good stuff and have put all the bad things out of their minds."

House number four was a small bungalow. It was painted dark gray and had a porch that looked almost as big as the dwelling. A paper-thin man answered the knock on the door immediately. He stood about six feet tall. Although, his scarecrow-like features made it difficult to tell. He spoke in a deep voice that belied his stature. "What can I do for you, Sheriff?" he asked. This suggested he knew who Al was.

"I know you're aware of Marcus Smith's death," Al said. "We're just trying to talk to the neighbors to determine if they noticed anything unusual going on. How the family got along. That sort of thing."

The man stroked his sunken face, which caused his dark brown eyes to appear gigantic. They completely dominated his appearance. He stepped out onto the porch and closed the door before speaking.

"I'm not one to denigrate the dead, Sheriff. Seems to me death is denigration enough. Then again the truth lives on. Doesn't it?" Not waiting for an answer, the man continued. "I don't mean to imply the Smiths fought constantly. I'm confident they didn't, but I've heard quarreling between husband and wife on more than one occasion."

"When? And under what circumstances?" Jim asked without bothering to introduce himself. No introduction was necessary, however.

"Deputy Lucas," he said with what appeared to be the faintest of smiles, "I suffer from chronic obstructive pulmonary disease. Probably caused by all the coal dust I breathed in working in the mines. It's so bad I seldom sleep more than two or three hours a night. And I am always up by four every morning. Being up that early means I am privy to what goes on when others leave for work. The Smiths always left at about the same time every day—five o'clock in the morning. I don't know if they waited until they got outside to scream at each other out of fear of waking everyone if they argued in the house, but scream they often did."

"What about the morning Marcus disappeared?" Al asked.

"A particularly loud morning," he said, and he scratched the top of his nearly bald head. "Maybe I thought it was louder because I was standing about where I am standing now. Here on the front porch."

"Could you hear what they were yelling about?" Al asked.

"Money. She wanted to know where it had all gone. He kept telling her he would get it back. But he didn't seem repentant. More like it was his to lose, so she should get over it."

"Was this usually what they quarreled about?" Al asked.

"Not until recently. You might say money was but the latest topic about which they disagreed," the man said.

"What other things?" Jim asked.

"I can't recall everything, but most arguments revolved around his not sharing information with her. She seemed to always be in the dark about things that affected their family, and you could tell she didn't like it."

"Why do you think none of the other neighbors we've talked to mentioned any of this?" Al asked the thin man.

"To get the complete answer to that, I suggest you talk to them again. I could speculate, though, it might be because most are retired, older folks who choose to sleep late. When they are up early, they don't hear well. Of course, that would be merely speculation on my part," he said. Again there was just a wisp of a smile.

"Did you call our tip line to let us know about their arguments?" Jim asked.

"I most certainly did not. Would never think of doing such a thing. That's not to say my wife didn't, though. I would think she might have tired of my complaining."

"Could we speak with her?" Al asked.

"I'm sure you could, Sheriff, if she was here. But Amy Marie left early this morning to visit family in Michigan for Thanksgiving. She's not due back for a week or so, but I'll let you know when she gets back into town. Tell her you want to ask her about that call."

No one else Sheriff Whitaker and Deputy Lucas visited had anything bad to say about the Smiths. In fact most were positive if not laudatory.

It became apparent that the thin man, whose name they learned was William Conover, had not only been right in describing the neighbors they had spoken to before coming to his house but in describing this last group as well. Most were elderly, and at least three of them had to ask him or Jim to repeat a question.

As he thought about it, things began to make more sense. The house the Smiths lived in had originally belonged to Marcus's parents. He had purchased it several years ago from his mother, Beulah, done extensive renovations, and invited her to live with him. Individuals about Beulah's age owned most of the other homes on Pine Street.

Of course, all of them, including the Smith matriarch, were young when they first came to Pine Street. Most had come from the hills and hollows around the region. Now, like her, they had grown old.

"You know, Jim," Al said, "many of those individuals we spoke with were old and hard of hearing, but I'll bet something else was at work too. They've known Beulah's family for thirty of forty years and weren't about to say anything bad about her son or his wife."

"Usually one negative report out of a dozen wouldn't be enough to sway me," Jim said, "but I think in this case, I'm coming down on the side of Conover. Although, he had to be one of the strangest individuals I've ever talked to."

Now they most likely had confirmation that all was not sweetness and light in the Smith family, as many had said and some might have genuinely believed.

He knew of other cases like this one where the husband was the only one in the family who worked for years. By virtue of bringing home the paycheck, he felt he was entitled to make most, if not all, the family's decisions.

The trouble started when the wife, as was the case with Trudy Smith, went out, got herself an education, joined the workforce, and often made as much or more than her husband. At that time things began to change. The wife started thinking that since she was also a breadwinner, she was entitled to share in decisions—that it was no longer just the husband's purview.

He wondered if this had been the case with Trudy. She might have felt powerless until she became a registered nurse. Getting the college degree alone would have bumped up her self-esteem, and when she started bringing home a hefty paycheck, she undoubtedly would have felt even better about herself. At that point she might have felt entitled to be a full and equal partner in the marriage.

What effect this had on their relationship beyond simply inviting quarrels was what Al and his fellow investigators had to find out. *But not today*, Al thought. By the time he and Jim had spoken with their last neighbor, the clock had climbed past 6:00 p.m. They would put off talking to Viktoria but not for long.

Jim dropped Al at Carlotta's. He had left his car there, and the sheriff headed home. His joints ached. Spending several hours on his feet was not good for his arthritis.

CHAPTER 28

Gloria Strong and Frank Davidson left Harlan at 8:30 a.m. for a 1:00 p.m. flight from Bluegrass Field in Lexington to LaGuardia in New York City, which was only about fifteen miles from Hoboken, New Jersey, where they would meet with the FBI to inquire about the Star Mortgage Company, the owner of one 2012 Ford Sedan Al Whitaker had seen at Aleksander Sepp's funeral.

The travel time from Harlan to Lexington was right at four hours—more than three times as long as the flight to New York City. Both had flown before for official police investigations, but this was the first time they had traveled together. Al had made Gloria aware of Frank's past hostility toward the sheriff's department, and Hartford told the sheriff he had cautioned Frank to be on his best behavior.

Perhaps because their supervisors had spoken to them, Gloria and Frank were the epitome of decorum on the ride to the airport. It was a clear, cold day. The roads were in great shape, and they made good time traveling on US 119 to Pineville, where they got on US 25 East, a major corridor connecting the region.

When they exited US 25 East for I-75 in Corbin, they had pretty much covered family histories and were beginning to search for topics of discussion when they began to talk about what they expected in Hoboken.

"I know Captain Ford called the FBI in NYC to get a read on our trip up there," Gloria said. "Any idea what their reaction was?"

"He didn't say. Not much they can do to stop us from snooping around some. That is, if we can't get the information directly from their field office in Hoboken."

"If they have information we don't have, why haven't they shared it with us already?" Gloria asked.

"Sometimes unless you're face-to-face with someone and can look him or her in the eye, you don't ask the follow-up questions that need to be asked. You don't know to," Frank replied.

"I sure hope that's the way it turns out when we get up there. It would save us a lot of time and trouble. I don't want to be up there any longer than we have to."

They spent the remainder of the trip to the airport reviewing the evidence—much in the same way they had done yesterday morning in the sheriff's office. They drilled down on the two strangers at Aleksander Sepp's funeral and the vehicle they were driving. Gloria had the tag number for the Ford Sedan along with descriptions of the two individuals.

Both men were around six feet tall, but one was a little on the heavy side. Al had estimated he weighed 220–230 pounds, while Al had said the other probably carried 180–190 pounds.

One thing Al had remembered about the larger one was his hair. He had described it as "jet-black, thick, wavy, and combed straight back." Gloria had written down his description word for word on her notepad. The smaller one, according to the sheriff, was pretty nondescript, with the exception of being bald. There was nothing about him that would make him stand out in a crowd.

They exited I-75 in Lexington onto Newtown Pike. The noon rush hour was in full swing, and traffic was bumper-to-bumper for a few miles until they turned right onto New Circle Road, a four-lane thoroughfare. As the name suggested, it circled the city. Built in the 1950s, it fell below the standard of highways being built today, but it remained one of the best ways to get in and around Lexington.

The exit for Bluegrass Field was Versailles Road. It was in the heart of some of the nation's most beautiful—and productive—horse farms. Once off New Circle Road, the farm to their immediate right was one of the best known in the region. It was the famed Calumet, where Triple Crown winners Whirlaway and Citation were sired.

An avid race fan, Gloria told Frank about how the farm's success had begun in the mid-1930s when the owners purchased the stud career of an English Derby winner and a yearling colt at a Saratoga sale.

"That got Calumet started," she said, "and in the thirties and forties, it was among the best in America."

"I don't know too much about racing," Frank admitted. "I do know the Triple Crown consists of the Kentucky Derby, Preakness, and Belmont. Am I right in recalling there has not been a horse to win all three in several years?"

"You're right. In 1978 Affirmed won the last Triple Crown. And you know what's so very interesting about that?" Not waiting for an answer, she continued. "A Kentucky jockey named Steve Cauthen rode Affirmed. Cauthen was and is the youngest rider ever to win all three races. At the time he was teenager. I forget his actual age," Gloria said.

It was obvious Gloria was in her element—so much so Frank resigned himself to listening.

"And you know something else? Alydar finished second to Affirmed in each of the Triple Crown races. Do you know who owned him?"

"Nope," Frank said with a big grin on his face, "but I bet you're going to tell me."

"Calumet Farm. In fact Alydar went on to become one of the best-known second-place finishers of all time," Gloria almost shouted.

"I hear you. I hear you."

Frank laughed as he entered the turning lane to take them to the airport. By that time any mistrust that might have been lingering when they left Harlan had disappeared.

Since they were carrying concealed weapons, Gloria and Frank knew they would not go through the normal check-in process.

Yesterday at noon both the state police and sheriff's office had filed letters of intent with the National Law Enforcement Telecommunications System advising the TSA that Detective Davidson and Deputy Strong would be carrying concealed weapons on their persons en route from Lexington to New York City as well as on their return trip.

Gloria and Frank identified themselves at the ticket counter and later to the TSA, who checked their credentials carefully before giving them the OK.

With two turbofan engines, the Bombardier CTJ700 regional jet cruised at just over 515 miles per hour. Helped along by a favorable headwind, the plane landed at LaGuardia ten minutes early.

Gloria, perhaps worn out by getting up well before 5:00 a.m. the last couple days, had dozed the entire way. Frank read—something he did regularly when flying.

Much to their surprise, the FBI met them at the gate. Standing at baggage claim was a tall, lean man with a big smile on his face. He held a hand-lettered sign with the names "Davidson" and "Strong" written in bright-red letters.

When they approached him, the immaculately dressed young man grabbed Gloria's hand with both his and shook it enthusiastically. He then did the same thing with Frank. The looks on both their faces spoke to the surprise they felt at being met in the first place and then for such a warm, enthusiastic greeting. Al Whitaker and Hartford Ford had told them not to expect the FBI to receive them warmly.

"They will probably see you as nuisances at best and incompetent hicks at worst," Al had said.

His error could not have been more obvious. The big man introduced himself as Agent Roland Maggard. He spoke with an accent, which Frank and Gloria had expected. What they hadn't expected was a mountain accent that clearly labeled him as a product of the Kentucky-Tennessee Cumberland Plateau.

"I sure have been looking forward to meeting you all. Don't get the chance to see home folks often," he said. The huge smile still covered his face.

"Where are you from?" Gloria asked with an equally big smile on her face.

"Grew up in Harrogate, Tennessee, just across the line from Kentucky. Been up to Harlan County many times. My daddy's family was from Coldiron. We moved to Tennessee just before I was born. He got a job with the Tennessee Valley Authority as a coal buyer. Since he had worked in the mines for several years, they figured he'd be good at that."

By this time Frank and Gloria had obviously relaxed. It was evident in their mannerisms and the good-natured chitchat taking place. As it turned out, the three of them knew many of the same people and had run in some of the same circles.

Agent Maggard told them he had taken a special interest in their case—now cases—since Captain Ford had called the FBI's Pikeville office asking for help.

"I got my start over at Pikeville," Roland Maggard said. "Spent almost five years working under a New Yorker, Agent Ed Dampier. When he took over the Hoboken office a year ago, he got me transferred up here. Didn't think I'd like it, but you know what I've found out?" He laughed. "People are just people regardless of where they live or how they talk."

"Anything new from Estonia about the court order giving the Sepp kids' fishery to their uncle?" Gloria asked.

"Yes, ma'am. We got it from Interpol earlier today. And it looks as if it's what all of us kind of expected."

Agent Maggard went on to tell them the specifics of what looked like a very good deal that had been handed to Aleksander and Viktoria's uncle. He said the value of the fishery, which most objective appraisers would have set at $8 to $10 million, was listed as $3.5 million. The fishery had been sold lock, stock, and barrel to Gunnar Sepp, provided a trust fund be established for Viktoria in the amount of $1 million, which she would receive when she turned twenty-one. No information was provided when, or if, Viktoria would get the additional $2.5 million to which she was rightfully entitled.

"Unless he intends to give Viktoria more money, it appears that Gunnar Sepp will gain ownership of the fishery for something like ten to twelve percent of its real value," Maggard said.

" And on top of that, Marcus Smith was set to receive a hefty one hundred fifty thousand dollars, payable in advance, for serving as the trust administrator," Maggard almost shouted.

"Do Al Whitaker and Hartford Ford know about this?" Frank asked.

"We sent a copy of the official court order to them just a couple hours ago."

"Looks as if Gunnar Sepp came out smelling like a rose," Gloria said.

"And Marcus Smith, had he lived, would not have done all that bad either," Maggard added. "I've never heard of anyone getting fifteen percent of a trust fund's value to serve as administrator. And getting all of it up front? That's just not done—at least not in this country. It looks as if things are handled differently in Estonia, though."

CHAPTER 29

At about the same time Agent Maggard was telling his new friends what was contained in the Estonian court order, a package arrived via UPS to the Tallinn residence of Administrative Judge Lekvov, whose signature was affixed to the order. He signed for the parcel and tried to tip the female driver, who politely declined.

He took the package, a fifteen-inch square box, to his study, closed the door, and laid it atop his eighteenth-century mahogany desk. He used a letter opener to slice open the box and carefully removed a securely wrapped object. He peeled away the layers of Bubble Wrap to reveal a startling beautiful crystal vase, which he turned on its side so he could see the markings on its bottom. He wrote down three letters: the second, ninth, and twelfth characters of a fifteen-letter sequence forming the hyphenated word "midnight-blossom."

Taking a small black book from a bottom desk drawer, he turned to a listing of the English alphabet. Opposite each letter was a number, all of which he wrote down in sequence. He then turned to an Apple computer and pulled up what appeared to be a web page for international travel. In reality it was a portal for an offshore bank in the Caribbean. He entered seven numbers, 4186257, each of which corresponded with every other letter, excluding the hyphen, in "midnight-blossom." For no more than five seconds, the sum of $250,000 flashed in red at the bottom of the computer screen. Then it disappeared. Information about travel packages to New Zealand and Australia replaced it.

He smiled before destroying both the vase and the black book.

CHAPTER 30

After leaving the airport, Agent Maggard stayed on Grand Central Parkway for a couple miles before getting on I-278 West, the Brooklyn Queens Expressway, which he continued on for about ten minutes before taking Exit 32A to Hoboken.

The late-model Dodge van they were riding in bounced some as Maggard cut in and out of traffic like a seasoned city driver. All the while he talked nonstop about the disposition of the Sepp Fishery as well as other cases he had worked on while attached to the FBI's Pikeville office.

By the time they reached the FBI's Hoboken regional office on Washington Street, where several city offices were also located, Frank and Gloria had a pretty good idea of what had taken place with the courts in Estonia and what Maggard had done in Pikeville. However, he had yet to mention the reason they had come to Hoboken—the Star Mortgage Company. They knew that would come.

The FBI's offices were located on the second floor of an older, nondescript brick building. At ten stories it towered above most of the nearby buildings that housed city offices.

Agent Maggard led the two Kentucky law officers into an open area that contained several cubicles, all of which appeared to be identical. Standing in the way of access to the cubicles was a large, ornate mahogany desk that seemed completely out of place in what was an otherwise modern office filled with functional, inexpensive furniture that could be found in similar offices around the country.

It turned out the mahogany desk was not the only thing that stood out in the office. Seated behind it was an immaculately dressed older woman.

Her gray hair looked as though a beautician straight out of the 1950s had styled it. Not a single hair appeared out of place. Agent Maggard and his office mates figured she used at least a can of hair spray to keep it looking that way.

However, none of them ever said anything like that to her face. They knew Margarita Petroski would let loose with a verbal salvo that would render them speechless.

Roland Maggard had told Frank and Gloria what to expect and how to behave around Margarita. "Just smile a lot and say, 'Yes, ma'am,' or 'No, ma'am.'"

After he had introduced them to Margarita, Maggard stepped back as if to get out of the line of fire. She looked them over carefully while smiling. "I trust your trip here was both pleasant and uneventful," she said, and she continued to smile.

Although both of them probably found her more comical than intimidating, Gloria and Frank did their best imitations of Southern decorum and replied almost in unison. "Thank you, ma'am."

They quickly followed Agent Maggard through a maze of cubicles to a lone glass-enclosed office situated near the back of the building. Maggard knocked twice on the door before entering and introducing Gloria and Frank to Edward "Ed" Dampier, special agent in charge for Hoboken. The small-framed man appeared no taller than five eight or five nine, and he wore his hair in a military-like crew cut. He didn't exactly smile when he stuck out his hand to greet them with a voice that was surprisingly uninflected with Northeastern influences. "It looks as if you got through Margarita," he said, and a smile began to emerge.

"We expected much worse," Gloria said. "I found her very sweet."

Both Agent Maggard and his boss looked at each other before breaking out in laughter.

"Looks as if the old girl has decided to be on her best behavior today. She usually straightens up some before her annual evaluation, but that's at least three months away. Must be something else going on. I'm not going to try to find out what. I'm just going to enjoy this lull before the storm," Dampier said.

"What exactly is her role here?" Frank asked.

"Margarita's employment began a year or so before J. Edgar Hoover died in 1972. It's rumored the director himself hired her. She has a contract that explicitly says she can work as long as she wants, and that's now well beyond forty years," Maggard said.

"But what does she do?" Gloria asked.

"I'm tempted to say whatever she wants, but her job title is administrative assistant to the agent in charge. Long before I came here, the office had hired another individual to do the actual work of the administrative assistant," Dampier said.

"We give Margarita some typing to do, which she is pretty good at, but that's not nearly enough to keep her busy. The rest of the time, she's become what the staff refers to as 'intimidator in charge.' You're not here for me to tell you about the exploits of Margarita, though. Are you?" Dampier laughed. "I told Agent Maggard to fill you in on what we found out about the court ruling in Estonia. I assume you did that, Roland?"

Maggard nodded.

"Let's talk then about the operation of the Russian Mafia fronted through the Star Mortgage Company here in Hoboken. The only mortgage work the company is involved in is buying up dilapidated houses in run-down sections of both New York and New Jersey and supposedly rehabilitating them before putting them up for sale. If the houses don't sell quickly, many mysteriously burn to the ground. And the burnings occur after large insurance policies have been taken out on them. They insure the houses with different agencies, so nothing much was said about the first four or five that burned. In the past couple weeks, though, at least two of the insurance agencies held up payments, and arson investigations have been started here in New Jersey and are contemplated in New York."

Dampier said it was apparent that dealing in real estate was nothing more than a front for prostitution, drugs, and several other nefarious undertakings in which the mortgage company was involved.

"And these people don't hesitate to use muscle to get what they want," Maggard chimed in. "Traditional Mafia operatives have become less violent in the last few years, but the Russians who run the rackets are just the opposite. They are suspected of several killings in and around this area, but they are also good at covering their tracks. It's hard to pin anything on them."

"So it would not surprise you if they were involved in the two killings in Harlan County?" Gloria asked.

"Not at all," Maggard said. "Our office thinks it's even likely. We've determined that some of the mortgage company's higher-ups have ties to Estonia."

"How so?" Frank asked.

"Interpol gave us a list of individuals with known criminal backgrounds who have emigrated from Estonia to the United States in the past few years. At least two are connected with this bunch in leadership roles, and we suspect several others are involved in handling day-to-day activities. One of these appears to have attended Aleksander Sepp's funeral, based on the description we received from your sheriff."

"Any idea where this guy is now?" Davidson asked.

"Nope. None whatsoever," Maggard said. "He hasn't been seen around here lately, but that doesn't mean he's not in the area. One of the things we've discovered they're doing is having their heavies switch jobs on a regular basis. It might be prostitution for a few months before they are switched to illegal gambling or some other mob activity."

"What's the guy's name? What was he involved in when he was last seen around here?" Frank asked.

"His name is Grigory Smirnov. He has no known aliases, and he was into collecting gambling debts—one of their bloodiest undertakings. If he hasn't been seen around here, it might well be that he's in Kentucky, holed up somewhere in Harlan County."

"But a guy like that would stick out like a sore thumb," Gloria said. "It would probably be difficult for him to escape notice for long."

"Not if he has some local folks fronting for him," Maggard replied, "and I wouldn't be surprised if that was the case. What we are finding out about this bunch is, violent as they might be, they are not macho about it like past Mafia operatives might have been. They hide in the shadows and change their MOs regularly."

"We want to visit the offices of the mortgage company," Frank said.

"Sure, but you have to know exactly why you are going there and what you are hoping to accomplish," Dampier replied. "These guys are smart. They'll know if you're there simply on a fishing expedition."

"It won't be hard for them to tell why we're here. We want to find out about the two guys that were present at Aleksander's funeral," Gloria said. "Apparently you think this Smirnov might be one of them."

"I know it won't come as a surprise to you to learn we have already asked about these two. We told Anatoly Varennikov, who appears to be in charge of the mortgage company, that a car registered to Star was present at the funeral of Aleksander Sepp," Maggard said.

"What was his response?" Gloria asked.

"That he had no idea why their vehicle was in Kentucky and that our descriptions of the two individuals at the funeral sounded as if it could have been several of their employees, but without photographs he just couldn't tell."

"But you had already concluded, based on Al's description, that one of the two was probably Smirnov?" Frank asked.

"Yeah, but we didn't push it with Varennikov," Dampier said, "because we already knew Grigory Smirnov had not been seen around here in at least three weeks. That gave us cause to think that at least he, and maybe both of them, are still in Kentucky."

"You said the company's operatives are switched around a lot from racket to racket if their names become closely associated with particular activities."

"That's right," Maggard said. "And they can afford to do that since they have at least forty-five to fifty people working their rackets at any time. Unfortunately they seem to keep coming from Russia primarily but also from Estonia, the Ukraine, and other former Soviet-controlled countries in the region."

Dampier asked Roland Maggard to accompany Gloria and Frank to the Star Mortgage Company, which he said was housed in what appeared to be a down-on-its-luck strip mall near the intersection of Ninth and Hudson Streets. It was several blocks north of the FBI offices.

As they left the suite of offices the FBI occupied, Gloria and Frank nodded their appreciation to Margarita Petroski, and both told her how good it was to meet her. She returned their pleasantries with a nod of her own and a smile that showed her perfect white teeth.

Roland Maggard took Washington Street north to Ninth Street. Traffic was relatively light and moved at a much slower pace than on the interstate. There was a look of relief on the faces of both Kentuckians—the opposite of how they had appeared on the trip from the airport. Their FBI friend probably didn't notice. As he had done on the trip to Hoboken, he talked nonstop.

The shopping mall might have seen better days, but there was no absence of vehicles in the parking lot. Agent Maggard wedged the SUV into a spot that looked as though it had been designed for a compact car.

The three managed to get out of the SUV, despite the little space between vehicles. Maggard was all smiles once they made their way to the sidewalk in front of a seedy liquor store two doors down from Star Mortgage Company. "You guys let me get things started, and then I'll turn it over to you. Remember to look whomever you are speaking to in the eye. Don't flinch. These guys will try to intimidate you." Realizing how this might have sounded to the two experienced law enforcement officers, Roland Maggard rephrased his statement. "I don't mean to suggest you haven't dealt with situations like this in the past. I know you have, but I predict this bunch at Star Mortgage is different from most you have dealt with before."

"Roland, I learned a long time ago you are never too old to learn from others, and there's a whole lot I don't know," Frank said.

"Amen to that," Gloria said.

Agent Maggard smiled and nodded before leading the way to the Star Mortgage Company three doors down. They walked into what appeared to be the front office. However, it was unclear from the mismatch of furniture whether it was a place to conduct business or lounge around and enjoy the big-screen television.

Two men sat in front of the television. They were slumped so far down on a huge faux leather sofa that their backs were all that touched its surface. Their legs were propped up on a wooden crate that looked as though it might have once held fruit or vegetables. Both men appeared fully engrossed in the reality television show.

One of them looked around thirty years old and was completely bald. Frank and Gloria exchanged looks that suggested both were thinking the same thing. This man fit the description of one of the two individuals Sheriff Whitaker had seen at Aleksander Sepp's funeral.

A scantily dressed woman in her late teens or early twenties looked up from reading the *New York Post*. "Can I help you?" she inquired in a not-so-friendly, New York City-inflected tone.

Agent Roland Maggard was quick to flash his FBI identification badge. Deputy Strong and Detective Davidson, who had equally as impressive badges, quickly followed.

"I'm Roland Maggard with the FBI, and this is Gloria Strong and Frank Davidson, law enforcement officers from Harlan County, Kentucky." He took his time to clearly articulate where the officers were from.

No sooner had Maggard identified himself than baldy on the sofa suddenly sat up straight. His attention was no longer focused on the show. Again Gloria and Frank exchanged knowing looks.

"Hey, Anatoly, the FBI's out here," the receptionist hollered loudly. As if aware of how loud it must have sounded, she quietly and almost apologetically said, "Our intercom's broke."

She directed them to a hallway directly behind the lounge and then to the third office on the right. Agent Maggard opened the door and stepped into an office that was the exact opposite of the last room. The furniture matched, and it also appeared expensive. The art, if not expensive, was at least tasteful.

Apparently the expensively dressed man sitting behind a cherry desk was a fan of Frederick Remington. His Western-themed statues and paintings were prominently displayed throughout the office. It was doubtful anything was original, but with the Remington Museum located not too far away in Upstate New York, anything was possible. The curator there would probably be well advised to check the inventory.

"What is it I can do for you?" the man said with just a trace of an accent.

He spoke clearly and slowly, but there was no disguising that he was not a native speaker. Anatoly Varennikov had been in the United States for over twenty years. He had emigrated from Russia with his family as a twelve-year-old in the late 1990s. Agent Maggard introduced Frank and Gloria to Varennikov and asked Gloria to explain why they were there.

"Mr. Varennikov, we are from Harlan County in Eastern Kentucky. In the last two weeks, we have had two homicides—"

"You have my condolences," Varennikov interjected, and he looked her directly in the eye. "But how does that involve me?"

"Well, for one thing, there were two individuals present at the funeral of one Aleksander Sepp, the first to be killed. They were driving a car Star Mortgage Company owns, and I think I might have seen one of the two in your outer office. I noticed as we were coming in here to see you that he hurriedly exited to the street."

Varennikov shrugged his shoulders, took a drink from a bottle of water, and suggested there were several reasons why this might have been the case.

"I'm sure your friends at the FBI have told you some of the employees of the Star Mortgage Company come here from Estonia. And I am also sure you know," he continued while almost smirking, "that the young man to whom you refer, Aleksander, was a native of Estonia. Is it not reasonable to assume some of my employees might have known him before he came to this country?"

"So you're saying the two at the funeral knew Aleksander in Estonia?" Frank asked. He was obviously surprised. "And they were there simply to pay their respects?"

"You can believe what you want, Detective. That would be your prerogative. Wouldn't it?" Varennikov said, and he smirked.

"If that was the case, allowing them to go to the funeral in faraway Kentucky would certainly be a magnanimous gesture on the part of Star Mortgage Company," Agent Maggard said. His look of disdain easily matched the facial machinations of Varennikov. "And this story doesn't jibe with what you told me just a couple days ago—that you didn't know why your car was there."

"I didn't know at the time we had allowed two of our employees to travel to the funeral, but that is consistent with the way we operate. We're a respected company that always tries to do the right thing by its employees. I'm sure each of you knows we could not keep good people if we treated them badly."

"Tell me, Mr. Varennikov, was the employee who just bolted from the premises when Agent Maggard mentioned Kentucky one of the individuals who paid his respects at Aleksander's funeral?" Gloria asked.

"Could have been. I'm not sure. We have so many who work here. I did not see this man. I'll ask my office manager to check our travel records and get back to you. Would that be to your liking?"

"Yes. It would. And if he was one of the two at the funeral, we want to talk with him. Soon. While your office manager is checking your records, please find out the identity of the other individual who traveled so far to pay his respects," Gloria said. Sarcasm dripped from every word.

"We will be happy to comply with both requests, Deputy," Varennikov said.

"They are requests—at least at this point," Agent Maggard said. "But if we don't get that information and get it soon, you can expect we will be back here with a court order. Is that understood?"

"Oh, indeed. And now, as much as I would like to continue discussing this with you, I have other important matters to attend to. I will notify my office manager to get you the information you want."

As the three walked back to the front office, they noticed the office manager was listening to the supposedly inoperative intercom and saying to whatever she was told to do, "Yes. I'll do that."

She looked up, smiled, and told them she would have the information they had requested no later than close of business tomorrow. She said she could not retrieve it any quicker. A New York firm the company had hired to handle most of its personnel work housed the company's travel records.

As they left the offices of Star Mortgage Company, it was apparent from their conversation that all three were convinced the individual who had bolted from the lounge was one of the two present at Aleksander Sepp's funeral. They didn't know what he was doing back in Hoboken, but they were definitely hoping to find out.

By this time Gloria and Frank were bone-tired and ready to get some much-needed rest. Reservations had been made for them at the Hillary Hotel on Riverway Street. It was not far from where they were. Agent Maggard dropped them off at what appeared to be a well-kept property—probably a three-star hotel. He told them to rest up and that he would be back to pick them up for dinner around 7:30 p.m.

They both looked forward to dinner. Roland Maggard had promised to take them to a top-notch Italian restaurant. First, though, they would shower and rest. Tomorrow would be an important day. It could provide much-needed answers to the two homicides they were working.

CHAPTER 31

Sheriff Al Whitaker arrived at work just before 6:00 a.m. He was just in time to talk with Gloria Strong before she and Frank Davidson left for Hoboken.

Then at 7:30 a.m. a courier from Post Ten delivered a multipage document on which Hartford Ford had scribbled a note: "Good reading, Al. I hope this will answer several of our questions. Have to be out of town for a couple days. Be in touch with you soon."

As Al hurriedly skimmed through page after page of information relating to Smith, he quickly formed an opinion. It was the treasure trove that could be the key to unlocking the two homicides under investigation.

The sheriff asked Blanche Halcomb to make a copy for Jim Lucas, who had holed up in the conference room to go through his copy of the report while Al did the same in his office.

The first few pages detailed the autopsy conducted in Frankfort on what it referred to as the decedent, Marcus Smith. It revealed that Smith appeared to have been killed by a slug similar to one that took the life of his young cousin, Aleksander Sepp. The black markings on the round suggested it had been fired from a nine-millimeter Makarov pistol. The round would be sent to Quantico to determine if it matched the gun that killed Aleksander Sepp.

Al put a big check mark next to this finding. If it was the same pistol, there was a strong likelihood the same individual killed both Aleksander Sepp and Marcus Smith.

As had been true in Sepp's case, the cause of death was attributed to "devastating and irreparable internal injuries resulting from a gunshot wound to the chest."

That's a fancy way of saying the poor guy's heart, lungs, and most other organs above the waist were blown to bits, the sheriff thought. *But like Aleksander at least he didn't suffer.*

Remembering that the funeral would be soon, Al hollered to Sylvia to check on the time and location of the services. He figured it would be at the small Pentecostal church the Smith family attended.

The sheriff would be at the funeral—and not just in an official capacity. Marcus had been a friend of his, and Ruby would accompany him because of her friendship with Trudy Smith.

"They say it's gonna be at ten thirty in the morning, Sheriff, and it be at the Pine Mountain Pentecostal Church over on Line Fork in Letcher County," Sylvia said as she came into Al's office with fresh coffee.

The location surprised Al. He figured they had moved the funeral there to accommodate a larger crowd. Marcus was well known and liked throughout the area. Al nodded his thanks for the information and coffee.

The remainder of the official autopsy report revealed little more than what could have been determined on-site. All those present at the Smiths' mountain cabin already had a good idea of what to expect. Jack Thornberry probably could have written the same report without performing an autopsy. The findings were that obvious.

It was what the state's IT experts had found on his computer that caused Al to sit up straight and exclaim, "Well, I'll be darned." This was as close to cursing as he ever got.

It was not technically Marcus's computer. It belonged to the coal company he worked for. As his wife had made clear, though, it was where he kept most of the family's financial records, and that was just the tip of the iceberg, according to the report. It was as though Marcus's alter ego, safely hidden away most of the time, came bursting forth when he turned on this computer. It was easy to figure out how he had masked his time spent on the computer. As a supervisor he often worked long days. Some stretched ten to twelve hours. Trudy and his family never would have known he was not actually working late, and the coal company would have believed he was working on a job-related project.

As the sheriff read the report, he was simply amazed. About three years before, Marcus had discovered that several universities offered free online courses, and he had decided to take advantage of their offerings. His choice of courses surprised Al, who thought he would have been taking classes related to his work.

Not so. He first enrolled in literature and philosophy classes. He struggled to tie them together as he wrote about Albert Camus's *L'Étranger* and delved into existentialism. *Not something he was likely to discuss at the supper table with Trudy and Beulah.* Al laughed to himself. He wondered if Marcus's dissatisfaction with the company he worked for had grown out of the existentialist emphasis on the struggles of an individual in a hostile environment. Al would never know now.

Marcus had also successfully completed courses in introductory astronomy and physics as well as what Al considered other esoteric subjects. It seemed as though Marcus had developed an unquenchable thirst for a classical education. Then he abruptly stopped taking courses about a year and a half before.

At that time he began dabbling in online poker, and unlike the college courses, there was nothing free about it. *At least not once the gambling gets its hooks into you,* Al thought. According to the report, it had worked that way with Marcus Smith.

Initially he was offered free instruction that promised to "make you a big winner in the exciting field of competitive poker." Once the so-called free instruction was over, however, Marcus Smith was taken to the proverbial cleaners. The system allowed him to win—not much but enough to keep him playing—for the first few weeks.

Probably, Al thought, *until he began to think there was nothing to this game.*

Then the losses started. It was not too much initially, but by the end of six weeks, Marcus Smith had lost over $40,000. Like many others he felt the need to get it all back in one game, so he started raising the stakes. By the end of nine months, his losses were a staggering $103,000, which was just under 50 percent of his savings at the bank.

For a month or so, he stopped gambling. Maybe he believed then there was no way to beat the system. During this lull he didn't go back to taking college classes. Instead he started researching his genealogy. Using one of the online programs that charged a small fee, he was able to trace everything on his father's side of the family back to his great-grandfather Jakob after he came to America.

Apparently, though, Marcus had found there were few records that could be accessed to trace one's ancestry in many foreign countries—Estonia being one of them. So the first and last mention of his great-grandfather Jakob was after he came to the United States.

Perhaps this dead end had led Marcus to start an online conversation with a distant relative in Estonia, one Gunnar Sepp. Marcus had done several Google searches for Sepps in Estonia before hooking up with Gunnar a little more than a year before. The first e-mail suggested the initial contact had been by phone.

> 10/1/12 @ 5:30 p.m.
> Gunnar,
> Great talking to you. Thanks for agreeing to help me track down Estonian relatives. As I get older, family means more to me.
> I will send information about Great-Grandfather Jakob in America.
> Marcus Smith

It was exactly a week before Gunnar Sepp responded to his distant cousin. When he did he seemed excited to make the family connection.

10/8/12 @ 8:30 a.m.
Marcus,
I am pleased to hear from you in America. I will make copies of genealogy to send to you soon. Maybe we can visit each other as you say.
Gunnar Sepp

Al walked out of his office and headed to the coffeepot for a refill. After thanking his two administrative assistants for keeping the pot full with fresh brew, he detoured to the conference room to say a word or two to Jim Lucas about the report the two of them were reading.

"Jim, this is mind-boggling. This is a Marcus I never knew."

"Me either. Of course, I didn't know him nearly as well as you did. How do you think Marcus found out about Gunnar to begin with? Finding him online would be like finding a needle in a haystack. I would think his mother probably had some contact information. It could also be that his father had reached out to some of his relatives before he died."

"That seems plausible to me. We'll need to ask Beulah. Not that it is that important how their relationship got started. Let's get back to work, Jim. Hartford said he hoped the report would answer a lot of our questions, and his wish appears to have been realized."

"It's amazing what people reveal about themselves on computers. It's as though they completely discount the possibility that any of it will ever see the light of day," Jim said.

"That's exactly why I try to use the telephone for most of my communication. No social media and very little e-mail for me and Ruby," the sheriff responded.

Al walked back to his office with a fresh cup of coffee and continued poring over page after page of information about Marcus Smith.

Two days after Gunnar Sepp's initial e-mail to his cousin in America, another came. Then there was another a day later and another two days after that. From the content of the e-mails, it appeared he simply wanted to establish a relationship with his newfound relative. E-mail number four read as follows:

> 10/13/12 @ 9:12 a.m.
> Marcus,
> I think to establish our friendship as relatives is most important. We should not let miles between us be a barrier. Let us work together to get a bridge in place!
> Gunnar

Marcus always responded similarly, but neither he nor his cousin came up with any ideas about how the long-separated family members could get together. However, they did continue to share information about their respective families, and Al noticed both men spent some time explaining what they did for work.

Not that unusual, he thought, *since one's vocation is often worn like a badge of honor.*

The week or so before Thanksgiving 2012, Gunnar introduced a new wrinkle. He brought up Aleksander and Viktoria for the first time and explained how they were living with him after the disappearance of their mother and father, Gunnar's brother.

> 11/14/12 @ 8:43 a.m.
> Marcus,
> In Estonia we do not celebrate your Thanksgiving. But my wife and I are thankful for being able to take into our home the son and daughter of my brother. They are teenagers. They are Aleksander and Viktoria.
> They come to live with us because my brother and his wife, who were from Tartu, have disappeared. Aleksander and Viktoria, they have no place else to go.
> Gunnar

From the chronology Viktoria had given him, Al figured she and Aleksander would have been with Mr. and Mrs. Gunnar Sepp for a few years by the time her uncle introduced them in this e-mail. *Why did he wait to tell Marcus about them?*

However, from the moment the two youngsters were first mentioned, Marcus seemed to take a genuine interest in them. As might be expected, he expressed his curiosity about what had happened to their parents.

11/16/12 @ 6:02 p.m.
Gunnar,
What on earth happened to the kids' parents? What a tragedy! I can't imagine how difficult it must be for them, poor things. Especially at this time in their lives. As I have told you, I have two boys, so I can definitely relate to Aleksander and Viktoria. They are lucky to have someone like you to be there for them.
Marcus

From this point forward, it was apparent to the sheriff what Gunnar Sepp was doing. He had not initiated contact with his cousin in America, but once contact had been made, he was fully intent on taking advantage of it to get what he wanted—control of his missing brother and sister-in-law's successful and highly profitable fishery in Tallinn.

The report revealed how he had reeled in Marcus Smith much like the anglers in Tallinn reeled in sprats and herring from the Gulf of Finland. Although, it was obvious that once hooked, Marcus did not appear to work hard at getting the hook out of his mouth.

Subsequent e-mails from Gunnar began to build the case against Estonia. He said it was not the best place for two bright youngsters like Viktoria and Aleksander to grow into adulthood and begin their lives.

"Everyone thinks things are OK in Estonia since Russia is no longer in control," Gunnar wrote, "but opportunities here are small compared to what would be available for them in the West—particularly in the United States."

Contending that he and his wife wanted only what was best for their niece and nephew, Gunnar wrote the following plea:

2/12/13 @ 8:47 a.m.
I do not know how to say this to you, Marcus, but would there be a way they could come to America? To live with you and your wife? I know it is much to ask, but I fear for their futures in Estonia. I want for them what is available in "the land of opportunity," your US of A.
Gunnar

The e-mails between Gunnar and Marcus continued unabated. While not exactly opposed to the idea, Marcus wasn't enamored with it either. The best way to describe his attitude concerning his young, distant cousins living with him was "someone will have to convince me this is a good idea." By "good idea," Marcus seemed to mean "good for him."

Near the end of February, one particular e-mail from Gunnar seemed to grab Marcus's attention and suggest to him that maybe his young cousins coming to live with him might not be a bad idea after all.

2/27/14 @ 7:58 a.m.
Marcus,
When the fishery is sold, there will be funds for Viktoria and Aleksander. The $$$ will be in a trust. I think it would be good for you to be the trust administrator. Could you do that? All legal documentation, of course, will come from here in Estonia.
Gunnar

Marcus wasted no time in responding. Al thought his quick reply probably indicated to Gunnar that his American cousin was interested in money.

2/28/14 @ 8:30 a.m.
Gunnar,
I am not a lawyer. You are. So, of course, you know more about this kind of thing than I do. How much money would the kids receive, and when do you think they would have access to it?
Marcus

Al shook his head as he read Marcus's response. He bet at this juncture his old friend's thoughts were not focused on the financial well-being of Aleksander and Viktoria but on his own.

That notion proved true some two weeks later after a series of additional e-mails had established that Viktoria and Aleksander would each receive something in the neighborhood of $1 million and that the administrator of the trust, one Marcus Smith, would receive $150,000 at the time the trust was set up in Estonia. This revelation floored Al. He had never heard of an administrator receiving this much for a comparably sized trust.

"I am astounded," he whispered to himself.

The e-mail chain showed that within a week, Gunnar and Marcus had agreed that Viktoria and Aleksander would come to America to live with the Smith family. When Marcus inquired as to whether the kids were excited about coming, Al saw that Gunnar repeated pretty much what Viktoria had told him when she came to his house the day her brother was killed. Aleksander was very excited about the prospect of living in the United States. His sister was lukewarm to the idea, but it seemed to be growing on her.

Marcus provided information about Harlan County that Gunnar could share with the teenagers, and he laid it on pretty thick. "We have beautiful mountains, cascading streams, picturesque hamlets, educational opportunities, and a variety of wildlife." Apparently infatuated with the black bear that had returned to the area, he spoke glowingly of being able to see a mother and her cubs anytime they visited the state park.

Interestingly the report showed it was within a few days of the agreement being finalized that Marcus started gambling again online.

"Hmmm," Al said to himself, "it looks as if the promise of that hundred fifty thousand dollars pumped him up again to the point he wasn't too worried about already having lost over one hundred thousand. Chances are he now thought he could recoup his losses and maybe win a little."

Al knew that was how many gamblers thought. When they lost big, as Marcus had, they convinced themselves they would only continue gambling until they were even again. Of course, most never got even. They only went into the hole even further. That was exactly what happened to Marcus. It took less than a month for him to clean out all of the savings he and Trudy had amassed at the bank in Cumberland. It was well past lunchtime when the sheriff put a paper clip on the last page he had reviewed and walked to the conference room.

When Al opened the door and peeked in, Jim looked up and shook his head. "Al, can you believe this?" he asked. He was holding up his copy of the report. "What got into Marcus?"

"Darned if I know, Jim, but whatever it was, in all likelihood it contributed to his death."

The sheriff and deputy took a short lunch since it was already late. Then they returned to their offices in the courthouse to continue going through the report. They had decided over lunch that Al would join Jim in the conference room as they finished their review.

Throughout the afternoon they found several other surprises in the report that detailed the transformation of Marcus Smith and the online relationship he and his cousin Gunnar Sepp had developed. Without question the biggest surprise pertained to the gifts Gunnar had sent by way of Aleksander and Viktoria to Trudy, Beulah, and Marcus—particularly the gift Marcus had received. It was Jim who came across it first. He sat still with his mouth agape. He shook his head as he described the gifts to Al.

Gunnar had told Marcus in an e-mail that he was sending gifts to his relatives to express his gratitude for giving his nephew and niece a chance to live better lives in America. He was sending Trudy a tiered sterling silver necklace, and Beulah would receive a set of Siana vases. Then Jim paused before continuing. "You aren't going to believe this. He promised Marcus a pistol—and not just any pistol. A nine-millimeter Makarov. He wrote in the e-mail, 'This will be for when the mother of the bear cubs comes after you!'"

Neither man left the office until well after dark, and as each headed to the parking lot, Jim Lucas was still shaking his head.

CHAPTER 32

Gloria Strong and Frank Davidson were finishing up the complimentary breakfast provided by the hotel when Roland Maggard showed up to take them back to the Star Mortgage Company. Frank motioned for Maggard to come sit with them.

"Hey. Thanks for a great dinner, Roland," Gloria said.

On his recommendation they had each had cheese-stuffed ravioli, a lightly breaded baked chicken breast, and a mesclun salad on the side. A small glass of zinfandel was served with dinner as well.

No sooner had they given their orders to the server at Ristorante Stagnolia than Gloria's phone vibrated with a text message from Al. It told her to call him when she could. What caused her to finish the meal a little more quickly than she usually would have were these words, "Important information to share!"

They left the restaurant in such a hurry that they passed on dessert. Instead they gathered in Jim's room to return the sheriff's call. Al was home enjoying supper himself when Gloria got through to him.

"I have Frank and Agent Roland Maggard here with me," she said, and she pushed the speakerphone button so everyone could hear.

By the time Sheriff Whitaker relayed all the pertinent information from the report, the three were shaking their heads in much the same way Jim Lucas had done throughout the day.

Gloria Strong asked the same question her fellow deputy had asked. "What on earth got into Marcus Smith?"

After finishing breakfast, Gloria and Frank grabbed their bags, and Roland Maggard pulled the government-issue Dodge van to the front entrance. Their bags were quickly loaded, and the three headed for the Star Mortgage Company. They did not know exactly what to expect.

The news from Sheriff Whitaker about Marcus, particularly the Makarov pistol from Gunnar Sepp, had kept them talking into the wee hours of the morning, and it continued to be the topic of conversation on the short trip to the so-called mortgage company.

The receptionist with whom they had spoken yesterday met them at the door. Unlike yesterday she was dressed conservatively in an attractive ensemble of black slacks and a wool blazer. She had a sugary smile on her young face as she wordlessly pointed them to Varennikov's office.

As if the surprises of the last twenty-four hours hadn't been enough, another one awaited them. Baldy, who had skedaddled out of the office yesterday when he had heard the mention of Harlan County, Kentucky, was seated on a leather sofa beside another individual who looked to be about his age. Unlike the bald man with whom he shared the sofa, this one had a head full of jet-black hair. It was combed straight back and looked as if it had been sprayed stiff.

"I would like for you to meet Viktor and Grigory Smirnov. They are brothers," Anatoly Varennikov said before Gloria, Jim, or Agent Maggard could say a word.

In a cool and seemingly calculated way, Varennikov went on to say the Smirnov brothers had been at the funeral of Aleksander Sepp. They had been there to pay their respects to the family of the young man they had met while working on the fishing docks in Tallinn, Estonia.

"Why didn't you tell my office this when we first asked you what the vehicle owned by your company was doing at the funeral?" Roland Maggard asked.

"As I explained to you yesterday, Agent Maggard, I do not know all our employees personally. I had to check with the company that handles our personnel functions to find out myself."

"We're going to want to interrogate these two," Frank said.

"You are welcome to do so, but please know they do not speak or understand English very well."

"Why don't you translate for us, Mr. Varennikov?" Maggard said. When the Russian agreed, the FBI agent pulled a recorder from the briefcase he carried. "I'm sure you won't mind if we record the conversation so we can verify the accuracy of your translation."

Whether the motley pair could speak and understand English was uncertain, but it was clear they were not going to tip their hand one way or other. Their answers were usually some variation of "not understand" as they constantly looked to Varennikov to interpret for them. Not surprising he spoke Estonian fluently. Through Varennikov they learned the boy's father had employed them to keep the dock surrounding his fishery clean and clear of debris and to haul away fish parts left over from filleting.

"Ask them what kind of work Aleksander did," Gloria requested.

Varennikov mentioned the name "Aleksander." Something in Estonian followed.

They both smiled before saying something Varennikov translated. "Although he was very young, he did almost everything we did."

The brothers vehemently denied having anything to do with the deaths of either Aleksander Sepp or Marcus Smith.

"Our records will show they did not leave for Kentucky until after the boy, Aleksander, was killed," Varennikov said.

The company's travel records also indicated, according to Varennikov, that the Smirnovs were back in Hoboken the day after Aleksander's funeral.

The interrogation continued for another thirty minutes or so before Agent Maggard, Deputy Strong, and Detective Davidson decided to call it quits. They had gotten everything of substance they could.

Back in the van, however, they spoke animatedly about what they had learned—provided Varennikov had given an accurate translation, which would be checked.

"Did you see the brothers' faces light up when Aleksander's name was mentioned?" Frank asked. "Do you think it's possible the Smirnovs did work for his dad and that Aleksander worked alongside them?"

"We learned from our investigation in Kentucky that Aleksander was a good worker and a good student. There is no reason to think his parents would have pampered him in any way," Frank noted. "Although, he would have been awfully young."

"But what we will probably never know," Gloria said, "is whether or not they started working with Aleksander once he came to Kentucky to introduce heroin into the drug picture in the mountains. I would bet the three of them worked the drug trade together."

"There had to be something going on. If they weren't spending time in Kentucky, how would they have learned of Aleksander's death? I don't buy their explanation they heard it from a mutual friend."

"Unless," Frank said, "the mutual friend was Marcus Smith."

"Or Viktoria Sepp," Gloria added. "This case just gets more complicated by the hour."

Despite not believing the Smirnovs were choirboys—Agent Maggard had too much evidence of their activities locally to prove otherwise—Gloria and Frank were now ready to head back to Kentucky. They believed it was possible, if not probable, neither of them was involved in the homicides they were investigating.

Agent Maggard promised he would have a validated translation of the Smirnovs' conversation with Varennikov typed and available to them by noon tomorrow.

However, before asking Maggard to taxi them back to the airport for a 4:00 p.m. flight to Lexington, there was one other thing on Deputy Strong's agenda. "I want to visit Rockefeller Center to see the Christmas tree and all the other decorations. I've watched the lighting ceremony on TV since I was a kid."

"You're in luck, Gloria," Roland Maggard said. "Usually the tree lighting occurs after Thanksgiving. Not sure why they decorated it so early this year, but they did, and it's one heck of a beautiful tree."

CHAPTER 33

Although Sheriff Al Whitaker wanted to question Trudy Smith in the worst possible way, he would not do so until after the funeral of her husband. Recent events had changed the way he felt about Marcus—and about her—but he was determined to keep all that bottled up so the services could be conducted with as much dignity as possible.

With everything that had transpired, he doubted it would be a normal funeral. In fact he doubted if anything would ever be normal again for the Smith family.

Friends and relatives started gathering at the Pine Mountain Pentecostal Church at around 9:15 a.m. for the funeral scheduled to begin at 10:00 a.m. Pentecostals were a very gregarious people, and they frequently visited other churches in their denomination throughout the area. Chances were Marcus Smith was known in several counties in the region, and Al was certain parishes from several outlying counties would be represented. Some might have even been located in neighboring Virginia or Tennessee.

The large brick building that housed the Pine Mountain congregation had been built almost entirely by church members. Many had worked in the coal mining industry and possessed myriad construction skills.

Called charismatic by some, Pentecostals were generally more open and spontaneous in their worship services than some of the other Protestant churches in the area.

But not by much. Al knew several Baptist churches had picked up at least some of the Pentecostals' worship practices. That included raising the hands when the singing or preaching particularly inspired a church member and adopting a more contemporary approach to singing hymns. Sometimes the use of musical instruments beyond the piano and organ accompanied these hymns.

The congregating crowd was larger than the group that had come to pay their respects to Aleksander Sepp. The large parking lot was almost full by 9:45 a.m., and Al noticed several cars parked alongside the highway.

Al and Ruby had arrived early enough to find a spot in the parking lot, and they walked with several others into the church's sanctuary, which he estimated seated in excess of two hundred.

If anyone thought the nontraditional manner of the building's construction would result in something substandard, he or she would have been mistaken. Having the members in charge of construction might have had the exact opposite effect. Their faith meant so much to them they had used all their many talents to build something that was a testament to their love of God.

One of the most striking features of the church was its ornate baptistery behind which was a realistic painting of a mountain stream that seemed to be flowing directly in the baptismal pool. The Reverend Kenneth Hale—a tall, willowy man whose light blue eyes shone like stars beneath his bushy, white hair—was renowned for his no-nonsense approach in the pulpit. He preached the necessity for nonbelievers to be born again if they expected to live eternally in heaven, and Al fully expected this theme would be at the center of his funeral message today.

As was the case at the funeral of Aleksander Sepp, the Smiths were gathered in the front pews of the church. Trudy Smith and Marcus's mother, Beulah, sat in the first row. They were together with sons, Troy and Sean. Their wives and children were spread across the second pew. Sitting with them was Viktoria Sepp.

Other members of the family filled the next several pews. Al didn't know many of them and figured they must live outside the area. He also recognized several of the men and women Marcus had worked with at the mine. That included Superintendent Jeff Lockhart and his wife.

People from the surrounding area who knew Marcus and his family, including church members and residents of Cumberland, Benham, and Lynch, accounted for well over half the crowd. There was no way Al would be able to follow up on the strangers in the crowd as he could at Aleksander's funeral.

Pastor Hale's message focused only briefly on the deceased. "He has gone on to be with the Lord, and the only way you can see him again is to accept Jesus Christ as your Lord and Savior. We are on this side but for a minute, dear friends, and eternity awaits. The question Marcus Smith would have me ask each of you is, where will you spend eternity?"

No one from the audience spoke.

Many of the hymns sung throughout the service had sad and mournful qualities, but then the last of the songs, "Ain't No Grave Gonna Hold My Body Down," bellowed forth like an anthem of victory.

Al had learned years ago that Claude Ely, a singer, songwriter, and preacher, wrote the song in the early 1930s. Ely was born in Southwest Virginia but grew up in Kentucky and was well acquainted with Harlan County.

When the song was finished, the funeral director allowed those present to move forward pew by pew to pay their last respects. Almost everyone hugged Trudy, Beulah, Troy, and Sean. Al could hear them whispering condolences as they tried mightily to console the family.

He and Ruby did likewise. His wife spent more time with Trudy and Beulah while he spoke of old times with the two boys. Al told them their father was a good man, but no sooner had he gotten the words out of his mouth than he regretted saying them. He wasn't sure that was the case anymore. In fact he was almost sure it wasn't.

The funeral procession traveled over a road that twisted and turned to the top of a knoll where Marcus Smith's body would join those of many of his relatives in the family graveyard. That included his great-grandfather Jakob.

After the burial Al and Ruby said their final good-byes to the family and slowly made their way back to the main highway.

"Al, did you notice Viktoria?" Ruby asked. "She seemed almost in a daze. Lost in her thoughts. She was obviously grieving, but it seemed as though she had cried so much there were no more tears left."

"That might be an apt description," Al said. "When you stop to think about what she has been through in the past few years, of the members of her family she has lost, it's a wonder she hasn't had a nervous breakdown."

"You're right," Ruby said.

They rode silently the remainder of the way home.

CHAPTER 34

The funeral of Marcus Smith had not had the same impact on Al as Aleksander's. Maybe it was because Aleksander had been so young, or maybe it was because of what he had learned about Marcus's involvement in what he could only describe as shady dealings.

In any event Al had gotten up that morning and driven to his office in Harlan. He was not in high spirits, but at least feelings of how unfair life could be did not consume him.

The drive had given him the opportunity to plan the day's activities. The new evidence from the report combined with the information from Interpol and what Gloria Strong and Frank Davidson had found out at the Star Mortgage Company had changed things considerably.

No longer did they have the Russian Mafia at the top of their suspect list. Al, however, was sure the Smirnov brothers had had a presence in this area peddling drugs, and he was not enitrely convinced they were not around when Aleksander was killed. Gloria and Frank Davidson didn't think so. He would accept that for the time being.

He had also been flabbergasted to learn Gunnar Sepp had given a pistol to his cousin Marcus Smith—a pistol that happened to be a nine-millimeter Makarov, which was the same kind of firearm that had taken the lives of two individuals within in a two-week period.

Coincidence? Al didn't think so, and he was sure no one on his staff or on the staff at the Kentucky State Police's Post Ten thought so either. As he pulled into his assigned parking space beside the Harlan County Courthouse at 7:45 a.m., the sheriff knew he still had a whole lot of unraveling to do to solve these mysterious killings.

Al noticed a light in the conference room, and he stuck his head in.

"Good morning, Al," Jim said, and he lifted his coffee cup in greeting. "Woke up early and couldn't get these cases out of my mind. While you were at the funeral, I spent most of the day yesterday continuing to review the report."

"Find anything else of interest?" Al asked.

"Well, yes. The information detailing how the one-hundred-fifty-thousand-dollar payment to Marcus was going to be made was pretty interesting," he said.

"Are you going to save me the time and trouble of poring over the report to find that information?" Al asked, and he laughed.

Jim opened the report and pointed to an e-mail from Gunnar Sepp telling Marcus what he needed to do to get his money. "You will notice there was a condition attached to Marcus getting access to the money."

> 3/11/12 @ 9:33 a.m.
> Marcus,
> The funds for you will be deposited as I have told you in my letter. Be sure to use information about account number to access. It is important not to make slipups. But funds will not be put into account if Aleksander and Viktoria do not agree to selling fishery. And it must be done soon.
> Gunnar

"The surprises just keep coming," Al said. "No wonder you were up early thinking about this stuff. When Gloria gets here, we need to get on over to Post Ten for a powwow with Hartford Ford and Frank Davidson. I know they've gone over this report with a fine-tooth comb just like we have. We've got to figure this thing out."

"I agree," Jim said. "If we don't get some answers soon, I'm afraid something else will happen, and somebody else will end up dead."

Before getting everything together for a trip to Post Ten, Sylvia came into the conference room to inform them they would not need to go after all. "Captain Ford and Detective Davidson are out in the lobby, Sheriff. You want me to send them in here?"

"Please. Tell them to come right in, and when Gloria gets here, send her in too, Sylvia."

"Will do, Sheriff."

The two state police officers walked in carrying coffee cups from McDonald's.

"Hey, guys. You don't like our coffee here? Better not say anything to Sylvia. She's liable to get her feelings hurt."

"We knew we would be pushing our luck a little with Sylvia, but she didn't say anything to us. Did roll her eyes a little, though," Frank said.

"How did it go up in the Big Apple?" Jim asked.

"Actually we spent almost all our time in Hoboken, which most folks would not liken to NYC, but we got what we went after, thanks in no small part to Agent Roland Maggard."

"I understand he's a local boy," Al said.

"Yeah. His family is from Harlan County. They moved to Harrogate, Tennessee, after his dad started working as a coal buyer for the Tennessee Valley Authority." Frank laughed before he continued. "Boy, were we surprised to see a homeboy waiting for us when we got off the plane in LaGuardia—especially since you guys had us scared to death about how snobbish the FBI can be."

"You were lucky," Hartford said. "To be able to work with Maggard and also a boss who knew something about our region."

"I wouldn't have predicted the treatment you got in a hundred years," Al said. "Like Hartford says, you were lucky."

Gloria walked in midconversation. She raised her eyebrows and then winked at Frank. Everyone in the room broke out in laughter. Al stood up from his chair and motioned for Jim to go to the whiteboard.

"Let's go through what we know and don't know like we did a few days ago. A lot has happened in three days."

"Let's talk about the murder weapon," Gloria said.

Al had called her last night to bring her up to date on what they had found out from the IT report. Jim added another note to their running list:

> ✓ Ballistics determined the murder weapon was a nine-millimeter Makarov pistol in both homicides, and markings on the slugs came from the same gun."

"Never thought we would get a report back from Quantico so quickly, but once we told them the two homicides might be related, they got right on it," Hartford said. "And I'll bet they were also a little more interested in this case because a Russian weapon was involved."

"A few days ago, we believed the shooter, or shooters, might have been involved with drugs in some way, and we believed Star Mortgage Company in Hoboken, New Jersey, employed that person or persons," Al said.

"We now believe that to be unlikely," Gloria said, "since the two suspects Al saw at Aleksander Sepp's funeral admitted to being in attendance but were there because they had known Aleksander in Estonia. In fact they say they worked for the fishery owned by his mother and father."

"You believe that?" Al asked.

"Yes. We do," Gloria said.

She looked at Frank, and he nodded to concur. "It is unlikely—highly unlikely—Anatoly Varennikov would have allowed us to talk with them if they had been involved in killing Aleksander or Marcus," Frank said. "From what Agents Maggard and Dampier told us, had they been involved in any way, they would have been hidden away somewhere or maybe sent back home to Estonia."

"He could have known that was how we would think. Maybe this guy's good at poker. Bluffs a lot. You know?" Jim said.

"Could be, but we were there and looking them in the eyes. Don't believe they were involved in either killing," Frank continued.

"But," Gloria said, "that doesn't mean they have not been in Harlan County selling drugs. I would say they were definitely peddling heroin, and their local contact was Aleksander Sepp."

"OK. If everyone is in agreement, let's write that down, Jim," Hartford said.

✓ The mortgage company suspects moved from the top of the suspect list to the bottom.

"If not these guys then who did the killing?" the sheriff asked.

"If we were just dealing with Aleksander's death, I would point the finger directly at Marcus Smith, since Gunnar Sepp got him a Makarov pistol as a gift," Jim said. "It appears Aleksander was not going along with selling the fishery, and that meant Marcus probably would have had to say good-bye to that hundred fifty K. But we know he didn't kill himself. Whoever left the cabin on the ATV probably killed Marcus and maybe Aleksander as well."

"And we are certain he did not kill himself because there was no powder residue on Marcus's hand or sleeves. And our examination showed no indication they had been wiped clean," Gloria said.

Jim added another bullet point to the board.

✓ Marcus Smith did not kill Aleksander Sepp or commit suicide.

"Who else would have access to the pistol?" Hartford asked. Answering his own question, he said, "I would think the entire Smith family, since Marcus apparently got the gun at the same time his mother and Trudy got their gifts. The pistol would have been at the Smiths' since Aleksander and Viktoria showed up."

"How did they get a pistol through customs?" Frank asked.

"I've wonder about that too," Gloria said. "That's something we'll have to ask Viktoria."

Al had said they would head back to Benham tomorrow to interrogate Trudy, Beulah, and Viktoria, and the pistol would be just one of the many things they needed to ask about.

"We've got to find out about the letter Gunnar wrote to Marcus—the one where he supposedly gave his cousin instructions about accessing the money he was to get for serving as trust administrator," Gloria added.

"That's key," Captain Ford said. "Getting access to that much money could have motivated several people to pull the trigger."

"What else do we need to find out when we question the women?" Al asked.

"That's about it until we get Trudy and Marcus's phone records. Judge Wilson gave his OK, so we should have something soon," Frank reported. "We'll share this information as soon as we get it."

With only a few additions, their list had not gotten much longer since earlier in the week. That meant they were finding answers to their questions and narrowing down the list of suspects. Al likened the investigative process to pouring information into a special funnel with multiple holes. They started at the top of the funnel with a lot of facts and figures, and as those facts worked their way down the funnel, the information that could be discarded leaked out of the holes along the way. By the time the remaining facts and figures came out of the narrow end of the funnel, they had their answers.

The problem, Al knew, was sometimes there were either too many facts being put into the funnel or too many leaking out along the way, and when that happened getting answers took a long, long time.

CHAPTER 35

After Hartford and Frank left, Al, Gloria, and Jim remained in the conference room to strategize. They decided Al and Jim would head back to Benham to continue questioning Trudy, Beulah, and Viktoria. Gloria would stay behind to go over the IT report to make sure Al and Jim had not missed anything important.

The information gleaned from Marcus's computer had once again dropped Viktoria to the bottom of the suspect list, and Al saw no need to bring her to Harlan for interrogation, which earlier in the week he had intended to do.

Before leaving, Al spoke with other detectives to get updates on the cases they were working. They reported nothing new had come up since their last briefing—at least nothing of importance, according to Deputy Andy Harris.

"That's good news, but with Thanksgiving coming up, let's keep our eyes and ears open for counterfeiting. Blanche, you might want to give the merchants association a call to alert them as well. I remember last year we discovered some out-of-town visitors had passed counterfeit five-dollar bills before an alert clerk noticed their color wasn't quite right."

"Sheriff, I know it won't surprise you to learn we have already done that very thing," Blanche Halcomb said. "We also told them to pay close attention to lower denomination bills, as the large denominations—twenties and fifties—are always examined carefully."

"Blanche, sometimes I get to thinking you folks don't need me very much." Al laughed. "All I can say is keep up the good work."

A short time later, the sheriff and Deputy Lucas were in Jim's Crown Victoria and headed back up US 119.

"We are keeping this road hot," Al said, "but I think we are closing in on whoever killed Aleksander Sepp and Marcus Smith. At least I hope so."

On the way they agreed they would interrogate each of the women separately as they had done in the past. They would start with Trudy. Viktoria would follow, and they would end with Beulah.

When they got to the Smith home, they were not surprised to find Trudy, Viktoria, and Beulah waiting on them. Trudy's sons and their families were also present.

"I am very sorry to have to be here so soon after Marcus's funeral. I know you are still grieving, and if there was any way to get around this, I would," the sheriff said.

"We understand, Al. It is difficult for us, but the boys being here has helped a lot," Trudy said. "I don't know how I would have done it without them."

Al spoke to Sean and Troy and their wives and introduced Jim Lucas. Both the sons looked drained. Their faces were pale. Sean, the oldest, looked to have been crying, while Troy appeared to have his emotions in check.

Try as he might, it was hard for the sheriff to get beyond the obvious pain the family members were experiencing. That being the case, he and Jim took their time. In situations like this, the worst thing a police officer could do was rush. If that happened the officer's behavior would be interpreted as callous and indifferent, and it was unlikely that those being interrogated would be cooperative. Irrespective of whether it was good police procedure, it was the right thing to do.

For the next twenty minutes, the sheriff and deputy simply visited with the family of Marcus Smith. When it was obvious enough had been said and to some small extent the pain had been lessened, Al and Jim began questioning Trudy Smith about the death of her husband.

"Trudy, I know you are aware of the Makarov pistol Gunnar Sepp gave to Marcus as a gift," Al asked.

"Yes. I am," she said. "He also sent me and Beulah gifts as well."

"Didn't you find it strange that a pistol would be given as a gift?"

"Initially yes, but then Beulah told me about how Great-Grandfather Jakob had been fond of guns. We all thought it might have stemmed from that. That included Marcus."

"Do you have access to the gun?" Jim asked.

Trudy Smith looked as if all the blood had drained from her face. She shook her head. "I have no idea where it is. Marcus took it from the house some time ago. I assume it is in his office at the mining company."

"The office was searched thoroughly when the state police went up there to get his computer, and there was no sign of a gun," Jim said.

As soon as Jim uttered the word "computer," there was an abrupt change in Trudy's manner and an almost imperceptible gasp. She had been looking directly at Jim, but now her eyes darted back and forth across the room. She appeared to recover quickly, however, and she expressed her surprise the pistol had not been found in the office.

"You told me earlier you were surprised your savings account at the bank had been almost completely depleted. Is that right?" Al asked.

"I was flabbergasted to learn our savings had disappeared."

"And you were not aware Marcus was gambling online?"

Again Trudy's eyes darted back and forth before she replied. "How would I have known that, Sheriff?"

"You knew nothing of this then? Did you know anything about Marcus taking college courses online?" Al asked.

"I think I recall him telling me something about that. He said that was why he spent so much time up at the office."

"Did that surprise you, Trudy, that Marcus would be taking courses online?" Al continued.

"Maybe a little, but I always knew he was interested in literature and philosophy. Stuff like that," she said.

"I didn't mention he was taking literature and philosophy courses. Had he told you that?" Al asked.

The eye movement seemed to increase, and Trudy began rocking back and forth in her chair. "He must have told me. That's the only way I would have known."

"Did you know, Trudy, about the one-hundred-fifty-thousand-dollar advance Gunnar Sepp had promised Marcus for serving as the trust administrator for Viktoria?" Jim asked.

Trudy was now clearly nervous. The rocking increased, and she would not look at either Jim or Al. When she didn't answer, Jim asked her the question again.

"I don't know. I don't know. All of this is so confusing to me. My husband is dead. Aleksander is dead. What do you want from me?" she almost screamed.

"We are not trying to be difficult, but it's important you tell us what you know," the sheriff said softly.

"I think I might have known something. Didn't you tell me when you questioned me earlier?" she asked.

"We told you about the trust being set up. Initially it was for both Viktoria and Aleksander, but I did not tell you about Marcus receiving the cash up front to serve as administrator," Al said.

"Maybe Marcus told me. I don't know. I just don't know," she said.

"And you are not aware of a document, probably a letter, from Gunnar Sepp to Marcus with information about how he could access the money?" Jim asked.

"No. I don't know what you're talking about. I just want all this to be over. I can't believe what's happened," Trudy said.

Al thanked her for answering the questions, and Trudy left the room. She moved directly into the arms of her son Sean. The entire family gathered around to console her, and more than one of them directed angry looks at Al and Jim. The sheriff understood their emotions were raw. He figured he would have looked accusingly too if the roles had been reversed.

Viktoria Sepp came into the room. Although she was still distraught, she seemed more composed than during her last interrogation. Al and Jim had agreed on the way to Benham that Jim would take the lead in questioning the young woman. They had specifically talked about the information they needed to elicit from her.

Al had mentioned on more than one occasion that he hoped she came out of this mess in the clear. She had already lost more than anyone should in a lifetime. Jim began by telling Viktoria how sorry they were for her losses. He then asked many of the same questions he and Al had asked Trudy. She affirmed, as she had done previously, that she knew of the trust that would be set up for her. She also understood that Marcus would be the administrator. She did not know, she said, he would have gotten one hundred fifty thousand dollars to serve as administrator.

"And I did not sign to give approval to sell the fishery," she said.

"Did you know about the pistol your uncle Gunnar gave to Marcus?" Jim asked.

"Yes. We all know. I was not surprised. Guns are often given as gifts in Estonia."

The information she had volunteered seemed to surprise the sheriff, and he began questioning the young woman. "Did the gift seem to surprise others in the family?" he asked.

"Not Beulah. She said it goes all the way back to Great-Grandfather Jakob," she said with just a trace of a laugh.

"What about Trudy?" he asked.

"I think so. She might have been surprised. She asked why you need pistol when you have other guns. Rifles, I think."

"How did you and Aleksander get the pistol into this country without it being confiscated and without being arrested?" Jim asked.

"We did not bring the gun with us on the plane," she said.

"Then how did it get here?" Jim almost shouted. This new revelation was obviously surprising.

"Aleksander, he knows friends from Estonia here in America, and Uncle Gunnar, he gives him money to buy it here."

"Here in Kentucky?" Al asked. His curiosity was piqued.

"I think from the same men who sell drugs. The same men I think he go to see the day he is killed. The same men I tell you about when we talk before."

Al knew the men Viktoria spoke of—the Smirnov brothers—and he was sure Jim was thinking the same thing. This was yet another twist in the case. *Did they do the killing after all?*

"Did you know them?" Al asked.

"They come to Aleksander one day when we are in the park. Aleksander walks away from me to talk with them. He tells me later that they work with him for our mother and father when he was small. I ask what they do in America, and he says only that they have good jobs that pay big salaries. I ask him if it is selling drugs. He says no. That in America money can be made in a lot of ways. But I don't believe him."

"I think you were right not to believe him," Jim said. "We are sure these two were selling heroin and probably using your brother as a local distributor."

Viktoria looked crestfallen. "I was sure he is involved in drugs," she said sadly.

"Did you not give Marcus the pistol when Trudy and Beulah got their gifts?" Al asked.

"Yes. We wait for two weeks before we give anyone gifts. We tell them we have gifts from Uncle Gunnar, but we will wrap them properly before giving the gifts to them. When my brother acquires gun, we give them the gifts all wrapped in pretty paper," she said.

"Let's move on to another subject. You told us previously you did not sign a release for the sale of your mother and father's fishery. Is that right?" Jim asked.

"That is what I just tell you. I never sign anything. I never send anything to Uncle Gunnar in Estonia."

"You're sure? Did you sign any kind of document you can recall?" Al asked.

" The only documents we sign, my brother and I, was when we come first to live with Uncle Gunnar in Estonia. I tell you about this earlier."

Al shook his head to acknowledge he remembered. Satisfied, he decided to move to a new subject.

"Did Trudy and Marcus argue a lot, Viktoria?" the sheriff asked, and he smiled as he did so.

Viktoria waited for several seconds before replying. "They argue some. No more, no less, I believe, than my uncle and aunt in Estonia."

"What did they argue about?"

"Trudy, she is concerned Marcus is never here. That he spends too much time away in the office or at work."

"Did they ever argue about their finances?"

"Sometimes she say she needs more information about accounts at the bank. She say she makes a large salary as a nurse. She is entitled to know how much there is," Viktoria replied.

Jim then nodded to Al that he had finished his questioning. He knew there was a final question the sheriff had to have an answer to. He wasn't sure it was relevant to determining how or why Aleksander Sepp was killed, but he knew Al wanted to know. "Viktoria, when you found your brother's body, did you position his right hand under his chin?"

"I am sure that you ask this," she said. She suddenly looked as though she would cry. "And I will tell you. It was the only thing we had, Aleksander and I, that connect us with our mother and father."

"And how was that?" Al asked.

"When we were young, our favorite TV program was from America. It was *Mister Rogers' Neighborhood*. He, Mr. Rogers, would say to always keep our chin up. Not to let rainy days get us down. So when things did not go so well, our mother and our father would say, 'Remember to keep your chin up. The rain, it will not last forever.' And they would lift our chins up when they say this.

"When they go missing, we are so lonely. No one can take their place. We try to cheer each other up. I would lift my brother's chin up and say, 'The rain will not last forever, Aleksander,' and he would lift my chin up and say, 'Viktoria, the rain, it will not last forever.'"

Then she began to cry. Al and Jim gave Viktoria enough time to compose herself before rejoining the Smith family. Al was once again leaning toward the young woman's lack of involvement in either homicide. He believed she was telling the truth. By the same token, he and Jim both agreed Trudy Smith had acted as though she had something to hide.

Beulah Smith, the family matriarch and, as Marcus had often said, the power behind the throne, looked anything but powerful when she walked into the kitchen and took a seat. The tough facade she always projected to the world had disappeared.

Her years, Al thought to himself, *are catching up with her.*

As they had with the other two women, Al and Jim once again expressed their condolences and apologized for having to interrogate members of her family.

"We wouldn't be here, Beulah," Al said, "unless we absolutely had to."

The old woman didn't speak but nodded that she understood. She told them she knew nothing about the selling of the fishery in Estonia or the setting up of a trust to the benefit of Aleksander and Viktoria. She said if Marcus was involved in any way, it was news to her. "Sheriff, Marcus and Trudy lived their lives independent of me. I often felt like an intruder here—although this had been my house."

"Did you know anything about their finances?" Jim asked.

"Not really. I heard them talk from time to time, especially after Trudy finished school and began working as a nurse. It seemed as if she wanted more information than Marcus was providing her about their finances. When they had these discussions, I tried to move out of earshot. Didn't want to get involved. Anyway, I recall that Marcus's father and I sometimes had squabbles about money too. I told you, Al. He lost a lot of our money in the stock market."

"What about the pistol Aleksander gave to Marcus as a gift from Gunnar? Do you know why he would have wanted him to have a pistol?" Al asked.

"No, but I didn't see it any differently than I saw the necklaces and vases he sent Trudy and me. I remember my husband talking about how his grandfather, Jakob, had brought a pistol with him from the old country when he came here. I thought it might have had something to do with that," Beulah said.

"Where did he keep the pistol?" Jim asked.

"I think at the mine office. That was where he kept a lot of other stuff, Deputy. I've heard him say there were a lot of wild animals that showed up around the mine portal. I recall him telling me one of his friends had killed a wolf that kept hanging around outside the mine," she said.

"Did you know Aleksander got the pistol from some men he had known in Estonia after coming here?" Al asked.

"No. He and Viktoria gave Marcus the pistol at the same time they gave me and Trudy our gifts," she said.

Al looked at Jim to determine if he had additional questions. He shook his head.

The sheriff got up from his chair and walked to Beulah's side of the table. He thanked her for her cooperation and reached down to help her up. She shook her head. She did not want to move from the chair, and like Viktoria had done before her, Beulah Smith began to cry.

CHAPTER 36

The discussion Sheriff Whitaker and Deputy Lucas had on their way back to Harlan focused primarily on Trudy Smith. They both were of the opinion that neither Viktoria nor Beulah had acted in any way suspicious.

"Viktoria unquestionably made some bad decisions. Especially being at a murder scene and initially not telling us. It's also obvious she wasn't completely forthcoming about what she knew about Aleksander's involvement with drugs. The story about the way she positioned his hand under his chin and why she did it might seem far-fetched, but when she told us how all that had evolved, I found it believable—and very sad," Al said. "Beulah looked like a grieving mother to me. I don't believe she knows any more than she told us. She did try to put the best face on things, though. But did you notice she never said Marcus and Trudy were close?"

Both agreed the answers given by Marcus's widow and her behavior were suspect.

"She seemed put off by our questions. Maybe angry would be a better word. I've got the feeling, Al, she definitely has something to hide."

"Agreed. I believe she knows more than she's letting on too. And Viktoria corroborated the reports we have heard about the quarrels with Marcus. I think Marcus spending so much time away from home also speaks to their less-than-loving relationship. We haven't seen anything to indicate infidelity at this point, though. Maybe it was just a case of them growing apart over time."

"We definitely need to keep an eye on her. That's about all we can do unless we get something incriminating from the phone records," Jim said.

Back in the office after a quick lunch at El Charrito's, one of several Mexican restaurants that had come to the mountains in recent years, the two law officers headed to the conference room to check in with Gloria.

"I don't know that I found anything of importance that you two haven't already laid out, but it's what I didn't find that interests me," Gloria said.

Al and Jim looked at each other after this puzzling comment.

"Do you recall that once Marcus and Gunnar Sepp started e-mailing each other, it was a regular occurrence—almost daily—until March eleventh? Then they abruptly stopped. In that last e-mail, do you recall Mr. Sepp told his cousin he was sending him information about accessing the money for serving as trust administrator 'by letter'?" Gloria said. "Perhaps one or both of them was thinking someone other than Marcus had access to his e-mail account."

"Maybe that's why Trudy was so nervous when we questioned her," Jim said. "Do you think she could have gotten access to his account?" Jim asked.

"Superintendent Lockhart said no one other than Marcus and members of his staff were ever in that office. I don't think she would have had access to his computer without them knowing it. If she did have access to the office, how would she have gotten into the computer? Marcus kept so many things secret from her. I am almost certain he would not have given her his password," Al said. "I think you are right, Gloria. It certainly is suspicious the e-mailing would have stopped so abruptly—and just before his cousin gave Marcus information to access the money."

The three were continuing their discussion about why the e-mails might have stopped when Sylvia walked in with news. "Al, we got the phone records you been asking for. I just got the report a few minutes ago," she said, and she handed a stack of papers to the sheriff.

Al went through Trudy's records page by page. When he finally laid the last of twenty-one pages down on the conference room table, he related only one thing that seemed interesting. "For the past several months, up until Marcus's body was found, Trudy called the mine office almost daily during the week and occasionally on Saturdays. Each call was made between eleven o'clock and noon. That's a time I don't think Marcus would have been present—at least most of the time. Until about the same time the e-mails stopped between Marcus and his Estonian cousin, many of the calls lasted for several minutes."

"She could have left messages for him when he wasn't there," Gloria said. "It's not unusual for couples to establish a routine of calling at the same time each day, even if only to leave a message."

Hollering to his administrative assistant, Al asked Sylvia to call the offices of Mineral Mountain Resources to determine the owner of the number Trudy was calling.

Within minutes Sylvia was back with the news. "That number be assigned to Marcus, Sheriff."

"Looks like another dead end if the calls were going to her husband," Jim said.

"Maybe not," Al said. "Let's find out who has the office next to Marcus. Gloria, why don't you go up to mine office and tell Superintendent Lockhart you need to check through Marcus's office for other personal items that might help us with the case? See who else works close to the office Marcus occupied. When Marcus wasn't in the office, it could be someone else was answering his phone."

Before leaving for the evening, Al asked Jim to head over to Post Ten to bring Captain Ford and Detective Davidson up to date on their latest findings.

CHAPTER 37

Gloria returned to the Harlan County Courthouse the following afternoon and headed straight to Sheriff Whitaker's office.

"What did you find out?" Al asked.

"Marcus's office is between those of two other foremen, who probably wouldn't have been present any more than he would have. Also when the foremen were gone, the offices were locked," she said.

"Darn it," he said, and he scratched his head.

With Thanksgiving coming up in a few days, Al told everyone in the office they would take some time off from the two homicides.

"Hartford Ford and I agreed if we didn't find anything that could help us by today, we would let things settle down a little before continuing our investigation. A lot of times you can get too close to the evidence, and it becomes a case of not being able to see the forest for the trees," he said.

Putting the two murder cases on the back burner didn't slow things down in the least. The heads-up law enforcement officials had given the merchants association proved prophetic. There were three arrests on Black Friday alone, two of which involved individuals from out of state trying to pass counterfeit ten-dollar bills at Walmart.

Unfortunately that was not the worst of it. On Saturday morning an ATV accident up near Pathfork had taken the life of an eleven-year-old boy. Like many other such accidents, the kid had been traveling at a high rate of speed when he hit something in the road and was thrown off the vehicle. The EMTs said he died instantly of a broken neck.

Al rode along with Deputy Adyn Banks to the scene of the accident. There was little they needed to do except offer condolences to the family, but Al really wanted to ask them why. Why was a kid this young allowed to get on an ATV in the first place? He had seen far too many accidents like this involving children. Parents who were otherwise protective of their kids didn't seem to see the danger in allowing them to ride these fast and powerful off-road vehicles.

As he rode back down KY Highway 72, Al noticed several houses were already decorated for Christmas. The festive lights contrasted, he was sure, with the pain and anguish one Pathfork family now felt.

The time off for Thanksgiving had done little to combat the feeling of fatigue that seemed to have overtaken Al recently. He attributed it to his age, but Ruby suggested it was more likely due to not being able to solve two homicides.

"And she's probably right," Al whispered.

His thoughts wandered as Deputy Banks crossed the bridge over the Cumberland River and headed north on US 119 to Harlan.

"Did you say something, Al?" he asked.

"Just talking to myself, Adyn, and hoping we can solve these two murders before Christmas," Al said.

CHAPTER 38

On Sunday Al enjoyed a thoughtful sermon from Reverend Johnson on the tradition of gift giving at Christmastime and its tie to the coming of Christ, which he said was the greatest gift ever given to humankind. Carols resounded throughout the sanctuary, and the faces of parisoners shone with a joy seen at only this time of year.

That afternoon, Al and Ruby also had the opportunity to catch up with the kids and grandkids via FaceTime on the iPad. The visit was heightened by the grandkids' exuberance at the expecation of the Christmas presents which awaited them. The day could not have ended better.

In all likelihood because Sunday had gone so well, Al came into the office on Monday morning feeling much more refreshed than he had on Saturday.

He was ready to get back to solving the two homicides.

As was his custom, he listened to reports from the deputies who had been on weekend duty. There were a couple more counterfeit attempts on Sunday as well as an arrest for driving under the influence following a rear-end collision on the bypass.

He asked Deputies Andy Harris and Adyn Banks to represent the sheriff's department at the funeral of the young man who had been killed in the ATV accident.

Since tax collecting was now taking up most of Sylvia and Blanche's time, he spent a little over an hour with them. They reported taking in well over $700,000 from individuals who had taken advantage of paying their taxes early for discounts. He made sure they were accompanied when depositing the funds, most of which came in the form of checks.

Jim and Gloria also spent their mornings catching up. Entries were made in their journals, and evidence logs were brought up to date. The sheriff was a stickler for timely, accurate record keeping, and each of the deputies, along with Sylvia and Blanche, had learned not to procrastinate.

Jim and Gloria also appeared to be feeling better after a few days away from the cases they had been working on for almost a month. Al motioned them into his office, and then he dialed Captain Ford at Post Ten. He put the call on the speakerphone and told his friend that Gloria and Jim were also present.

"And I've got Frank Davidson here with me, Al. Let's get this conversation started," he said.

"Too bad we can't take advantage of that whiteboard in your conference room." Detective Davidson laughed.

"Guess we'll just have to depend on our memories today," Jim replied.

What followed, sans the writing on the whiteboard, was a complete review of the double homicide in northeast Harlan County.

As they talked Al Whitaker could envision the answers they were looking for slowly but surely working their way down the evidence funnel.

"We are at a point, I believe, where everything is pointing to Trudy Smith's involvement. If not the killer, I would bet she knows and is complicit with whoever did the shooting," Al said.

When everyone agreed they hatched a plan to put Marcus Smith's widow under twenty-four-hour surveillance.

"We are going to see where she goes, who she is with, and what she does," Hartford Ford said. "But we've got to be careful that she doesn't know we are watching her."

A schedule was devised for an eight-person rotation. It involved six different automobiles. That included one each from the Cumberland and Benham Police Departments, both of which had also assigned a police officer to the rotation.

At 11:30 p.m. on Friday, December 21, Trudy Smith came out of her house with her cell phone in hand. It was a windy but warm day. Her jacket was unfastened and revealed her white hospital scrubs underneath. Cumberland Police Chief Jason Hightower and Al Whitaker could see her clearly from where they sat in a nondescript 2005 Chevrolet Impala. They were parked above the Benham School House Inn.

"She's probably been called in to work," Hightower said. "This would be the second time this week."

"Well, Jason, since we're both off tomorrow, there's not a reason in the world we shouldn't follow her." The sheriff laughed.

Trudy Smith did not go to the hospital. An hour and a half later, she pulled into the parking lot of a motel in Barbourville and parked beside a black Lexus. She took an overnight bag from her trunk, walked up a flight of stairs, and knocked on a door on the second floor.

The door opened immediately, and someone embraced her. Both Al and Jason identified the man as Willard Stanton, the IT officer at Mineral Mountain Resources. Seeing Stanton there with Trudy came as no surprise to them. Their investigation had revealed that in all probability he was Trudy's contact at Mineral Mountain Resources and the person she had been calling daily.

The day after beginning their surveillance of Trudy Smith, Al had gotten a call from Superintendent Lockhart regarding the key to Marcus's office. When Gloria Strong inquired about who might have one, Lockhart had confirmed that only he had a master key, which he kept in a safe in his office. Later he realized his mistake.

"I got to thinking after she left," Lockhart explained. "Our IT guy, Willard Stanton, gets that key several times a year so he can go in and update all the computers."

He went on to say that most of the work could be done from Stanton's workstation, but on some occasions he had to upgrade individual computers. "He was in and out of offices several times a year," the superintendent said. It was at this time that Stanton became "a person of interest," and Al had asked Benham police to keep an eye on him during the day. He thought they might discover him rendezvousing with Trudy.

Remembering that Viktoria had seen a shiny, new black car speeding away from her brother's crime scene and after determining that Stanton drove a black Lexus, Sheriff Whitaker had arranged with the superintendent to have the lines repainted in the company's parking lot. This required all employees to park in a nearby overflow lot. The damp December day had rendered the unpaved ground soft and pliable—just right for taking tire prints. Jim and Gloria then drove to Benham and used a quick-drying rubber substance to get prints from each of the tires on Stanton's car. One of them was a perfect match for a print found near the location of Aleksander Sepp's murder.

Al had wanted to interrogate Stanton but had decided to wait until his deputies surreptitiously gained access to his fingerprints and prints from his work boots. Those would then be compared with the prints left around the cabin.

The Benham police officers hadn't found him anywhere near Trudy. Maybe it was just a matter of letting their guards down, but they definitely were together now.

Jason Hightower hollered, "Police! Open up!"

The law officers then waited for a few minutes before knocking again. A disheveled and seemingly embarrassed Stanton finally opened the door, and Trudy Smith sat crying on the bed.

"We're arresting both of you for the murder of Aleksander Sepp," Al said, and he advised them of their Miranda rights while Jason handcuffed the two.

Trudy appeared indignant and demanded to know what evidence they had. She threatened to sue for false arrest.

"We've got enough evidence to convict both of you," Al said. Then he added, "You can be sure of that."

He noticed as he spoke that Stanton was shaking his head from side to side as if he couldn't believe what was going on. *I think he wants to say something*, Al thought, *and I'm going to try to make it easy for him.* His experience told him it was sometimes not the quality of evidence but its preponderance that led to an admission of guilt—especially if the individual was sorry for what he or she had done.

Al rattled off fact after fact in what he knew was a circumstantial case and added other facts he was less sure of that seemed incriminating. "Someone could get the death penalty," Al said.

Before Al continued Stanton looked directly at Trudy, and he said, almost too quietly to be heard, "I killed Aleksander, Sheriff." He paused for just a second or two. "And I also killed Marcus Smith."

Al and Jason didn't get a chance to express their surprise before Trudy, with her hands behind her back, broke loose from Jason's grasp and lunged headfirst at Stanton.

"Keep your mouth shut, Willard," she screamed.

Her head hit Stanton in the chest and knocked him backward.

CHAPTER 39

It was a couple days later when Stanton's lawyer worked out a deal with the commonwealth attorney to take the death penalty off the table if he became the state's witness. Stanton agreed, and arrangements were made for him to give his statement.

Unlike what Trudy Smith wanted, he was not going to keep his mouth shut.

Deputy Gloria Strong, Deputy Jim Lucas, and Detective Frank Davidson accompanied Sheriff Al Whitaker to the Harlan County Detention Center to take Stanton's statement. Initially he checked with his lawyer before answering any of their questions. After a while, though, it was as if a dam had broken, and information came pouring out of him without prompting.

Trudy Smith had came to him over a year ago asking for help. According to her she and Marcus Smith no longer lived together as husband and wife, and Marcus had become secretive and standoffish.

"I don't know anything about what's going on with our finances," she'd said. "Marcus takes all our money and does what he pleases with it."

Stanton explained how Trudy had cried when she told him she had gone back to school to help out the family financially, but once she started drawing a salary, she still had very little control over her money. At that point he began to feel sorry for her.

"I thought she was going to have a nervous breakdown," he confided, "and I guess I wanted to comfort her. But that led to other things. Before I knew it, we were in a relationship."

Not long after their first tryst, which was in the same Barbourville motel where they had been arrested, Trudy began asking him if he could access her husband's computer.

"She said Marcus spent most of his time when he wasn't working or sleeping on the computer in his office, and she wanted to know what was going on. So I rigged a fault in Marcus's computer to deny him access without resetting his password. I told him to be sure everything was working OK, he needed to give me his password so I could enter it in my console, which controlled the network."

Once that was done, Stanton said he gained remote access to Marcus's computer and could access all his information from the computer screen in his office.

"Trudy was elated and started calling the office almost every day to find out what Marcus was doing online. I had set it up so Marcus could use his computer as a phone, so once I got access, I could take her calls. They came at the same time every day. She suspected he was viewing pornography and seemed disappointed when I could not find any evidence of that. She seemed vaguely interested when Marcus started taking online courses, but she dismissed it as a waste of time. I was concerned when I had to tell her about the online gambling. I thought she might confront him and tell him where she was getting the information."

Stanton thought she might have done that very thing had he not suggested she go to the bank and demand they tell her about their savings accounts. She forged a note from Marcus giving her permission to get copies of the bank statements. He never understood why Trudy's name was not on their bank accounts.

"Once she got the financial information, she confronted him," he said, "and Marcus stopped gambling for a month or so."

Having talked nonstop since they sat down with him, Stanton asked to take a bathroom break. When he returned he requested a cup of coffee. He ran his hands through his hair and shook his head from side to side as if trying to rid his mind of the repugnant information he was revealing.

"Mr. Stanton, how did Trudy react when Marcus and Gunnar Sepp began e-mailing each other?" Frank Davidson asked.

"She didn't pay much attention to it at first, but once Sepp mentioned having Aleksander and Viktoria come here to live, she got very interested. Of course, he had to discuss this with her and his mother and I believe also with their boys. She didn't like the idea initially, but when everyone else thought it was OK, she agreed for them to come."

"And what happened when she found out about the trust and the funds Marcus would receive to serve as the administrator?" Al asked.

"Then she got really interested," he said.

"Did Gunnar Sepp and Marcus figure out someone had access to one of their computers?" Al asked.

"They must have. Around March the e-mails stopped, and they apparently started communicating through the mail."

"Gunnar said in the last e-mail that information about how to access the funds would come to Marcus by mail. Is that right?" Gloria asked.

"Yes. Once we—I mean, Trudy—found out about the letter, she made sure she was always home before Marcus to go through the mail. She intercepted the letter and got the information she needed to gain access the account in the Cayman Islands."

"But the last e-mail also said no money would change hands until Gunnar Sepp got a signed release from Viktoria and what turned out to be a death certificate for Aleksander. How did she get Viktoria to sign, and how in the world did she get a death certificate for Aleksander so quickly?" Al asked.

"She didn't get Viktoria's signature. Gunnar had sent a copy of the release to Marcus. Trudy intercepted it and forged Viktoria's signature."

"What about the death certificate?" Jim Lucas asked.

Stanton appeared hesitant. He ran his hands through his hair and shook his head again before responding. "I lost my father a little over a year ago. I made a nearly exact copy of the death certificate on some publishing software I have, put in all the relevant information, and then notarized it. She sent it to Sepp," Stanton said.

"You notarized it?" Al asked.

"Yeah. I've been a notary public for several years."

"How did Trudy get the release and death certificate to Estonia so quickly?"

"The old fashioned way She faxed them from Marcus' phone number and wrote on the form that the originals would follow. Apparently it didn't cause Gunnar any problems," Stanton replied.

"How did you keep Marcus from finding out Trudy had gotten his letter from his cousin?" Al asked.

"We steamed open the letter, copied the contents, and replaced it in the envelope. I used just a little glue to make sure the envelope was resealed. Marcus never knew the letter had been intercepted."

"Mr. Stanton, we appreciate you providing this information for us, but you haven't mentioned how and why you killed the two men," Al said.

"I am aware of that, Sheriff," Stanton responded. "I did it. I'm sorry for what I did. I haven't and I won't deny it." He paused. "Trudy was afraid Aleksander would not agree to Gunnar Sepp selling his mother and father's fishing business. And she knew if he didn't, the hundred fifty thousand dollars, which she intended to get her hands on, would be long gone—much like the money Marcus had lost gambling.

"Viktoria told Trudy she thought Aleksander was selling drugs supplied by two of his friends from Estonia and that Aleksander would be meeting these friends in the state park. Trudy took the pistol Gunnar had given Marcus as a gift. Marcus had said from the outset he didn't want it and had stored it away somewhere. Trudy found the pistol along with a box of ammo, and the two of us were in the park an hour before the meeting was to take place."

"How did you conceal yourselves?" Frank asked.

"There's an old logging road up on the knoll above a sycamore tree. We were able to back up the road far enough not to be seen. We saw two men drive up in a black sedan. They got out. Both were dressed well in suits, and they embraced Aleksander. They talked for a few minutes before he took a wad of bills out of his backpack and gave it to them. They gave him two large packages, which he placed in the backpack. They embraced again, and the two of them left."

Al looked at Gloria, Jim, and Frank. He knew they also realized Stanton was talking about the Smirnov brothers. The brothers were here when the killing took place after all, unlike what their boss at the Star Mortgage Company had told Gloria and Frank in Hoboken. *They may be innocent in this homocide*, Al thought, *but my instincts tell me there will be trouble from them in the future.* He could tell from their expressions that his fellow law officers shared this sentiment.

"What happened then?" Gloria asked.

"Aleksander looked at his watch, and before he could turn around—and before we could reveal ourselves—two young guys drove up behind him. Both were thin and appeared fidgety. Aleksander had obviously been expecting them. He took two small packages out of one of the larger packages he had placed in his backpack and gave it to the taller one, who handed him money. They immediately left."

The Eolia cousins, Al realized. From what Viktoria had said, after hearing shots, they must have returned to check things out and found the body. *Like the Smirnovs these two spell trouble ahead*, Al thought. *Especially now that they were taking heroin.*

"How did you make contact with Aleksander?" Gloria asked.

"Trudy stepped out of the car to where he could see her and hollered at him. 'Aleksander, what are you doing?' She acted as though she was concerned for him.

"'Stay right there,' she commanded. 'I'm coming down there.' We pulled down the logging road onto the Little Shepherd Trail. Aleksander appeared defiant and stayed in the middle of the road. Trudy jumped out of the car and confronted him. They argued. I slipped up behind him and called him by name. When he turned around, I shot him in the chest. He fell on his back. I knew he was dead." Stanton dropped his head. "I don't know why I got involved with her. I don't know why."

It was some time before he regained his composure. When he did, his story continued.

"We took his wallet, emptied his front pockets of change and a couple slips of paper, grabbed the backpack, and left him there. We got in the car and sped off. From what I learned from Trudy, Viktoria arrived at the sycamore at about the same time we were pulling away," he whispered.

"What happened to the backpack? You know, it probably was filled with heroin? Frank asked.

"We figured that it was full of drugs and that scared Trudy really bad. As I drove away, she rolled down the window and tossed the bag over an embankment."

Frank realized telling this sordid story was apparently having an effect on Stanton, and he asked Stanton if he wanted to take a break.

"If you don't mind, I'd like to stop for the remainder of the day," Stanton said.

Al asked Detective Davidson to step out in the hall with him.

"This guy seems to have finally realized what he's done. I can't see any problem with coming back tomorrow. I take it you are feeling the same way?"

"Yea. I don't see a problem with it, Al. I think you're right. He's committed heinous crimes, and now he's sorry for it. Should have thought about what he was doing before he fell under Trudy's spell."

The four law officers left Stanton to his remorse and told him they would reconvene at 10:00 a.m. tomorrow.

Before leaving, they spoke with the detention center guards about putting Stanton under a suicide watch.

CHAPTER 40

When they arrived early the next morning, the guards said Stanton had not eaten supper and had eaten very little of his breakfast. He had requested to be brought back to the interrogation room and asked for a pen and paper.

"Knowing he was under a suicide watch, we decided to have someone in there with him. I think he's finished writing, and his lawyer's in there with him now," one of the guards said.

The four of them walked in, relieved the guard, and prepared to start asking questions about the murder of Marcus Smith. Before they could do so, Stanton said, "I have written letters I would like for you to deliver for me."

He handed them to Gloria. Both letters had been folded in half. He had written Beulah Smith's name on one and Viktoria Sepp's on the other.

"We will have to check with the commonwealth attorney about whether or not we can do this, but I don't think there will be a problem," the sheriff said.

Stanton nodded his head and said thanks.

Frank began the questioning. "Please tell us how you were involved in the death of Marcus Smith."

"I wasn't just involved, Detective. I killed Marcus Smith," he said. As with the confession he had given yesterday, Willard Stanton began a step-by-step explanation of what had happened. "By the time Marcus went missing, Trudy was beside herself. I have never seen a person so mad. She said Marcus had gambled away their savings, and she deserved the hundred fifty thousand he would have received as trust administrator for Viktoria, and she intended to keep it."

"But why was she mad if he was gone? Wouldn't he be out of the way then?" Al asked. "And you said she already had the money from the Cayman Islands account."

"She thought when he found it missing, he might figure out what she had done and go to the police. She had planned all along to kill him, or I guess to have me kill him, and now he was missing. She thought that somehow he must have found out what she had done, and she was frightened.

"When Beulah told you, Sheriff Whitaker, that Marcus might be at a family cabin near Slope Holler Road, Trudy went into a panic. She was sure he was there and that he might he hiding out before going to the police. We agreed I would go to the cabin, and if Marcus was there, I would kill him. Once it was done, she said we could take the money and build a life together."

"Where would you have gone?" Al asked.

"I don't know, Sheriff. I was so caught up in this vicious cycle. I wasn't thinking rationally," he said. "It was almost as though once I took the first step, something compelled me to take another and another."

"How did you get to the cabin in all that snow?" Jim asked.

"I knew the mining company had built a road a few miles from the cabin that ran parallel to Slope Holler Road. It was used to get to a coal seam we were mining high up on the mountain. I went up there regularly to calibrate the scales used to weigh the loaded trucks. I checked out a half-ton four-wheel-drive truck from the motor pool. I told them I was going to check on the scales. Instead I drove to Cumberland, and I loaded an ATV I kept in a garage down there into the back of the truck."

"How did you do that?" Jim asked.

"Used ramps I attached to the tailgate. Fairly simple to do. I've used company trucks to transport ATVs before. They are really handy around a strip mine site," he said matter-of-factly.

Al Whitaker motioned for him to continue.

"I drove up the strip mine road with little or no difficulty. Actually, it is easier to travel on a gravel road in deep snow than on the blacktop. Not nearly as slick," he said.

Al noticed a difference in Stanton today. He seemed at ease. *Maybe the operative words are "at peace,"* Al thought. Al laid his hand on the letters the killer had written to the closest relatives of his victims.

Stanton took a sip from the coffee Gloria had asked the guards to bring to the interrogation room and continued telling the story of the second killing. "I unloaded the ATV and headed toward the cabin."

"How did you know where the cabin was located?" Al asked.

"Some of the workers had discovered it last summer. After a shift, two of them had stayed on the mountain to hunt quail and spotted it. They asked around. Marcus heard about it and told them it belonged to him. We even used a bulldozer to open up an entrance for ATVs. Someone told Marcus what they had done, and he wasn't too happy about it. But we left it the way it was."

"How long did it take you to get to the cabin?" Gloria asked.

"Probably no more than forty-five minutes. I gunned the ATV a little—probably a little too much. I started leaking oil on the way back," he said.

"What happened when you got to the cabin?" Al asked.

"I parked my ATV alongside the one I supposed Marcus had ridden, walked up on the front porch, and knocked on the door. Marcus cracked the door just a little to see who it was. Obviously he recognized me and opened the door. He looked distraught—as if he had the weight of the world on his shoulders. I didn't say anything. I just pulled the pistol out of my jacket pocket. He was startled and asked me what on earth I was doing. I told him not to make any trouble and motioned for him to sit down in the chair beside the stove. I pulled up a crate and sat down facing him.

"'Did Trudy send you?' he asked. When I replied she had, he started nodding. He said he figured I might have been in cahoots with her when he noticed someone had access to his computer. 'Couldn't have been anyone except you,' he said. Then he asked if she had stolen his hundred fifty thousand from Gunnar Sepp. I told him she had. He just shook his head.

"We talked for more than an hour. He had come to the cabin, he said, to think through what he needed to do now that 'his way out of the mess he had created' had been blocked. He said he had decided to go to the police and admit to everything. 'But not to killing Aleksander,' he said. 'I know they probably think I was involved in some way, but I had nothing to do with that.' I told him I knew he had not killed the young man. 'How did you know?' he asked. 'Because I killed him,' I said.

"The look on his face was unlike anything I have ever seen before. It was a look of utter disbelief fueled by uncontrollable anger. He started to get up from the chair. But before he could get up, I shot him in the chest. About the same place I had shot Aleksander Sepp. He fell back into the chair, and his head dropped to his chest." Willard Stanton ran his fingers through his hair just as he had yesterday before continuing. "It was a near blizzard outside. With the ATV leaking oil, it was too risky to leave. Didn't want to break down in weather like that, so I decided to spend the night in the cabin. Actually slept some on the cot. Not much but enough to get a little rest. When I got up the next morning, I loaded the stove with as much coal as I could pack into it and left," he said.

"Why did you put so much coal in the stove?" Frank asked.

"I'm not sure. I guess I hoped the cabin would catch fire and destroy the evidence of what I had done."

"If you wanted the place to burn down, why not set the fire yourself?"

"I'm not sure, Detective. I don't know how to explain what I've done or why I did it. I wish I could turn back the clock," he said.

There would be no turning back for Willard Stanton. Regardless of why he had killed two people, he had done so willingly. He would kill no more, but returning to the life he had known just a few weeks before would be impossible.

"There has been too much bloodshed," Al said to himself. "Too much bloodshed to turn back now."

CHAPTER 41

The cases had finally been solved—and before Christmas. On learning of Willard Stanton's confession, Trudy Smith also took a plea deal. Both would serve life in prison without the chance for parole. Given her grievances against Marcus Smith, the commonwealth attorney had figured Trudy might appear sympathetic to some jurors, so he was happy with life without parole.

Knowing them both as he did, Al thought Stanton was the more sympathetic of the two. At least he was remorseful and and at least outwardly genuinely sorry for what he had done. Trudy, on the other hand, was defiant. She blamed her late husband and Willard Stanton for everything.

The investigation had revealed that the fifty-five year old Stanton had never been married and his relationship with Trudy Smith was his first in several years.

"Some of his friends said his life revolved around technology, especially working with computers," Gloria had told Al. "They said he didn't seem to have time for anything else."

Too bad he didn't stick with computers, Al thought. *If he had two people would probably still be alive and a lot of others would not have had their lives ripped apart.*

Four snows had already fallen, but there would not be a white Christmas in the mountains. Al was glad. Ruby would worry less about the kids traveling home. All three would be there for the first time in several years.

Al took out his three-ring binder, and under the sections marked "Kingdom Come Homicide" and "Slope Holler Homicide," he wrote in bold letters: "CASES CLOSED."

EPILOGUE

Six Months Later

Sarah and Alonzo Stuart opened the doors to their pickup truck, but before getting in, they stood hand in hand on the warm June day and looked at the cabin that had been their home for more than fifty years.

"We air a-goin' to be a-missin' this here place, Lonzo," Sarah said.

The old man bobbed his head up and down to indicate his agreement.

"And it ain't just this here cabin," she continued, "but this here holler too. It's been air home in the good times and the bad fer most of air lives."

Again Alonzo nodded.

"We be a-leavin' air kin buried up and down these here hills. May God be a-blessin' their souls," she said, and she wiped away tears that had welled up in her eyes.

Alonzo put his arms around his wife and whispered to her. "I know you air right," he said.

The two—the last to leave what had once been a thriving community—got into the truck and followed the winding path down the mountain. Some two hundred yards in front of them was a Buick Rendezvous. Thelma Mattingly, accompanied by Ruby Whitaker, was transporting the Stuarts' daughter Roady and great-granddaughter, Annabel, who was fidgeting in her car seat.

Roady was singing. Having won her confidence with frequent visits since their first meeting in the fall, Thelma and Ruby sang along with her when they knew the lyrics.

The Stuarts were moving to Evarts. They had purchased a relatively new, two-thousand-square-foot house not far from the post office. They had paid cash with the funds they received from the sale of their cabin and their hundred-plus acres to an energy company from Oklahoma that planned to sink several natural gas wells in the area.

Fracking, or hydraulic fracturing, had come to the mountains as energy companies drilled in the Appalachian Basin. The Stuarts were just a few who sold or leased their property.

They had initially agreed to lease the mineral rights and retain ownership of their property, but they had been unable to get an ironclad guarantee that the well supplying water to the cabin would not be contaminated. They balked on a lease and agreed only to an outright sale.

"When you don't have water that be fit to drink, you ain't got a place worth a-livin' in," Sarah had said.

Thelma and Sheriff Whitaker had stood side by side with the Stuarts during the negotiations to make sure they got out of their land what it was worth. In addition to the up-front money, they were guaranteed a percentage of the sale price of the gas until the gas field was depleted, which could take several years. Others had not fared as well.

While the Stuarts felt the energy company had treated them fairly, having to leave the only home they had ever known was traumatic. Sarah's tears today were but a few of those she and Rhoda had shed since the negotiations began in late March.

Alonzo tried mightily to appear stoic, but there were times when his strong facade almost crumbled as well.

"The old man, he don't say much, but we all be a-knowin' he be a-hurtin' inside," Sarah said on more than one occasion.

When the SUV and pickup truck pulled into the driveway of the Stuarts' new house, Al was inside awaiting their arrival. He wasn't alone. The prodigal son had come home.

Frank Stuart was heavyset and had curly salt-and-pepper hair. He appeared to be in his late fifties and looked a lot like Al figured Alonzo would have looked at his age. He and his wife, Beth, had shown up about a month after the Stuarts signed on the dotted line to sell their land.

Al and most everyone else figured Frank had heard about his parents' money and came running home to get his share. Frank told everyone who asked that he had been in Cincinnati for the past several years. He and his wife had worked in a plant that made plastic moldings for the automobile industry.

"We made a good living. Even got a little money saved. I ain't here to live off my family," he said.

Al wasn't sure that was the truth, but it really was none of his business. He told Ruby as much. Anyway, he was glad someone younger would be around to help Sarah, Alonzo, Rhoda, and the baby, Frank's granddaughter.

"There was just no way the family could have made it on their own much longer," Al had said. As evidence of his vacillation concerning what he might or might not do in regard to Frank Stuart, he then whispered to himself, "But that son of theirs had better not take advantage of Sarah and Alonzo."

Frank had found a job within a week of coming home, and everyone knew it was no coincidence that the same energy company that had bought his folks' land had hired him. Some suggested Al had had something to do with it.

Sarah walked into the living room of her new home. Alonzo, Roady, and little Annabel, carried on her aunt's hip, followed.

Sarah looked closely at everyone who was there, and she shook her head as though she was remembering something special about each of them. Finally Sarah began to speak. "We don't be a-knowin' why things be a-happenin' the way they do. We will be a-missin' air old home place, but the memories in air hearts and minds will be a-helpin' us to go on." After a long pause, she continued. "We be thankful fer our new house and fer our boy Frank and his wife a-comin' home. The Lord, he has been a-blessin' us all, and we will be a-thankin' him fer as long as we be a-livin' on this good Earth, and then I reckon we will be a-thankin' him in heaven."

The sheriff of Harlan County walked out of the Stuarts' new house hand in hand with his wife, Ruby. Their longtime friend Thelma Mattingly followed.

Before they got to their cars, Sarah Stuart walked out to the porch and waved. "We be a-thankin' you," she yelled.

They didn't notice her crying as they drove away.

Made in the USA
Charleston, SC
11 July 2016